EMPIRES OF A STRANGE GALAXY

by
Shawn O'Toole

Cover Art Illustrated t
Shawn O'Toole

Empires of a Strange Galaxy
Copyright © Shawn O'Toole 2018
ISBN-13: 978-1717398215
ISBN-10: 1717398219

*****

EMPIRES OF A STRANGE GALAXY

*****

CONTENTS

Part 1

AMBIGUOUS CLARITY

Chapter 1
"City of the Nest"

The Age of the Six Empires was a balance of power among mutually alien natures and their mutually strange ways. Knowledge was mysticism or science. The power of knowledge was magic and or technology.

The races of the galaxy were either slaves or masters. Genocide was the fate of the useless vanquished. Prowess, cunning, industry, fecundity and the aggressive use of force decided the fate of all.

Ambiguous Clarity was head-and-shoulders taller than most humans. His eyes were deep blue and the irises so large the only white was at the very corners. His complexion was bluish beige and his long hair lustrous black. A long goatee without a mustache hung from his narrow chin. Every feature of his aspect was long and narrow. The hands that poked out of the long sleeves of his dark blue robes were only four digits each and one of the spindly fingers wore a ring set with a blue crystal.

Ambiguous Clarity was a Mystic of the magically advanced Mystic Confederacy. He was a professor of divination for its esteemed Academy of Magic. He was an agent of the Ministry of Vigilance though he travelled as an envoy from the Ministry of Alien Affairs.

Dr. Clarity was on a mission. He journeyed to the Nest World, capitol world of the One Hive Realm to negotiate a trade deal between the Mystic Confederacy and the Hive. His secret agenda was to thwart the designs of rival powers: The cult of the Living Darkness hoped to render the Hive neutral should the Concubines of the Great

Seen Unseen and their ally the People of the Third Eye go to war with the Confederacy.

The City of the Nest was the capitol city of the united Hive race. A dweller was hairless, purplish gray and nigh humanoid save that it stood upon four spindly legs. A hand was three long digits and a foot three stubby toes. The head of the creature came to a rounded point behind its ears which looked as if gills. The eyes were black, vertical slits within purple irises.

Six-legged beasts pulling carts shared the streets with the crowds of pedestrians between huge edifices of concrete. The buildings had archways but no doors and round or triangular windows without glass. A right angle could not be found in any aspect of the architecture, as was typical of things built by races other than humanity.

Dr. Clarity was riding in a Hive carriage pulled by one of the indigenous beasts of burden. Lady Sees-Big-In-Small of the Hive was with him. Unlike the little wenches, she was as tall and heavy as a Mystic. She wore jewelry Dr. Clarity recognized to be charms. She said unto him in the reverberating voice of her kind, "The Mother sees Ambiguous Clarity from afar. The Mother shall see him with her own eyes."

"I am to meet with the Queen of the Hive?" Dr. Clarity was surprised.

"Yes."

The Queen Mother of the One Hive was the only mother of her race. Only the oldest of her kind were not her children. Few other than her own people had ever seen her.

It was believed by the Confederate Ministry of Vigilance that Her Maternal Majesty seldom, if ever, left the sanctity and security of the Palace of the Nest. As the mother of a race of billions it was supposed she could do little more than spend her life laying countless eggs. Dr. Clarity hoped his meeting with Her Majesty would be within her palace. He hoped to see things that would enlighten his people concerning this alien race.

Infertile females the stature and weight of human females were the labor cast of the Hive. They were the "wenches" and the vast majority of the population. In war they provided what the humans referred to as "cannon-fodder." The males of the race were the true warriors: though few they were as tall as a Mystic but heavier and stronger. These bucks of the Hive were the "knights" though they fought on foot. They wore armor and wielded powerful disruptor rifles.

The knights of the Hive, not wench conscripts, guarded the Palace of the Nest. They snapped to attention as the carriage bearing the royal banner rode onto the grounds. A lady of the Hive and an honor guard greeted Dr. Clarity as he stepped from the carriage. "Ambiguous Clarity," Sees-Big-In-Small introduced. The robed Mystic made a sweeping bow.

"I am Hears-Utterance-In-Silence," the awaiting lady introduced herself. "Ambiguous Clarity is welcome. The Mother tells her daughter he comes as a wary friend."

The Mystic arched an eyebrow. He mentioned, "I come in peace and friendship but for the sake of my own."

"Yes. Ambiguous Clarity is true to his hive though it is without a mother."

"Our many mothers teach us loyalty," the Mystic vouched for his people. "It is by our many that we are one."

"Yes," the Hiver smiled.

The Palace of the Nest was like the many other edifices that were the architecture of the city. It was heavily guarded, had gyroscopic shield emitters and was surrounded by a garden but otherwise blended in with the cityscape. It was the way of the Hive that wealth was impersonal but it did surprise the visitor that even the Queen Mother lived accordingly.

Ambiguous Clarity was brought into a vast chamber filled with clusters of eggs. The guards within the chamber were armed with staves rather than rifles. They glared at the alien as he entered. The unheard voice Dr. Clarity knew to be that of the Queen assured him, "Do not fear. My sons watch for love of me and their siblings, not in hate of you."

The eggs were as large as a man's fist and the translucent shell was soft but undoubtedly strong. An embryo or fetus was within the dark, grayish fluid that was the yoke. Wenches tended the eggs and helped open those that were hatching. They carried the newborns out of the chamber and undoubtedly to nurseries. "We show what few are allowed to see," the unheard voice of the Queen told Dr. Clarity. "Though we are aliens to you, we are family to each other. Know that a friend of the Hive is a family friend."

Dr. Clarity was brought before a huge, bulbous mass of purplish gray with purple veins. Though the thing was without an evident head or limbs the Mystic wondered if it was indeed the Queen Mother. "Yes," the Queen of the Hive answered the unasked question. "It is my body as the life of my people."

The bottom of the mass opened and grayish fluid gushed out. A Hiver dropped out of the mass. The creature was like any other lady of the Hive in aspect but her countenance was full of uncanny grace. Wenches came up to her and wiped the fluid from her. The visiting Mystic bowed. "Your Maternal Majesty," Dr. Clarity recognized this alien as the Queen Mother of the One Hive.

"Ambiguous Clarity," the Queen smiled. Her spoken voice was that which the Mystic heard without hearing. "You come as a spy but not as an enemy."

"Yes, Your Maternal Majesty." The Queen was reputed to be a powerful telepath and now an agent of the Ministry of Vigilance knew for certain that such was true.

"I knew you would come before you were chosen to be sent," the Queen confided. "I know why you come. I awaited you for my people. You have come in the service of your own people."

"Does Your Majesty know my every thought?"

"I shall not tell what is best not to tell you."

"Will Your Majesty forgive me if I am guarded?"

"Ambiguous Clarity, I am the Queen of this world but not of yours. There is no Queen of Numinous." The planet Numinous was the eleventh state of the Mystic Confederacy and the homeworld of Ambiguous Clarity.

"Your Maternal Majesty, I come in peace."

"Yes."

"Our mutual enemies hope to render you neutral should they assail my people."

The Queen sneered as she uttered, "The Phantoms murder my children and lay our homes waste! Come to our aid should they come again and we shall come to the aid of the Confederacy should they assail you."

"There are also the Concubines of the Great Seen Unseen to consider," Dr. Clarity reminded. "We hear tell that you are fond of them."

"Yes. The women of the Living Darkness are selfless and dutiful. Their ways are much like the ways of the Hive."

"You are the One Hive," Dr. Clarity reminded. "Your race was many hives and they warred until only one remained."

"Yes," the Queen of the Hive knew the history of her race. She reminded, "Your people were many tribes and nations. Your Confederacy is the many become one."

"The Concubines of the Great Seen Unseen are an order of nuns of the cult of the Living Darkness. Their loyalty is unto an idea, not a family, tribe or nation. Their empire serves what they believe to be a higher purpose than the defense and prosperity of their people."

"Yes," the Queen understood. "They are mortal and only human in the service of a Living Darkness."

"You have many people," Dr. Clarity turned the topic into economics. It was his understanding that the question of resources was the fundamental concern of every empire. "You grow plenty on this verdant world but there are herbs not to be grown anywhere other than Mystique or the unfriendly world Artemis. Allow us to trade herbs for your produce. We will also trade finely crafted crystals for use in your artifices. We may purchase such devices of your manufacture should you be inclined to sell them."

The Queen mentioned, "The humanity of Jingo and of Golgoth reject our things for their own technology. The Delvers have no use for our devices of magic in preference for their own. You would be interested in what we craft?"

"Your Maternal Majesty, we are fond of everything magical."

Separated from the extension of her body that grew and laid eggs, the Queen of the Hive was indistinguishable in aspect from the ladies. She personally led her guest out of the vast chamber and into a room with a table laden with bread, fruit and edible bugs, fungi and what looked like innards. Juices were within silver pitchers and to be poured into silver cups. The Queen and the Mystic sat on the floor at the table. They chatted, ate and drank while wenches danced and sang for their pleasure.

The music of the Hive was singing, clapping and the snapping of fingers. The singers would slap their own bellies and flanks and the hands of other singers. There were no artificial musical instruments to be played. "Do my daughters please you?" the Queen hoped.

"Yes," Dr. Clarity answered in all sincerity.

"My children are fond of singing and dancing. It is their pleasure to entertain."

"Queen Mother of the Hive, I am stirred by the grace and vigor of your children."

10

The Queen remarked, "All races sing and dance. It is something we all have in common."

"Indeed."

"Dr. Clarity, we know there are only four hundred million of your people. Why so few? The resources of your Confederacy equal that of the Hive Realm yet your population is only a ninth our number."

The actual population of the Confederacy was four hundred and *forty-four* million citizens, but it was not the way of Dr. Clarity to volunteer strategic information. "Your Maternal Majesty, it is my understanding that your people are most comfortable in crowds. It is the nature of my species to value privacy."

"It is your way to be alone?"

"Not always. We need our moments alone to calm our hearts and quiet our minds that we may see and hear all that we have seen and heard. We come together to share our insights and to work together on whatever is needful or interesting."

"The people of Ambiguous Clarity are interesting."

"As are yours, my hostess."

The Queen of the Hive gave Ambiguous Clarity a tour of the city. There was no fanfare: it was a quaint and pleasant tour. The Queen's children recognized their mother and smiled but never did they bother her with so much as a wave or a chat. It was the way of the Hive to stay busy and out of the way of others who were busy.

Parks and gardens were throughout the metropolis. Hivers who were not busy working were busy playing. They sang and danced or played feisty games of tag or catch. "All must toil and play that all may be happy," the Queen smiled. Dr. Clarity admired her for her maternal love of her people.

Big-Big was a megasaurian: a pseudo-reptilian humanoid with a hide of greenish gray scales. His yellow-within-orange eyes were close-set and his pupils were vertical slits. He had fangs that showed whenever he spoke or grinned.

Big-Big was as tall as a Mystic but much heavier with a broad frame of dense bones and powerful muscles. He wore only a loincloth no matter the climate and seemed always comfortable.

Big-Big was the manservant and bodyguard of Ambiguous Clarity. He washed and pressed the Mystic's clothes, prepared his meals and baths and on Confederate worlds drove his carriage. Dr. Clarity was an agent of the Confederate Ministry of Vigilance and Big-Big was his deadly assistant.

Big-Big was in the quarters given to Ambiguous Clarity for his stay in the City of the Nest. The accommodations were spacious but minimalist. There was a table but no chairs. The beds were round mats with pillows and blankets. The "doors" were mere curtains and the "windows" slits and holes in the walls.

Big-Big was sitting on the floor at the kitchen fire-pit when he heard Dr. Clarity pull back the curtain and enter the quarters. "Supper smells delicious," the Mystic complimented as he entered the kitchen. "Is your megasaurian cuisine for me as well?"

The megasaurian nodded. His gruff voice rumbled, "Big-Big will feed Dr. Clarity the good meat. Dr. Clarity cannot chew the good meat so Big-Big cuts it into tiny pieces."

"Thank you, my friend. You may partake of the good meat with me."

"No! The good meat is for Dr. Clarity. Big-Big wants to give what is good."

"As you wish." Megasaurians were gracious and graciously stubborn. The Mystic knew better than to argue. Besides: the professor did enjoy megasaurian cuisine… when he could actually chew and swallow it.

Ambiguous Clarity left the kitchen and went to his bedchamber. He disrobed down to his underwear shorts. He lit incense before sitting with his legs folded on the mat that was to be his bed. He would meditate until dinner was ready.

"Your cooking is delicious, my friend," Dr. Clarity complimented as he ate.

Big-Big grinned. He remarked, "Dr. Clarity always likes what Big-Big feeds him."

"Yes, I do."

"Strength is from eating good food."

"Indeed."

Big-Big ate the food native to his world in the native manner: with his bare hands, tearing with his teeth and chewing with his mouth full. He would slurp, snort, gulp and belch with unabashed relish. The crude manners of a megasaurian amused Ambiguous Clarity.

"The Queen of the Hive is a lovely entity," the Mystic remarked. "May my efforts win her favor." Big-Big said nothing but he was always listening. Dr. Clarity continued, "Her hatred of the Phantoms is especially promising."

"Hate is bad," Big-Big frowned.

"Not if it provides an army of millions in the defense of my Confederacy."

The Concubines of the Great Seen Unseen and the People of the Third Eye were an alliance with designs on Confederate territory. The Mystics were on friendly terms with the three other Galactic Powers but none of these relationships were militarily binding. The Mystic Confederacy could be at a distinct disadvantage should the Concubines and Phantoms move to seize disputed worlds. Any of the "friendly" powers may turn unfriendly should opportunities to exploit arise.

Dr. Clarity chuckled. Big-Big stared at him so he explained, "I failed in my negotiations with the Greater Humanity Empire. They believed my civilization was primitive because our weapons were swords, glaives, bows and arrows. We routed their army with its guns, vehicles and aircraft. In their desperation they sprayed us with poisonous gasses we easily rendered inert. They tried to blast us with devices that destroy by splitting particles. We manipulate the flow and balance of the subtle forces. We negated the cause of their desired effect quite effortlessly."

"Guns kill," Big-Big reminded. He was fully trained by the Ministry of Vigilance in the use of firearms.

"Of course," Dr. Clarity acknowledged. "Basic alchemy cannot be denied by simple enervation. Kinetic shielding is required to stay a bullet, by siphoning its momentum into energy to divert its trajectory. As for humanity's explosives: the concussive force is reversed and dissipated proportional to the power of the explosion. All that said; avoiding detection altogether is the best defense against any and every weapon."

Dr. Clarity mentioned, "The humanity of the Greater Humanity Empire called their early wars with us the 'Blue Blood Wars' though their own blood is red. We do not call these conflicts the 'Red Blood Wars' and our blue blood is shed in our every war."

Big-Big wondered, "What do Mystics call the Blue Blood Wars?"

"Oh, to those not of our kind they are the Blue Blood Wars. Among our own they are the Early Conflicts with the Greater Humanity Empire. Alas, it is the way of all races to use the names humanity gives us."

Ambiguous Clarity was given a tour of the planet for the next five days. As a spy he was delighted to get a good view of the capitol world of a rival power. Though he hoped to make the Hive an ally it was best to be prepared for the worst. "We are alien to you," the Queen of the Hive stated. "Aliens cannot be friends. I show you my world in friendship."

Ambiguous Clarity smiled, deeply moved by the sincerity of this alien. He was personally fond of her and now he trusted her wholeheartedly. "Your Maternal Majesty, I shall implore my Confederacy to favor the Hive."

"Thank you."

The Nest World was green with forests, yellow with grasslands and beige with deserts. Farmland surrounded the towns and cities. There were lakes and seas but few rivers and no oceans. The land was watered by venting from underneath it, as was most common among the habitable worlds.

The boats and ships of the Hive were wooden. Few of them had sails. Every sail was triangular. "You have ships but no navy," Dr. Clarity noted.

"Worlds are conquered on land," the Queen explained. "More sailors would mean fewer soldiers."

"Your Majesty, we have used the seas to decisive effect against our enemies. Our navy was our edge in our wars with the Delver Plutocracy. The Delvers may align with your sworn enemy." The Queen of the Hive fell silent. Dr. Clarity hoped she was considering his suggestion.

Ambiguous Clarity enjoyed his visit to the Nest World. He yearned to stay longer but alas, he had things to do on the planet Lith. He was in a carriage on his way to the City of the Nest Interstellar Teleport. Lady Sees-Big-In-Small accompanied him within while Big-Big rode on the outside with the driver. "Did Ambiguous Clarity enjoy his visit to the Nest World of the One Hive?" the lady of the Hive smiled.

"Yes," Dr. Clarity smiled back. "Your people are lovely and your Queen Mother the loveliest of them all."

The Hiver giggled. She blushed purple as if personally flattered.

Big-Big was fully loaded with luggage as he followed Dr. Clarity from the carriage into the edifice that was the interstellar teleport station. Though burdened, the brute strength of the megasaurian was hardly encumbered. He carried everything with tireless ease.

Dr. Clarity asked Big-Big, "Did you enjoy your visit to this alien yet quaint world?"

The megasaurian grunted. He grumbled in his gruff voice, "The little ones cringe when Big-Big gets close. Big-Big smiles and they run away."

Dr. Clarity chuckled. He explained, "My friend, you are a monster with fangs looming over them. Forgive them for their natural fright."

"Big-Big likes the big ones. The big ones like Big-Big."

"You would have loved the Queen," the Mystic assured, "for she is indeed lovely."

Shifting one vertical plane of two dimensions with another was the means of travelling from one world to another. On the other side of an arch of light was a chamber on the planet Lith in clear view and only a step away.

Chapter 2
"Metropolis Prime"

In the days of prehistory the living worlds were joined by natural portals that spanned from one end of a horizon to another and never closed. Life streamed into the worlds from one world and flowed freely between them. Every land was lush and every creature thrived. Alas, the perfect balance was imbalanced and the portals shrank and closed. The perfect and cyclic flow was broken by aimless tangents. Most worlds were laid waste.

Lith was the homeworld of a Great Race and the seat of its Galactic Power… yet the planet was barely habitable. It was a vast, rocky wasteland dotted with struggling life. There were trees but such were few and little more than tall shrubs. What little flora could be found was mostly brush and cacti.

The *Delvers* and the *Worklings* were the indigenous races of Lith. The strong, aggressive and industrious Delvers asserted themselves as the master race. The weak, timid and listless Worklings toiled in peace and safety as the slave race.

A Delver is nigh a head shorter than most humans but very broad, robust and heavy with a frame of stalwart bones and powerful muscles. His legs are short but thick, strong and steady. His arms are longer than his legs and even stronger.

A Delver's skin is a hide of fine, orange-beige scales. He is hairless but thick scales above his eyes have an aspect of eyebrows. His eyes are black dot pupils within brown irises that were within black at the corners. His face was hard and looked as if carved from stone. His earlobes were negligible.

The attire of a Delver was boots and a loincloth when he worked. He wore a helmet when his labors were construction or in the mines. Robes were his formal wear and the usual clothes of the merchants, bankers, lawyers and politicians. The females dressed as the males but without the boots and helmet. The robes were either brighter colors or pastels.

The Delver species is oviparous. They have neither breasts nor nipples yet the distinction between male and female is easily discerned. The females are smaller and their features softer. Their voices are more melodic and their mannerisms more graceful.

There were only two females for every three males of the Delver race. There were no sexual rivalries, however. It was the nature of their species to fancy work to play. Industry and comradeship, not sensuality and intimacy, were the preferences of male and female alike.

The Worklings are a cousin race of the Delvers and like them in most ways. They are smaller, weaker and their arms in equal proportion to their legs, however. Their hide of fine scales is darker and more brown than orange. Their eyes are more widely spaced and their features softer. A loincloth was the only attire of a Workling, though their shamans did wear charms and headdresses.

The Worklings were slaves but never bullied or oppressed. Their masters did the mining and heavy lifting. It was the menial and boring things left for the slaves to tend. The hours were seldom long and the labors hardly strenuous for them. There was never a thought of rebellion. Even in the days when their masters were feuding tribes and nations the Worklings lived easy lives.

Metropolis Prime was the capitol city of the Democratic Plutocracy of Lith. It was built into mountains and was the stone of the mountains. Railroads made entirely of metal in segments connected much like the spine of creatures linked it to the neighboring towns and cities built into the surrounding hills and mountains.

For security reasons, the Delver Plutocracy forbade alien portals from opening within the capitol, those initiated from Penumbra being the only exception. Dr. Clarity and Big-Big came to Lith by stepping into the city of Twin Mountains. They boarded a train and were two of several alien passengers, most of these others being human merchants of the Greater Humanity Empire.

A Delver locomotive was sleek and unpainted titanium alloy. There was nothing of right angles in its design: everything was rounded or pointy. The machine was as modern in its aspect as those of humanity--yet its plasma engine was more like the steam engines of yore in its gist.

Big-Big sat by the window and stared out at the barren mountains. His gaze remained unbroken as the ride passed through tunnels. "Big-Big likes trains," he blurted. A human behind him chuckled.

"As do I," Dr. Clarity told his friend, manservant and bodyguard. "Though human trains are faster we are not in a hurry."

"The train is fast!"

"Not as fast as a Golgothite monorail or a Jingoan maglev train. Delver railroads are safer, however: The tracks bend without breaking. The wheels are leaned at opposing angles for better grip of the tracks. I believe a Delver train has never derailed."

The train stations were within the towns and cities built within the hills and mountains. The train echoed within the tunnel of stone as it slowed to a halt. Hissing steam let out as the engine vented.

A female Delver wearing an orange, yellow and black robe greeted the Mystic as he disembarked, "Ambiguous Clarity."

"Yes," Dr. Clarity recognized the dress uniform of a Delver soldier. Females were a fourth of the Confederate Army but only a twentieth of the Delver forces.

"I am Senior Lieutenant Glittering Gem, chief secretary for Colonel Grim Temper. I shall bring you to him tomorrow, when you have had your rest. Today I provide you with our hospitality."

"I shall follow your lead."

"This way," the female officer led the Mystic and his accompanying megasaurian into the depths of Metropolis Prime.

A Delver city was vaulted tunnels and chambers carved into the rocks and supplemented with fitted masonry. Shafts kept the air fresh and filled every nook with natural lighting. There was nothing wood for trees were sacred on Lith and not to be cut down. Whatever was not stone was metal, usually titanium alloy. There were no carriages or automobiles but rather cable cars and streetcars.

The largest cities of the known galaxy were Golgoth City with twelve million inhabitants, Anthropolis with four million and the City of the Nest with one million. Metropolis Prime was home to "only" seventy-five thousand—yet its cyclopean architecture within mountains was as awesome as the populations of these other cities were vast.

"Big-Big likes cable cars," the megasaurian remarked as he gazed down at the bustling crowds below. Sr. Lt. Gem believed he was a slave and was surprised to hear him speak without being solicited to do so.

"Yes," Dr. Clarity smiled, his response to his supposed slave surprising the Delver all the more. "Though not as fast as the train the view is more interesting."

Big-Big was Dr. Clarity's servant but willingly. They were friends. They met on Big-Big's homeworld. When Big-Big mentioned his yearning to visit other worlds Ambiguous Clarity offered him a job, promising him high adventure. Serving as the bodyguard of a secret agent did not disappoint the adventurous megasaurian.

Sr. Lt. Gem led Dr. Clarity and Big-Big onto a round platform with railings. The railings were too short for the stature of Mystics and megasaurians but this was a *Delver* city. The platform rose along a wall lined with walkways, doors and windows. It reached the tenth level before stopping. "This way," Miss Gem led the aliens along a walkway. She stopped to unlock a door and as she unlocked it she told, "Your stay is provided for. The staff has already been notified to accommodate you. You may dine in the cafeteria free of charge."

"Thank you," Dr. Clarity graciously accepted. Though he found Delver food bland and Delver beverages dangerously strong, he would enjoy his meals regardless.

Rugs were on the floor of the stone chambers that were to be Dr. Clarity's quarters here in Metropolis Prime. The furniture was metal tables, stools and benches. There was a metal book shelf full of books written by famous authors of every Great Race with a literary tradition. Dr. Clarity was disappointed to discover that every title available was one he had already read, some of them twice. "May you want for nothing," Miss Gem told the Mystic. "Ask and I shall make the effort to provide."

"Your poet Whistling Clamor is known to my people," Dr. Clarity mentioned. "May you provide copies of his work?"

"Dr. Clarity, he has published twenty volumes of poetry and an autobiography."

"Yes. I would appreciate any and every volume of his work."

The Delver grinned. "I shall lend you my own copies."

"Miss Gem, I thank you."

"Dr. Clarity, I shall return to these quarters at noon tomorrow. Should he not be delayed, I shall be accompanying Col. Temper. Tell reception should you need to contact me before noon tomorrow."

"Senior lieutenant, I hope to meet the colonel at noon. I am pleased you shall be with him."

Glittering Gem nodded. "By your leave," she waited to be dismissed. The Mystic nodded and she departed.

Big-Big prepared supper in a kitchen with stone counters and a titanium alloy oven. Titanium was the common metal used by the Delvers, though the particulars of the alloys differed according to the need of an artifice. Dr. Clarity intended to have his breakfast and lunch in the cafeteria, to satisfy the hospitality of the Delvers, but supper would be provided by his personal chef.

The Mystic and megasaurian were too tall to sit on the stools at the stone, round table. They sat on the floor on opposite sides of the table. "They have farms built into hills and use the water below to water their crops," Dr. Clarity rambled with a lecture. "Their agriculture sustains them but barely. They import food that they may enjoy abundance."

Big-Big wondered, "Where does other food come from?"

"They once purchased from the Confederacy and the Golgothite Empire. They have since favored the crops and meat from the Greater Humanity Empire."

"Why?"

"Jingoan agriculture is cheaper because automation can raise livestock and grow crops beyond the means of the Confederacy's farmers. The Golgothite Empire has become the Concubines of the Great Seen Unseen: the clones are the Many of One and have dedicated their agriculture to the production and sustainment of their many." Big-Big nodded.

Dr. Clarity claimed, "The balance of power is the possession and acquisition of resources. There are no weapons without materials to make them. There is no army without food to feed it. There is no influence with nothing to offer."

"Good must win," Big-Big insisted. The Mystic snickered. "Good must win! Good is good. Bad is bad. Bad must lose."

"Why? What is *good* without resources? What is *bad* about acquiring resources? My friend, I shall do what is best for my people." Big-Big snarled. The Mystics came to his world as invaders and the people of Big-Big fought back. The fighting ended when Ambiguous Clarity negotiated peace between the natives and the invaders. It grieved Big-Big to hear his friend voice the reasoning of an invader. Still, Ambiguous Clarity was a friend and Big-Big was true to his friend. Big-Big would not fret Dr. Clarity's bad comment.

Senior Lieutenant Glittering Gem returned… and Colonel Grim Temper was with her. They sat at the dinner table with Doctor Ambiguous Clarity and shared cups of hot tea brewed by Big-Big. "The Golgothites on Zygoth want to rebel," the colonel told the professor. "They hope to spark an uprising throughout their empire to take it back from their ruling slaves."

The Concubines of the Great Seen Unseen were the slaves who supplanted their masters. Dr. Clarity reminded Col. Temper, "The clones outnumber the naturally born Golgothites twenty-one to one. Their Many of One has the weapons and vantage points. An uprising would be quelled swiftly and brutally."

Col. Grim nodded. He explained, "We must assist if the Golgothites are to reclaim their empire."

"Your Plutocracy is asking for my Confederacy to join in support of an insurrection?"

Temper reminded, "In the Age of the Three Empires our empires were at peace with that of Golgoth. Prosperity was our mutual prosperity."

"Col. Grim, why are we discussing this, you and I? Your ambassador in the Confederate Middle or my ambassador here in Metropolis Prime is the proper channel for such discourse."

"Plausible deniability," the colonel explained. "We would be formally plotting subversion through the proper channels. Our personal and private conversation bears no such connotation."

It grimly amused Dr. Clarity to witness the sneaky side of the famously honorable Delver race. "Tell me your plan," he invited.

Col. Temper began, "Our empires are signatories of the Treaty of Zygoth. We are sworn to come to the defense of the Golgothite Empire should they come under attack from an unforeseen threat. We did not anticipate the rise of the Concubines of the Great Seen Unseen. Our direct intervention in the uprising would be legitimate. The revived Golgothite Empire would assume the mantle of the old. It would honor the old treaties and the lucrative trade deals would be reinstated."

"Our intervention would provoke the Scourge of the Galaxy," Dr. Clarity warned. "The Phantoms are a staunch ally of the Concubines and would surely be called to aid them."

Col. Grim smirked. He boasted, "My people have been itching for a fight with this *Scourge* of the Galaxy. We are eager to test our mettle against theirs."

"Oh? You are eager to imperil your frontier? You would relish the massacre of your colonies? You would risk invasion from an enemy known for genocide?"

"These Phantoms win by terror. We are fearless. They could not overrun us."

The Mystic leaned over the table and stared into the Delver's eyes as he warned, "Do not fancy your firepower would avail you against an enemy you shall not see till it strikes. Do not count your people safe within fortifications from a ghostly threat. Do not think my Confederacy, the Hive and the Greater Humanity Empire all cowards for fearing the People of the Third Eye. We were humbled at the expense of many." The Delver snorted. He did not argue and the Mystic hoped it was from terrible realization.

"The conflict would surely escalate." Dr. Clarity warned. "The other powers may join the fight and the fight could become a galactic war."

Col. Temper nodded. "Go to Zygoth," he suggested. "Glittering Gem shall accompany you... as a representative of the Heavy Duty Corporation. She will introduce you to a man who may change your mind."

"Is this a perilous quest?"

"The Concubines have not severed all trade with your Confederacy. You are a merchant when it suits you. Yet another merchant of your kind would not arouse their immediate suspicion."

Ambiguous Clarity and Grim Temper stared at each other for a long, tense while. "I shall meditate on this matter," the Mystic decided.

"Yes, divine. You are a professor of divination. We shall await your decision. You shall not hear from us until you contact us."

Dr. Clarity and Big-Big spent the next few days touring Metropolis Prime. They rode the elevators, escalators, cable cars and streetcars for the sheer fun of it. They listened to the singing, flutes, chimes, cymbals, whistles and drums played by the natives. They visited parks colorful and fragrant with flower gardens and bubbling with fountains and elaborate, artificial waterfalls. "We are underground yet it is nigh as bright as day," Dr. Clarity stared up at the lofty ceiling of stone. "The air is as fresh as that of an open field."

Delvers seldom smile but are never rude. When the Mystic smiled and nodded they nodded in return. When he spoke to them they responded warmly even if they were busy.

The Worklings were a more cheerful and curious race. They smiled at the sight of the Mystic but were especially interested in Big-Big. They waved at the megasaurian and "pestered" him with silly questions. "What are you?" a Workling asked.

"Big-Big."

The Worklings chuckled. "What are you?" a female of the race repeated the question.

"Big-Big is the people of Big-Big." The Worklings laughed. The megasaurian grinned. His fangs aroused interest rather than fear.

"Big-Big likes Worklings," the megasaurian told Dr. Clarity as they moved on.

"They are certainly fond of you," Dr. Clarity smiled.

Large, ovular screens were displayed throughout the city for public viewing. The image of a female newscaster told the listening crowds, "The Chairman is on Golgoth today meeting with the High Priestess of the Great Seen Unseen. He is negotiating the reinstatement of our deals and treaties with the Golgothite Empire. Wish him success for our peace and prosperity."

"Interesting," Dr. Clarity smirked. He told Big-Big, "They ask us to partake in their contingency plan."

"They trick us?"

"No. Delvers can be sneaky but they are never treacherous. I believe they mean to flow in a direction to tilt the balance especially in their favor."

"They are bad."

"My friend, every empire is friendly or unfriendly as a matter of selfish interest. Your people are not an empire so I do not hope for you to understand."

"Empires are bad!"

"They are security and prosperity in a universe dictated by cunning and the use of force," Ambiguous Clarity corrected.

Dr. Clarity was in his bedchamber meditating while Big-Big cleaned up after supper. There was a knock on the door. Ambiguous Clarity was a secret agent, thus, unexpected danger was to be expected. The uncanny instincts of a megasaurian made catching a megasaurian unawares nigh impossible, however. Big-Big answered the door without even the slightest fret.

Sr. Lt. Glittering Gem was the one who knocked. She wore a robe in pastel shades of green rather than her uniform as a soldier in the Army of the Plutocracy. Big-Big grinned down at her. "Is Dr. Clarity here?" the gruff yet feminine voice of the Delver asked. Big-Big nodded. "May I come in?" Big-Big nodded and stepped out of the way. He closed the door behind the guest. "I must speak with Dr. Clarity immediately." Big-Big nodded. He disappeared behind the curtain to the bedchamber and did not return.

Dr. Clarity came out. "Miss Gem," he smiled in greeting. "I saw you coming," he mentioned his powers of remote viewing.

"Do you know why I have come?"

"I can neither see nor hear your guarded thoughts. I do feel your anxiety."

"Our Chairman visited the High Priestess of the Seen Unseen."

"Yes, I know. I have been watching the public news broadcasts."

"What I am about to tell you is classified."

"I am listening."

"Dr. Clarity, need I remind you that the interests of the Plutocracy coincide with those of the Confederacy?"

The Mystic smirked. He corrected, "Your people are negotiating a secret pact with the Concubines of the

Great Seen Unseen." Miss Gem's eyes went wide and her mouth gaped. Dr. Clarity continued, "You have agreed to recognize their claims on Bosky if they recognize yours on Crux. Particulars of your secret dealings are a threat to my Confederacy." Sr. Lt. Gem was dumbfounded. Dr. Clarity told her secrets even she did not know. "Miss Gem, we know even what you do not tell. Speak freely that I may trust you."

"I am not a diplomat. We shall not be negotiating."

"Speak freely, please."

"Dr. Clarity, we must hurry to Zygoth."

"Why?"

Miss Gem hesitated before explaining, "Our situation on Zygoth is compromised. We require your expertise to rectify the situation."

"You are asking me to serve as an agent of your Intelligence Corps? That could be a conflict of interest. You must tell me everything."

The Delver hesitated before nodding. "My knowledge is limited to my own need to know."

"Yes, of course."

"I shall tell you all that I know pertaining to this mission." Dr. Clarity gestured for her to do so. Miss Gem told him, "A portal is soon to open. We must hurry. I shall tell you everything as we make haste."

"Big-Big!" Dr. Clarity cried out for his manservant to hear. "Pack our things! Make haste, my friend, for we are in a hurry indeed!"

Chapter 3
"Zygoth City"

Senior Lieutenant Glittering Gem told Doctor Ambiguous Clarity, "The Golgothite Ben Lucas is the leader of a secret movement to retake the empire of his people. His daughter was arrested by the Concubines of the Great Seen Unseen." The "Concubines" were clones used as slaves by the naturally born until they supplanted their masters. "We question the resolve of Mr. Lucas under such circumstances."

Dr. Clarity asked, "Is his daughter an adult?"

"Yes. She is adolescent, however, and remained in her father's care."

"Was she arrested in connection with his subversive activities?"

"No. She was arrested for engaging in correspondence with a citizen of the Greater Humanity Empire. Ben Lucas assures us that her intercourse with this foreign human was the continuation of an apolitical relationship."

Dr. Clarity asked, "Is this daughter aware of her father's doings?"

"No. Ben Lucas assures us that he was mindful not to involve his daughter in his secret activities."

"I fear the daughter may know more than her father intended," the Mystic considered. "The daughter will talk if questioned."

"Yes," Miss Gem agreed. "Our mission is to rescue her if able and terminate her if we are not."

Dr. Clarity warned, "We shall not win this man's favor by murdering his offspring."

The Delver agent explained, "Our primary objective is to maintain plausible deniability."

"My Confederacy has nothing to deny. I would be risking my people by acting against either party on this matter."

"Dr. Clarity, the Concubines offered the subcontinent of Vendya on Bosky... in exchange for our recognition to their claim to Rebus."

The Mystic blurted, "Vendya is neither theirs to give nor yours to take! The subcontinent is Confederate territory!"

The Delver smirked. She threatened, "The Confederacy shall be our ally or we shall be in league with the Concubines of the Great Seen Unseen."

"You have been getting closer to every Golgothite faction," Dr. Clarity noted. "You come to us to turn against them." Honor was the highest virtue among the Delvers. It stung Glittering Gem to hear such an accusation. Alas, as one true to the faith of her people, she was not at liberty to deny the truth.

Zygoth was the third planet in the Gol system. It was a desert world with a primitive indigenous population ruled by the advanced civilization of Golgoth. Zygothites and Golgothites alike were human. Their hair was black and their eyes typically brown but the breed of Zygoth was swarthier and less attractive.

Zygothites were traditionally nomadic and lived in tents. They became the cheap and unskilled labor of the Golgothite cities built on Zygoth. They lived in ghettoes furthest away from the pyramidal edifices of fitted stone and glass. They were kept out of the affluent suburbs lest coming to do menial jobs.

Zygoth City was a Golgothite city and the capitol of the colony world. Crowds of pedestrians, automobile traffic and monorails kept the population flowing in every direction. "So many people," Dr. Clarity mused as he watched the hustle and bustle from behind the window of a bus. "Mankind is such a prolific species."

Miss Gem mentioned, "Two million human beings inhabit this city now. It grew by two hundred thousand when the Golgothites were exiled from Golgoth."

"Interesting." Dr. Clarity dwelled on the numbers before remarking, "There are over seven *billion* human beings in the known galaxy." He thought for a moment before adding, "There were two *billion* Golgothites before the Culling. A mere two hundred million of the naturally born remain... but there are more than four *billion* clones." Dr. Clarity chuckled, "The Many of One are many indeed."

The Delver glared at the Mystic as if insulted. She stated, "Their numbers shall never overwhelm us."

"What if they do? There are only a hundred million of your people and only four hundred and forty-four millions of mine. The Scourge of the Galaxy is a mere three hundred and sixty million entities. The Hive, the greatest of all populations inhuman, is a mere three billion and six hundred million."

"Dr. Clarity, do you teach statistics at the university?"

"When one can divine from the numbers, yes I do."

"What am I to divine from your rambling?"

The Mystic grinned before stating, "Humanity enjoys a greater power of life than all other life shall ever match."

The red, white and black flag of the Golgothite Empire once fluttered from every pole in the city. The banner was recently replaced with the white, red and black flag known as the "Double X" of the Concubines of the Great Seen Unseen.

Barefoot clone women uniformed in skimpy red uniforms guarded buildings and patrolled the streets. These armed clones were Concubine Sentinels, the foot soldiers of the ruling Many of One. The bald heads of these women were covered with elastic hoods and black goggles fixed to the hoods. These Girls in Red were ominous despite their comely physiques. They were authorized to kill at the slightest provocation. "The Concubines are ready for an insurrection," Dr. Clarity surmised.

"Yes," Miss Gem agreed. "A rebellion is doomed to fail without our direct involvement."

Glittering Gem came in the guise of a secretary for the Heavy Duty Corporation. She was a secretary and her clan owned and operated the corporation so her cover was not a lie. Ambiguous Clarity came in the guise of a concerned stockholder. He did own stock in businesses that did business on Zygoth so his cover was not a lie either. Their stay on the planet would endure scrutiny until they made their move.

"The Concubines of the Great Seen Unseen are an order of nuns first and foremost," Miss Gem told Dr. Clarity. "They are uncomfortable interacting with infidels. They are trying to redirect their trade by favoring the People of the Third Eye."

Dr. Clarity understood, "We are tolerated in the midst of an intolerable transition."

"Yes."

The Mystic and his valet would be staying with Glittering Gem in a hotel that catered to Delvers. The lower levels of the establishment were a secret base of operations for the Intelligence Corps.

Dr. Clarity followed Sr. Lt. Gem into a chamber with consoles and monitors. A robed male of the Delver race greeted, "Ambiguous Clarity."

"Yes, I am. Who are you?"

The Delver rumbled a chuckle. He answered, "I am Chisel Spark."

"You are an agent of the Intelligence Corps, no doubt."

The Delver again chuckled. He would neither confirm nor deny the obvious.

Females were only two of every five Delvers yet they were four of every five soldiers serving in the Intelligence Corps. Males were in command, as was the way of the race, but the superior intuition of females was valued and employed. An anonymous female activated one of the monitors.

For all its advanced metallurgy and powerful machines the mechanical engineering of the Delver civilization was pre-industrial. Arcane geometry and mystical physics were used to generate electricity to power devices of amazing simplicity.

The Delvers had radios and televisions but these were meticulously handcrafted, thus, could not be cheaply mass-produced. The race was obsessively practical and would not squander the use of their marvels on petty entertainment.

A glass orb with a silver, gyroscopic core was already fitted into the panel fixed to an ovular monitor. The orb was a dome in its position and was to be touched to be activated. The core spun and the sphere filled with bolts that sparked on the surface upon contact. The user was stung by the touch but Delvers were a hearty people.

The image of a mansion heavily guarded by Concubine Sentinels lit the screen of the monitor. The image changed as a visual scan of the surrounding grounds was made. Dr. Clarity warned, "Golgothite technology can detect remote viewing and trace it to its source."

"Let them," Chisel Spark grinned.

"Discovery does not concern you?"

The Delver explained, "An active scan would alert the enemy. Our passive scan shall not."

Dr. Clarity arched an eyebrow. He would be mindful to learn all he could about the limitations of Delver and Concubine artifices. He questioned, "You cannot gaze into the interior?"

"No. Passive scanning is limited."

"Is this mansion the headquarters for the occupation forces?"

"No. It is the private residence of Ola Wolfsbane. She is a Golgothite witch and the appointed mayor of Zygoth City."

"Why are you showing me the abode of Ola Wolfsbane?"

"Miss Lucas was brought to the mansion under guard and has not been taken elsewhere."

"Was she brought to the witch for questioning?"

"We assume so."

"Mr. Spark, the Concubines take Miss Lucas seriously or else she would be questioned by the lowliest Concubine Priestess. Taking her to the mayor's mansion implies greater concern than a girl making benign contact with foreigners."

"We agree."

"Intruding upon the grounds of the mayor could provoke a diplomatic incident."

"Dr. Clarity, you are invited."

"When and how?"

"You own stock in the Arcane Artisans Guild. Use your influence and you shall be among their representatives at Ola Wolfsbane's party."

"Ola Wolfsbane is having a party?"

"She makes money from us all and wants to secure her business connections."

Dr. Clarity hoped, "The intentions of the Concubines to isolate the imperial economy may threaten Miss Wolfsbane's personal finances. We may have an opportunity to exploit."

Glittering Gem considered, "Maybe she had the daughter of Ben Lucas brought to her mansion because she is aware of the intended uprising. She may hope to make a deal."

"Let us not assume beyond our ken."

Dr. Clarity told Mr. Spark, "I shall be paying Mr. Lucas a visit. I must speak with him."

"We shall arrange a meeting."

"No. I shall visit his home."

"Dr. Clarity, his home may be under surveillance."

"Yes. What if it is? The Concubines may watch and listen as I hide in plain sight. Let them hear me whisper loudly and clearly in audible silence."

"What?"

"I am a Mystic. You must think mystically if you are to understand my meaning."

"Oh." Mr. Spark looked at Miss Gem, who shrugged.

Glittering Gem and Ambiguous Clarity were on their way to see Ben Lucas. Big-Big did not come along because megasaurians tended to be scary... even when they smiled—especially when they smiled. The agent of the Confederate Ministry of Vigilance asked the agent of the Delver Intelligence Corps, "Why am I involved in your matter?"

"I have already told you."

"Yes, but you did not tell everything."

Miss Gem answered, "You have always bested us. We need the superior acumen on this most delicate matter."

"Miss Gem, you have bested me. You persuaded me to join you against my better judgement." The female smiled as if flattered.

Ben Lucas was a handsome man. His wife was beautiful. Their daughter was beautiful. A picture of the parents and their offspring hung on the wall of the Lucas home. "Natural selection at its finest," Dr. Clarity remarked.

"Thank you," Mr. Lucas smiled. "Can your people drink our tea?"

"Yes."

"Would you like a cup of tea?"

"Yes, please."

"Miss Gem?" Mr. Lucas offered tea to the Delver. She nodded and accepted.

The human and his guests sipped hot tea. Dr. Clarity began the conversation, "Mr. Lucas, I took the liberty of divining before entering your home. You are not under surveillance."

"Good."

"Why is no one watching you? The Virgin Army is proficient in surveillance. Their excessive presence in the city implies martial law is pending. You are a prominent citizen. I hear tell you adamantly and openly opposed the mass-production of the Many of One. You should be a person of interest to them."

"Maybe I am."

"Yes. The enemy is the cult of the Seen Unseen. There may be a secret within the obvious."

The Golgothite snickered. He told the Mystic, "These clones were made from a daughter of Golgoth but they are *not* our daughters. They're more like golems. They obsess over procedures and routines and nothing else. They are witless beyond their programming."

"Mr. Lucas, I assure you, the Many of One are indeed many human beings. By Unheard Whisper or not they have become your empire by their own initiative. They are doing right what their sires did wrong."

Mr. Lucas said unto Miss Gem, "I thought your people were going to help us."

The Delver explained, "Our involvement would involve the Phantoms. We need the Confederate Army if we are to prevail."

The Golgothite asked the Mystic, "Are you going to help us?"

The Mystic ignored the question by asking, "Do you understand why your empire has become the Concubines of the Great Seen Unseen?"

"Yes. We replaced our proletariat and slaves with cheap and easily mass-produced clones."

"Your civilization was decadent," the Mystic accused. "The clone slaves were a symptom, not the cause of your fall from grace. Your civilization was doomed regardless."

"You're not going to help us?"

"Mr. Lucas, what is to be done to revive your culture? Pride for the sake of pride? Vanity became apathy and imbalance and stagnation. My Confederacy shall not squander its efforts on a cycle of futility."

The Golgothite sneered. The Delver warned him, "Dr. Clarity is not here as an envoy. He is ascertaining whether his people should bother to assist."

The Mystic assured, "My people were on friendly terms with the Golgothite Empire. We mutually prospered. We would rather the Golgothite Empire revived. We shall support what proves hopeful."

"Thank you," the human told the Mystic. "Thank you," he told the Delver. "Help us and we will make it worth your while."

Dr. Clarity perked as if he heard something. He told Mr. Lucas, "Your wife is nearly home. The sight of me and Miss Gem would exasperate her anxieties. We shall take our leave."

The Mystic and Delver were riding on a Golgothite monorail on their way back to the Delver hotel. Sr. Lt. Gem wondered, "Have you been dissuaded from helping us?"

"No." Dr. Clarity grinned, "Things have gotten very interesting." Miss Lucas was arrested for what should have been a minor offense… yet she was taken to the abode of a Golgothite witch. Ben Lucas was a man of influence and openly opposed to the very existence of his rulers… yet he was not under surveillance. When the likely was not and the unlikely was then something was amiss. There was a mystery to solve. The unknown was always perilous. Dr. Clarity was enjoying his visit to the planet Zygoth.

Golgothites, foreign humans and aliens were the guests of Ola Wolfsbane. All of them were rich. All of them were important.

Malicious Virtue was a merchant representing the Arcane Artisans Guild. He introduced, "Ambiguous Clarity, professor of divination for the Confederate Academy of Magic and a beneficiary of the Arcane Artisans Guild."

Ola Wolfsbane was the beautiful specimen of a most beautiful breed of the one race every race found comely. Her black hair was pulled up into a fancy style. She wore a silky blue gown embroidered with silver and opals. She wore expensive jewelry.

The woman looked up at the towering Mystic and smiled alluringly. She greeted in her melodic voice, "Welcome to Zygoth, Dr. Clarity. What brings you to my city?"

"I have concerns I must address."

"Concerns?"

Dr. Clarity ignored answering by saying, "I am delighted to be here. Your house is as grandiose as any to be found on Golgoth proper."

"Yes, it is," the woman immodestly agreed. Her brown eyes twinkled. "The indigenous architecture was mud-brick walls and huts. My conquering ancestors made drastic improvements on this wasteland of a world."

"Indeed."

"What are your *concerns*, Dr. Clarity?"

Ambiguous Clarity was a secret agent. He excelled at being secret by being unpredictable. He blurted, "The daughter of Ben Lucas is in your personal custody. I mean to know why."

Ola Wolfsbane tittered. She asked, "Who told you this?"

"Miss Wolfsbane, did you not hear that I teach divination? I may be asking you what I already know. Please tell me."

"What does it matter to you if Miss Lucas is in my custody?"

"I am a beneficiary of the Arcane Artisans Guild. We did business with this city while Mr. Lucas was mayor. We do business with you. I am concerned by the number of clone troops I see in the city: their Many of One is many more all of a sudden. I hope business here is not becoming an undue risk."

"Dr. Clarity, you have nothing to worry about. I am in regular correspondence with the clone High Priestess. Zygoth shall continue to serve as an open world for galactic commerce."

"The High Priestess had a meeting with the Chairman of the Delver Plutocracy."

"Yes."

"She has not met with the President of my Confederacy."

"Not yet, but she will."

"On favorable terms, I hope."

"Undoubtedly," the woman feigned a smile.

Dr. Clarity pressed, "The guild was on favorable terms with Mr. Lucas. Are you holding his daughter hostage?"

"No! No. Dr. Clarity, you don't understand."

"Enlighten me." Miss Wolfsbane simpered. Dr. Clarity told Malicious Virtue, "I shall be voicing my concerns to the chair of the guild."

Malicious Virtue knew Ambiguous Clarity was an agent of the Ministry of Vigilance. The guild did favors for the ministry in exchange for favors. Mr. Virtue played along, "It would be unfortunate if you dissuaded him from doing business with Miss Wolfsbane."

"Perhaps, but I distrust the unknown."

"Dr. Clarity, I am certain there is nothing to fret."

"You are certain of what you do not know." Dr. Clarity turned to his hostess. "Miss Wolfsbane," he bowed. "I thank you for your hospitality but I must be going."

"Wait!" the woman chased after him.

"Miss Wolfsbane?"

"The matter is a sensitive one here in Zygoth City."

"The city of itself is not my concern."

"Please. Come with me."

"Where are you taking me?"

"I'm going to show you what I shouldn't tell you." She muttered, "You'll be disappointed because it really is nothing to worry about."

"We shall see."

As Miss Wolfsbane led Dr. Clarity up the staircase she told, "I know you people are always polite. Please understand that it would be very discourteous if you betray my trust."

"I may trust you should you trust me."

Miss Wolfsbane knocked on a door. The door opened and a younger woman, Miss Lucas, poked her head out. She looked up at the visiting Mystic. Ola Wolfsbane told the girl, "We need to explain things to this gentleman."

Ambiguous Clarity stayed for the duration of the party. He mingled with the guests. He noted everything said to him. He was a spy, after all.

Dr. Clarity returned to the Delver hotel. He reported to Chisel Spark in the presence of Sr. Lt. Gem, "Miss Lucas is not a prisoner. Her arrest was feigned. Miss Wolfsbane is teaching her magic and Mr. Lucas would not approve."

Mr. Spark questioned, "Is Miss Lucas aware of her father's plans for an uprising?"

"There are no such plans, not really. Mr. Lucas is a romantic who mourns the loss of glory. He hopes we shall prevail for him."

Miss Gem reminded, "There has been a surge of clone troops in the city."

"Yes, but not to deal with the Golgothite citizenry. The Golgothites here tell me the indigenous Zygothites are restless, as they often are. The nomads are waging an insurgency, as they sporadically do. We have no use for Mr. Lucas."

Dr. Clarity had a late snack with Big-Big. The Mystic said unto the megasaurian, "You were out playing on the monorails and buses, were you not?"

The megasaurian rumbled a chuckle. He answered, "Big-Big likes trains and buses."

"Would you like to ride on boats and airplanes?" Big-Big nodded. "Good. You shall do so on the planet Farrago. Trouble or not, you will have fun."

A mission was always perilous but not always bloody. More often than not all was sights to see and secrets to hear. Ambiguous Clarity was the spy. Big-Big was the tourist. Things did get bloody on Farrago... but that is another story.

Part 2

MISADVENTURES

Story 1
"Sentries, Throngs and a Boss"

The Many of One were human females made from
the blood and memories of a living dead woman. As the
Concubines of the Great Seen Unseen they were nuns of
the Living Darkness. Having supplanted the Golgothite
Empire they seized the worlds, industries and technology of
a Galactic Power.

A Concubine of the Great Seen Unseen was bald
but had eyebrows. Her eyes were white-within-white. She
was ashamed of her unnatural aspect. She kept her head
and eyes covered when in the presence of any other than
her sisters.

The women of the Living Darkness were kept
chaste. As soldiers they were the Virgin Soldiers and their
military the Virgin Army.

The uniform of a Virgin soldier was an elastic
garment with an elastic hood. Black, singular goggles fixed
to the hood covered her eyes. The shoulders, buttocks, arms
and legs were kept bare. A Concubine was spawned as if an
elemental: she could tread on broken glass and hot coals
without harm but to wear shoes would pain her.

Blair Purple the Supercilious of the Thirteenth
Harvest was a Concubine Priestess. As a Virgin Soldier she
commanded the Sixth Research Battalion, Third
Expeditionary Force. Her command was housed and
operated in what was once a Golgothite monastery on Iris,
the ninth moon of the planet Oculus.

Because she was a Priestess Blair wore the purple
version of the standard uniform. Her armed Sentinels wore

red and her unarmed scientists and technicians (Keepers) wore blue. "What is it?" Blair asked her Girls in Blue.

"A sapient life-form of entirely corporeal physiology," a Keeper responded. "Its mystical signature quotient is at two hundred and twelve."

"What's the nature of its abilities?"

"Psychic and hyper-regenerative."

Blair hoped, "We have it inhibited?"

"Yes, ma'am."

"Male or female?"

"Male."

"Is this creature indigenous?"

"No."

Iris was frozen at its poles and scorched desert most everywhere else but it did have its forested regions. The old monastery was built in the wooded hills of Iris Region One. Rhonda Bonfire had come to the region... sneakily and uninvited.

Rhonda Bonfire was half-human and superhuman. Her father was a bounty hunter from the planet Jingo. Her mother was a warrior of the Vexite race. Rhonda was as tall and strong as her tall and strong mother. Her skin was as greenish gray and scaly. Her blood was green. Her hands were more like her father's, however, since her pinky was not a secondary thumb. The scales of her scalp were very much like a head of short and spiky hair.

Rhonda was as monstrous as her inhuman mother but as professional as her consummate professional father. She was as adventurous as either of them.

Iris was a world of the Golgothite Empire when the humanity of Jingo still believed its own world was flat. The Jingoans had since advanced, united and expanded into what became the Greater Humanity Empire. The young empire of Jingo challenged the dying empire of Golgoth for control of Iris. The Golgothites lost most of Iris but clung

44

to a few of its territories. The Concubines of the Great Seen Unseen fought to reclaim Iris only to litter its deserts with the bones and artifacts of their Virgin Army.

Rhonda's father was John Bonfire, a war hero who made his name fighting for control of Iris. Rhonda came to the moon to see the monuments with her father's name on them. She ended up making one of the settlements her permanent residence. "Keep out of the hills," Mrs. Rutherford warned. "The clones don't mind if we stay out here in the desert but they'll kill you on sight if they catch you in *their* woods. They have Girls in Green roaming around ready to snipe anyone not one of them."

Billy Wilder was a hermit who lived in the forested hills claimed by the Concubines of the Great Seen Unseen. Ironically, he lived in their hills to be left alone. He would come to town, however, for supplies. Though an extreme introvert he introduced himself to Rhonda when he heard that her father was John Bonfire, a man he met during the wars. Billy and Rhonda became friends.

"Those girls are always up to something," Billy told Rhonda. They were sitting side-by-side in the rocking chairs outside the Rutherford General Store.

"Like what?"

"They found something."

"What?"

The old man shrugged. "A person… and it probably wasn't human."

"That sounds interesting." Old Billy again shrugged. Rhonda asked him, "Did you see this person?"

"No."

"Why do you think it was a person?"

"They found it on the Silent Hill."

"The Silent Hill?"

Billy nodded. He explained, "There's a shrine up there to some dark god worshipped by the ancient Golgothites. Animals won't go near it. I've been up to it and the closer I got the dizzier I got. It was like vertigo, like I was climbing higher and higher with a sheer drop right under me. Rhonda, my girl, I was *walking* up that hill but I felt like I was climbing a sheer cliff."

Rhonda again asked, "Why do you believe what you did not see was a person?"

"I already told you animals won't go up that hill!"

"You didn't explain why what they found wasn't an artifact or anything other than a person."

"Fair enough," Billy conceded. He explained, "They brought a stasis pod and that's only to keep things in living captivity."

"Where did they take this 'person' they captured?"

"To the old monastery, I think. The entomopter flew straight in that direction."

"The monastery?"

"Yeah. There's an old Golgothite monastery in them hills. The clone girls turned it into some sort of military outpost or something."

"Why?"

Billy shrugged. He told, "I've been to it before the girls turned it into a base. I lived in it."

"Do you remember the layout?" Billy nodded. "Will you tell me everything about it?"

Billy again nodded. He told Rhonda, "I watched the girls renovate the place so I'll be telling you a lot."

A Concubine Sentinel was comely in her skimpy red uniform. She looked so serious behind those black goggles and wielding her little gun. "Yuliet Red, report," such a one was addressed.

The Sentinel touched the side of her goggles-communicator and responded, "All is well."

"Acknowledged."

As a girl on her own time a Girl in Red was as feisty and chatty as any other. While on duty, however she was a Sentinel and nothing but a Sentinel. She kept both hands on the vertical grips of her minicarbine and neither slouched nor fidgeted… until grabbed by the head and her face then *snapped* past a shoulder.

Rhonda lowered her twitching victim to the ground.

Two Sentinels were together staring into the surrounding forest… unnoticing the pair of large hands rising from behind… until struck by simultaneous chops to the neck. The sentries winced and dropped.

"Too easy," Rhonda derided her victims. She was glad there were so many of these useless clones. She hoped they would remain in mass-production.

Rhonda was bigger, faster and stronger than most humans. She had better instincts than these civilized clones. The huntress was wily and her prey witless.

An old monastery was converted into a military outpost. Rhonda scaled the wall of the largest building and dropped onto its top floor.

A Sentinel was alone guarding a corridor… when she heard squeaking. Assuming it was an animal that crept into the building, she went around a corner to investigate… only to be snatched by large hands. There was no one to hear her grunt and groan. Rhonda giggled: she was having too much fun.

Two Sentinels faced the shapeless mass of greenish brown flesh imprisoned within the upright, cylindrical vat filled with bubbling fluid. Whatever the creature was, it had what looked like closed eyes and a closed mouth. The women stared in vigilant silence… until their heads were knocked together. The two dropped. "You did not notice my reflection in the glass?" Rhonda was amused.

The "sleeping" creature opened its black, soulless eyes and its mouth clearly smirked. The eyes looked at the

47

bodies on the floor then back up at Rhonda. The mouth did not speak. "Can you hear me?" Rhonda asked the thing. It kept smirking in silence. "I will rescue you if you are innocent." The thing kept smirking, its eerie countenance making Rhonda wary. "Who are you? What are you? Why are you a prisoner of the Concubines of the Living Darkness?"

The shapeless entity grinned, its unfriendly smile showing its yellow teeth and fangs. "Release me... and I shall tell you."

Rhonda noted, "The Concubines had you sealed yet they added the precaution of having you under armed guard."

"I am their prisoner."

"Why?"

"They captured me."

"How?"

"They happened upon me."

Rhonda insisted, "I need a reason to trust you."

"Release me and you shall know." The amorphous prisoner closed its eyes and mouth.

"Are you awake?" Rhonda wondered. "Hello?" The entity was disturbing but was such because it was shapeless and mysterious? Rhonda would not release it from its confinement because that could be dangerous. She would not kill the thing either because it might be harmless. She would leave it in the care of the Concubines for better or worse.

Rhonda was making her departure... when she heard what sounded like a multitude of hurried footsteps making their way up the stairwell. She ducked around a corner only to happen upon a crowd of Sentinels. "Halt!" one of them barked. Rhonda drew a pistol and *blasted* her and several others. The crowd of Sentinels answered

Rhonda's bullets with a storm of glowing, bluish white plasma bolts.

The intruder darted around a corner, the Girls in Red in hot pursuit. Rhonda leapt over a railing into the hall below. The Sentinels stopped at the railing but kept shooting at her. A Girl in Red touched the side of her goggles-communicator and reported, "The intruder is on the ground floor and making her way into the east wing!" Sentinels poured into the east wing.

A pistol was not the weapon for contending with throngs. Rhonda unslung her submachine gun. She sprayed rounds into the crowds of Sentinels pouring into her corridor. They withered in droves but more kept coming.

Rhonda kicked in a door and took cover behind the desk in the room. She reloaded as Sentinels poured in after her. Rhonda popped up and blazed away. Women screamed and dropped. Plasma bolts *zipped* and *smacked* aimlessly. When the submachine gun went empty Rhonda drew her pistol and blasted what remained of the assailing group. She cringed as she heard more Sentinels coming. "How many of you are there?" she fretted.

Bodies in skimpy red uniforms littered the room and corridors. Throngs of the living scoured the grounds inside and out. "She exited the building through a window of the east wing," a Sentinel inside the building reported. The Girls in Red were apt trackers and those outside swiftly found the intruder's trail. "She's heading due east," a Sentinel reported. "Are we to pursue?"

"Negative. Secure the grounds."

"Acknowledged."

Concubine Scouts were the Girls in Green. They were even better trackers than the capable Girls in Red. They scoured the hills and forest for the escaped intruder. They followed her tracks only to lose the trail at a creek. "Let her go," Blair Purple commanded. "Resume your assigned patrols."

Azrella Red was the chief Sentinel of the Sixth Research Battalion. She reported, "Forty-eight dead, all of them Sentinels. No one is missing and all assets are accounted for and undamaged." Blair nodded. Azrella added, "The intruder was a human-Vexite hybrid armed with Jingoan firearms. She reached our prisoner but neither released him nor terminated him."

"Interesting," Blair was amused. "It seems our intruder was nothing but boldly curious."

"She murdered forty-eight of our sisters," Azrella fumed.

The Priestess shrugged. She reminded her Sentinel, "Our duty is to succeed, not survive."

Fransis Blue was the chief Keeper. She was a science officer and in command of research and operations. She voiced, "I don't like this Vexite hybrid lurking in our hills. Why aren't we after her?"

Blair explained, "I would rather our sentries were guarding our facilities than be out looking for an aimless nuisance."

"This hybrid is undoubtedly spawned or sired by a Jingoan," Fransis supposed. "She may be in the service of the Imperial Security Agency or an Imperial Army scout. The enemy may have sent a hybrid so as to claim plausible deniability for her actions."

Blair looked at Azrella Red and reminded her, "You are the head of our security. What do you make of our sister's concerns?"

"They are plausible."

"Are they likely?"

"Yes."

Blair Purple considered the worries of her sisters. She decided to handle the situation a way she had done before. Her plan was a proven plan but a dangerous one. Fransis was an archaeologist with only a minor in mystical physics. As the most proficient mystical physicist in her command, Blair herself was the only one qualified to operate the devices to be utilized. The danger was delightfully thrilling, however, and she would not assign the task to another even if another was available.

Rhonda Bonfire saw the top of a hill but she could not see what was upon it. She felt as if whatever she was not seeing was somehow very important. Rhonda awoke in the forest at night. She obsessed over the hilltop in her dream wondering what she was supposed to see. She would search for this hill in the morning and climb to its top.

Concubine Sentinels guarded the forested hill. These Girls in Red were easy to spot among all the green. Rhonda snuck past most of them. She snatched or pounced upon the few who were in the way along the way. Nine women were dead before Rhonda Bonfire found the mystery she was looking for.

The top of the hill was the Shrine of Silence: an altar of stone surrounded by thirteen pillars of black crystal. A Concubine Priestess was at the altar tapping the keys of the keyboard sitting upon it. A minicarbine sat next to the keyboard. The Girl in Purple looked up from her monitor and seemed not the least bit concerned to see the Vexite hybrid approaching. "You killed your way through my sisters to get here, didn't you? I'd rather you didn't but alas, sacrifices must be made."

"Who are you?"

"I am Blair Purple the Supercilious of the Thirteenth Harvest. I used this mystical array to bring you to it."

"You lured me?"

The clone smirked. "I didn't want you violating my base but I did mean for you to come to this Shrine of Silence."

"Why?"

"I'm going to use it to kill you."

"Surrender," Rhonda demanded.

The Concubine Priestess smirked. "I am not a witless Girl in Red. I am a science officer but not a cowardly Girl in Blue."

"Courage is not enough to win a fight," Rhonda warned. "You are no stronger than any other woman made from your template."

The Concubine Priestess asked, "Is your human parent Jingoan?"

"Yes."

The Virgin Soldier boasted, "I fought your human kin on this very world. I personally slaughtered fifty-four of your armed men by luring them up here. I outsmarted them. Vexites are mindless savages so you may prove my easiest kill." The human clone glared at the Vexite through those black goggles. The Girl in Purple eventually shrugged and challenged, "Well?"

Rhonda raised and aimed her pistol and demanded, "Surrender."

"Why would I do that?"

"Surrender and you shall not be harmed."

"I have a duty to perform."

"Surrender."

"No."

Rhonda squeezed the trigger—but Blair Purple vanished! The voice of the Priestess giggled as if that of an evil little girl. It echoed strangely, "Do you know what this place is? I wanted you to find me here."

The Priestess appeared behind Rhonda and raised a minicarbine. The target spun around and blazed away... but the Priestess again vanished.

Rhonda cried out, "Your trickery shall not avail you!"

"What if it does? I'll have your body on a table and its parts in jars."

The Concubine Priestess appeared and disappeared and never in the same spot twice. A different pillar lit up every time she did so. Blair shot glowing bolts at Rhonda and Rhonda shot bullets at her. The eerily resonant voice of Blair laughed. It taunted, "This is fun."

Rhonda swallowed. Her instincts warned her that the little clone had the advantage. Blair Purple was winning.

The Priestess reappeared and Rhonda again shot at her… and missed. The voice of the clone giggled.

Unlike the useless Sentinels, this Priestess was clever. Rhonda would be clever if she was to defeat this Girl in Purple. Rhonda had an idea. She ejected her magazine as if reloading. When Blair reappeared to take advantage, Rhonda slapped the magazine back into place and blazed away! The clone shuddered with every hit… and dropped.

Rhonda Bonfire enjoyed killing the armed and vigilant yet hopelessly useless Concubine Sentinels. She regretted slaying this Concubine Priestess. Though Blair was an enemy and meant to kill her, she proved a worthy opponent.

Rhonda knocked the monitor and keyboard off the altar. She then laid the body of Blair upon the altar and crossed its arms across its bosom. "I shall speak well of you, Blair Purple the Supercilious of the Thirteenth Harvest. Warriors shall know you were one of them."

Rhonda Bonfire found more than she sought but in vain. Still, she had yet another adventure to tell.

Story 2
"The Three Piddlings"

The natural humanity of Golgoth was exiled from their homeworld when their clone slaves rebelled and supplanted them. They were relocated to the colony worlds to serve as a conquered population in their own empire. Alas, the clones knew better than to expect loyalty and displaced natural Golgothites yet again when security was considered.

Quango was a desert planet on the frontier with the humanity of the Greater Humanity Empire. Fearing that the rival power would incite the disaffected Golgothites to subversion, it was decided the population should be relocated. The alien slaves would be kept on Quango but not the humans.

A *Lunk* was a hulking humanoid with broad shoulders and arms as long as its legs. The creature wore only its natural and shaggy gray fur. Its eyes were brown-within-black. Though as strong as seven men, it was gentle unless provoked. It was too stupid to ever develop an advanced civilization. The Lunks were the heavy-lifters of the slave races.

A *Piddling* was a small humanoid with a proportionately large head and big red-within-red eyes. Most breeds were brown-skinned with black hair worn in a topknot. Though a weak creature, it was nimble and its three-digit hands dexterous. It was somewhat intelligent, thus, useful for chores that required some thought. It was perfect for jobs that required numbers rather than brawn.

The *Piddlings* were a slave race only recently sold to the Golgothite Empire. Their highly prolific species was cheap to purchase in vast quantity. They were even cheaper than the cheap and easily mass-produced Many of One.

Lunks and Piddlings remained common and kept busy on the frontier worlds. The ruling Concubines of the

Great Seen had no intention of retiring these races from service. Lunks and Piddlings were made busy helping evacuate the human population on Quango.

Mozy, Plix and Bobo were Piddlings. The three whistled as they carried buckets to be delivered to a construction site. When Mozy heard sobbing, he stopped. Plix and Bobo walked into him and the three tumbled together. "Off of me, you fools!" Mozy, the leader of their trio slapped his fellows. "Take heed!"

"What heed?" Plix and Bobo asked in unison.

Mozy cupped his ears with his hands. Plix and Bobo imitated him and listened. "A child is sobbing!" Plix and Bobo realized aloud in unison.

"Yes," Mozy nodded gravely. "We must help!" The three Piddlings left their buckets as they ran off to find the sobbing child.

A little girl sat on a curb weeping. She was surprised by the shadow that fell over her. Looking up she saw three Piddlings staring down at her. "Hello," she greeted most politely. She was taught to always be polite.

"Hello!" the three smiled and waved together.

"We have come," Mozy told the girl.

"To the rescue," added Plix.

"Because we heard you crying," finished Bobo.

Mozy wondered, "Why are you sobbing?"

Bobo asked, "Who are you that we may know who you are?"

Mozy scolded, "You fool! We must tell before we ask!"

"Tell her what?"

"Our names!"

"But we already know our names."

Mozy bopped Bobo on the head before telling the little girl, "My friend who asked without telling is Bobo. He is Plix. I am Mozy."

The child answered the little Piddlings, "My name is Elzbeth Elsis Laurel."

The three Piddlings repeated in unison, "Elzbeth Elsis Laurel."

Bobo remarked, "You have such a big name for such a little creature."

Plix piped, "She is not so small. We are not much bigger."

Bobo argued, "But she is small though humans are big. We are common among our normalcy."

"You are fools!" Mozy accused. "Have we not come to deliver Elzbeth Elsis Laurel from her despair?"

"Yes!" Plix and Bobo cried with fervor.

"Let us help her then." Mozy told the girl, "Elzbeth Elsis Laurel, we are here to serve."

Bobo told her, "Elzbeth Elsis Laurel, we are here to help."

Plix asked, "Elzbeth Elsis Laurel, why are you so sad?"

"I dropped Polly when we were riding away."

Bobo was aghast, "You dropped Polly?! Not Polly!"

Plix hoped, "Is Polly all right?"

Mozy bopped Plix on the head and reminded him, "Elzbeth Elsis Laurel was sobbing! Would she sob if Polly was all right? You fool!"

"Polly is my dolly," Rachel explained. "I want her back but my mommy said I can't go back and get her."

Bobo asked, "Where is Polly?" When Rachel pointed the three looked as one.

Mozy swore, "Elzbeth Elsis Laurel, await our return for we shall return with Polly!"

Bobo added, "And Polly will be with us." Plix nodded. The three Piddlings ran in the direction the child had pointed.

A Concubine Sentinel stepped out in front of the three Piddlings. "What's the hurry?" she asked them.

Plix answered, "We must rescue Polly!"

Bobo added, "Elzbeth Elsis Laurel was weeping because she lost her Polly. She will smile when we return Polly to her."

Mozy told the Sentinel, "Call the other Sentinels and help us search."

The Sentinel wondered, "Who or what is this Polly? Who is this Elzbeth Elsis Laurel and why is she weeping?"

Plix and Bobo rolled their eyes. Mozy scolded the Sentinel, "We told you everything yet you ask us to tell you again? You fool! What is your name and who is your commanding Priestess?"

The Sentinel touched the side of her goggle-communicator. She called, "This is Melissa Red reporting, over." She waited but a moment before reporting, "Three Piddlings are in a hurry to find 'Polly' and return her to an 'Elzbeth Elsis Laurel.' I don't know and they just ramble when I ask them to explain."

The three Piddlings huddled. They whispered amongst themselves. "What are you doing?" Melissa Red questioned.

"Ready?" Mozy asked his fellows. "Ready," Plix answered. "Ready!" Bobo responded. The three slapped each other's backs before breaking their huddle. They grinned up at the Sentinel.

"You three are rather odd, even for Piddlings."

Mozy told the Sentinel, "We have something to show you."

Plix assured, "It will be fun."

Bobo added, "It will be surprising."

The wary Sentinel questioned, "Fun and surprising?"

The three Piddlings stated in unison, "It will be a fun surprise."

"What is it?"

Plix waved a finger and shook his head. Bobo did a little dance for whatever reason. Mozy told the Sentinel, "We must show you."

"Yes, you will. Show me."

Mozy turned and waved then Plix turned and waved then Bobo turned and waved for the Sentinel to follow.

The Piddlings led the armed woman into a shed. She looked about but saw only what one expected to see in a shed. She asked, "What are you trying to show me?" The door closed and she heard it latch.

"Surprise!" three Piddling voices cheered. Plix muttered, "That was fun."

The Piddlings ran off, ignoring the shouts and banging on the door.

"Attention, all personnel," the voice that was the voice of every Concubine of the Great Seen Unseen hailed via goggles-communicator, "Three naughty Piddlings are roaming in your sector. Hold them but do *not* harm them. Report when they are in your custody." Concubine Keepers were the Girls in Blue, the scientists, technicians, engineers and medical personnel of the Virgin Army. They resumed their tasks mindful to catch the Piddlings should they happen upon them. Concubine Sentinels, the Girls in Red, are too severe to allow unauthorized personnel to roam the grounds. They began a thorough search.

"Halt!" Mozy, Plix and Bobo were spotted. The three Piddlings fled, Bobo running in a confused circle before following after his friends. The Sentinels chased the naughty slaves into a building. "Search the rooms," a Girl in Red told the others.

A Sentinel heard whistling as she entered a lavatory. No one was at the urinals. She looked under the stalls and spotted three pairs of Piddling feet. The one foot was tapping to the tune of the whistling. The Sentinel touched the side of her goggles-communicator and reported, "This is Sharlene Red. I found the three Piddlings."

The Sentinel was armed but did not raise her weapon. Though ordered not to harm the Piddlings she would not unless actually ordered to do so; they were such silly and harmless creatures. Sharlene barked, "Step out of the stalls!"

"May we finish?" the voice of Mozy asked.

"Yes, let us finish!" Plix blurted.

Bobo warned, "We would be messy not to finish."

The three resumed whistling. The one foot kept tapping. Sharlene sighed. She tapped her goggles and a chronometer lit up within. She watched the time as she waited.

A pair of feet lifted out of view. The feet did not return to the floor. Sharlene peeked under. As she crouched to do so, Mozy climbed over into the next stall.

The next pair of feet lifted out of view. Sharlene looked under this stall and it too was now vacated.

The Sentinel was startled by the *flush* in the third stall. Two Piddlings dropped onto her back and she flattened to the floor. The third stall opened and its feet ran out. Sharlene could hear the three Piddlings scurrying out of the chamber.

Mozy, Plix and Bobo hurried out of the building. They scaled a fence and dropped to the other side. They hid and watched as the Sentinels came out looking for them.

"Mozy," Bobo whispered.

"Shhh," Mozy implored without turning to face Bobo.

"Mozy," Plix whispered.

"Shhh!" Mozy turned for emphasis. He found his friends pointing... at a doll lying on the ground. "Polly!" the three Piddlings cheered together.

A Sentinel glimpsed the three Piddlings dart out of hiding and snatch up a doll that was lying on the ground.

Elzbeth Elsis Laurel remained seated where she sat for it would be rude to leave when she knew her friends were soon to return. Rachel did so hope the friendly little Piddlings could find Polly. The girl smiled and clapped as the three returned, Mozy holding Polly as if cradling a babe in his arms. "Polly!" Rachel smiled.

"Polly," Mozy handed the doll to the little girl.

"Polly!" Plix and Bobo echoed in unison.

"Thank you, thank you, *thank* you for finding her!" Rachel told each of the three. The Piddlings smiled as the child snuggled and kissed her dolly.

A shadow fell over the three Piddlings. They turned and were startled to see a squad of Concubine Sentinels looming over them! "Uh, hello," Bobo tittered.

The one Sentinel asked the Piddlings, "Is this what all your mischief was about?" The three nodded together. The Sentinel sighed. She touched the side of her goggles-communicator and hailed, "This is Ursula Red, reporting, over." There was a pause before Ursula Red reported, "We found the Piddlings. They were looking for a little girl's lost doll." Elzbeth Elsis Laurel was cringing as the Sentinels loomed over her and her friends. She feigned a smile. Ursula resumed her report, "They found it and returned it to her. I believe they are eager to resume their assigned duties." The three Piddlings nodded. The Sentinel smiled. The Piddlings cringed. She told them, "Get back to whatever you were supposed to be doing… and stay out of trouble."

The Piddlings answered in unison, "Yes, ma'am!"

Ursula Red waved her arm and led the other Sentinels back to their sector. Bobo was surprised, "They do smile, the ones in red."

Plix remarked, "Her smile scared me."

"You fool!" Mozy scolded Plix. "She smiled because we did her job for her."

Bobo agreed with Plix, "Seeing a Sentinel smile did scare me too."

"Yes," Mozy actually agreed with his friends. "The smile of the scowling ones is scary."

Elzbeth Elsis Laurel was happy. Ursula Red the smiling Sentinel was happy. Mozy, Plix and Bobo were happy. The three Piddlings whistled as they went back to work.

Story 3
"Ships of Wood or Steel"

The Greater Humanity Empire was the youngest of the Galactic Powers. It was the first to discover the planet Bosky. Though the empire laid claim to the world, the Mystic Confederacy, the Democratic Plutocracy of Lith and the Concubines of the Great Seen Unseen hurried to lay claims to whatever regions they could snatch. The Bosky Wars began.

The Imperial Navy roamed the seas of this verdant world. Submarines launched cruise missiles armed with enervators and aircraft launched from carriers bombarded enemy positions.

The Delvers were a race indigenous to a world dry and barren. Their conquests were dry worlds or covered in snow and ice. There was no Delver navy. Though the Delvers had dirigibles, these were unsuitable for combat so they had no air force.

The Imperial Humanity Ship *Unity* was an aircraft carrier on the prowl. Its airpower hammered the strongly shielded and heavily armored Delver fortresses that held the Isle of Green. "They're digging in and assembling shield arrays," Capt. Douglas told his officers. "We need to take those babies out before they're operational." He gestured at points on a holographic map of the island as he explained, "Submarines are already firing on them but it'll take precision strikes from above to take these sites out."

"Sir," the female operations officer addressed the captain. "A Mystic fleet was glimpsed circling the Cape of Confusion and seems to be heading straight towards our group. The ships did cloak."

The Confederate Navy was wooden sailing ships. Not only were the vessels tiny, slow and fragile compared to the steel warships of the Imperial Navy, but when detected, they could be destroyed without so much as a fight. Unfortunately, the ships could "hide in plain sight" from both eyes and sensors. Divination allowed the Mystics to maneuver their fleets on intercept courses. The aliens would open portals and board human ships. Confederate marines would slay crewman with curved daggers and make their way to sensitive areas to plant enervators. These magically advanced but technologically primitive aliens had rendered frigates and destroyers dead in the water before. Submarines had gone missing only to be found enervated from within.

Commander Zhirik assured, "The Mystics and Delvers are not allies."

"The enemy of my enemy is my friend," the captain quoted an ancient proverb. He reminded his officers, "We're already fighting the Mystics on the other side of this world. Helping the Delvers helps them too. Be ready."

"Yes, sir."

A crystalline orb with a glowing blue core was in the bowels of a Confederate warship. A lens above focused sunlight into the device to keep it powered. The orb was called a "cloaking device" by the Jingoans. To the Mystics it was an "orb of concealment" and the most expensive part of a warship.

A squadron of sixteen vessels was sailing on an intercept course with an Imperial carrier group. The I.H.S. *Unity* was to be boarded by two hundred fifty-six marines and enervators carefully placed and activated within. The marines were to make haste both in their quest and in their escape lest they be overwhelmed by the enemy crew of thousands.

A Mystic is slender but lithe and head and shoulders taller than most humans; bigger, faster and stronger. Every Mystic was a magician and their every warrior skilled in either hiding in plain sight or in channeling one's aura into an invisible cone pointed out to deflect ranged attacks.

A Confederate marine wore black boots and blue trousers. A black sash was worn around the waist, the ends of which dangled from the right hip. His weapon was a curved dagger. A wizard held a slender wand in his right hand and a straight dagger in his left. A priest's blade was also straight but his wand was a gnarly rod.

The marines were topside as their sailing ships neared the giants looming on the horizon. "Success is unlikely," a captain told her marines. "Do what you do quickly or do not bother."

A marine reminded, "We fulfilled our task on a ship below the water. We may jump from this one at least."

"Not to avail," the captain warned. "The height of your jump would be to your death. Should you somehow survive hitting the water, the mighty propellers would pull you in and grind you."

The crew and marines were mindful not to stare at the enemy frigates and destroyer as they neared and passed them for staring could dispel the concealing glamor.

Portals cannot be opened near reactors due to interference. They cannot be opened within an enemy's spatial dominance lest opened from within. The bridge was within the eye of the Unity's shield umbrella. The Confederate marines would board where they could as close to their objectives as they dared. They would enter at different points so that if one party was blocked another may reach a target.

Mystics are taller than what was meant for the low and narrow corridors of a human vessel. Mystics are limber, however, and even stooped prove swift and nimble. The boarding parties tiptoed past busy sailors or hid from them as they passed. Those in the way or who happened upon them were snatched and quietly silenced.

Imperial Marines guarded the engine rooms and main reactor. One of the men glimpsed a form looming over him and *blasted* it with his shotgun. The hapless

Mystic bled blue as he was knocked to the floor. A fellow behind the human cut the human's throat and it bled red.

Shouts were followed by the blasts of shotguns and the deep and loud tapping of rapid fire. An alarm sounded. The daggers of Confederate marines met the firearms of Imperial Marines in close quarters. "More are coming," a Mystic warned his officer, "too many more."

The boarding parties hurriedly planted their devices: a crystal orb with a yellow core. The core would glow when activated but enervation negated talismans and inhibited spells: there would be a delay before the devices activated. The Mystics made their escape. Their devices illuminated and lights throughout the enemy ship went out. Everything electrical within the effect went out. The intruders could not breach where they were tasked to go, however, thus the targeted systems were unaffected.

Two sailing ships were spotted and obliterated. The others were sought but escaped detection.

"We've cleared the ship," Cmdr. Zhirik reported to Capt. Douglas.

"Don't be so sure about that," the skipper warned. "Even one of those bastards can wreak havoc."

A Confederate marine was stranded aboard after failing to reach his portal of escape. He hid but was happened upon by sailors and chased by Marines. When cornered and demanded to surrender, he brandished his dagger and lunged. A barrage of gunfire torn him open and sent him sprawling to the floor.

Part 3

BATTLE OF THE SIX ARMIES

Chapter 1
"Concubines and Phantoms"

Crux was a world so barren its native population was less than a million human beings. It was poor in all but the most common resources. Save that the planet was directly linked to every realm, it would be deemed worthless. Alas, its one merit made it the most prized world in the galaxy.

The *Concubines of the Great Seen Unseen* were an empire of women made in the likeness of one woman and endowed with her formative memories. Their *Virgin Army* was a vast force of light infantry wielding plasma weapons and supplemented by bug-like aircraft and two-legged fighting vehicles.

The *People of the Third Eye* were an androgynous race of partially material entities: the *Phantoms*. Their warriors were stealthy, fierce and masters of sensory manipulation. Their weapon was a sword with a broad, curved blade, a long counter-curving grip and a heavy pommel. A warrior could leap by stretching ahead of itself and bring the blade or pommel to bear with tremendous force.

The Concubines were clones of a human female and the Phantoms a terrible race of sexless, inhuman specters. They had only three things in common: they were Galactic Powers, they prized loyalty above all else and they worshiped the Living Darkness.

The Concubines were an empire disinterested in war if conflict could be avoided. The Phantoms were a warlike species too restless to find comfort in peace. The

Concubines were obedient in their loyalties whereas the Phantoms were impulsive and dangerously passionate in their devotion. To the Concubines the *Living Darkness* was the *Great Seen Unseen*, a loving father whose wisdom was beyond all mortal ken. To the Phantoms the Living Darkness was the *Great Shadow*, a mighty spirit of will and passion beyond the thoughts and feelings of every mortal creature.

As Galactic Powers the Concubines of the Great Seen Unseen and the People of the Third Eye were staunch allies. Not only did they serve a common cause but they accepted and loved each other. The Concubines found the passionate sincerity of the Phantoms endearing. The People of the Third Eye admired the clones for being selfless.

The Virgin Army and the warriors of the Third Eye invaded Crux as a joint expedition. Concubine airpower would pummel distant positions and hardened targets. The Phantoms would raid and ambush relentlessly and on a grand scale. The vast numbers of Virgin Soldiers held territory and waged fixed battles.

The Hive, the Mystic Confederacy, the Democratic Plutocracy of Lith and the Greater Humanity Empire were the rival powers. All of them laid claim to Crux. All of them had forces and colonies on the planet already. They reinforced their positions and took opportunities. They provoked each other by snatching territory. "We must avoid uniting them against us," General Ilea Purple the Astute warned. She was in command of the Concubine forces on Crux.

Wisely-Adamant, the commanding general of the Phantom warriors, chafed at the idea of not pressing an advantage. "Yes," it reluctantly conceded to wisdom.

Ilea asked, "May I assure the Delvers in your name that your forces shall not enter their claimed territory?"

Though the Phantom seethed at the idea, it trusted Ilea the Astute. "Yes. Your promise shall be my own."

A general of the Virgin Army wore the purple one-piece of a military Priestess but without the elastic hood and black goggles. A short, white cloak with a hood denoted her rank.

The Concubines of the Seen Unseen were human females but bald and their irises faded ghostly white. The women were sensitive about their unnatural look and preferred their heads and eyes covered when in the presence of outsiders. Ilea's hood was pulled back and her eyes and head exposed as a gesture of trust. The gesture was not lost on the Phantom, nor unappreciated.

The generals were in the command-and-control room of a Virgin Army command station. Girls in Blue were busy at consoles or otherwise handling operations. A holographic globe of Crux was in the middle of the room and marked with updating indicators of troop positions and movements. "The Jingoans are the biggest threat," Ilea told Wisely-Adamant, "not only to us but to the others. Let us focus our efforts on dislodging them from the planet."

The Phantom discerned, "The others will let us be as we rid them of but one rival."

"Yes."

Ilea pointed at the globe and suggested, "Sneak your legions into Region 13 while we harry Region 6 with airstrikes. My legions will invade 6 suddenly and relentlessly. When I give you the word, take 13."

Wisely-Adamant disapproved, "Troops may be pulled from Region 13 to reinforce Region 6."

"Yes, that is the idea."

"Your women will do most of the fighting."

"Yes."

The Phantom voiced, "My warriors shall not be shamed letting others do the fighting."

Ilea explained, hoping the logic was explanation enough, "We have the numbers. We'll absorb the enemy's firepower so you can fight them warrior-to-warrior." The Phantom was agreeable with the idea that its people would be allowed to meet the enemy at close quarters.

Portals opened midair and swarms of dragonfly-type bombers flew through. The aircraft shot glowing yellow enervation missiles at shielded targets then showered caseless rockets or dropped loads of bombs.

Portals opened throughout the north of Region 6. Concubine Scouts followed by columns of bipedal main battle tanks followed by throngs of Girls in Red stormed positions. The war machines erupted into fiery chunks and the waves of foot soldiers withered as the cannons, rockets and machineguns of the Imperial Army slaughtered them. Alas, the Virgin Army kept coming: The Many of One proved many indeed.

Locust-type entomopters led beetle-types loaded with Girls in Green and Girls in Red on air assaults behind the lines.

"Region 6" was called "Drytopia" by the Jingoans but regardless of its names, it was being overrun. Jingoan troops were being called in from other regions in a desperate hope to hold the line.

Rocky Nowhere (Region 13) hurried every man and woman it could spare to bolster Drytopia's defenses. Its airpower was out on sorties over the beleaguered region... as the warriors of the Third Eye moved into position all across Rocky Nowhere.

Phantoms do not become "invisible" per se. They hide in plain sight. Material senses, whether natural or artificial, are sensitive to effect rather than cause. The effect is interpreted and the cause discerned. To corrupt the effect is to render it indiscernible. To do so subtly is to allow or manipulate misinterpretation.

The Phantoms were masters of sensory manipulation. The "sniffers" and motion sensors detected "animals" and "wind" as throngs of spectral warriors crossed their threshold. Imperial snipers watched as "dust clouds" blew through the valleys. Sentries felt uneasy but dismissed the unease as "nerves" because of all the troubling news and rumors. Dogs smelled "wet grass" and were too stupid to note that all was dry and barren here.

Magic cannot match the firepower of technology but is more than a match in its power to negate by antithesis. Swords are useless against wheeled or tracked fighting vehicles but such machines are useless without electrical power. Phantoms assembled crystalline devices and warlocks readied to activate them. Swordsmen moved into position and waited for the signal to assail.

An inhuman *shriek* made every man, woman and animal jump and cringe. Heads were suddenly lobbed off or smashed. The screams and shouts of men and women were followed by sporadic gunfire. A helicopter overhead lost power and crashed.

Corporal James Redriver was an Imperial Ranger. He chafed at being left out of the action in Drytopia. He seethed in righteous indignation as his skills were wasted on roaming patrols in the desolate hills of Rocky Nowhere... until action came his way.

James was riding point on his four-wheeler when his engine suddenly died. The jeeps behind him slowed to a stop. "Enervation!" a voice warned. "Take cover!" The nine Rangers jumped from their vehicles and took cover behind rocks.

James activated the bio-scanner fixed to his assault rifle. The vehicles had been hit by a directed enervation pulse and his inert device was unaffected. He calibrated the sensor to focus on detecting Phantom signatures. He swept the area with a quick scan. "Phantoms?" Lieutenant Smith supposed.

"Yes, sir: Six ahead on the high ground and seven to the rear, also on the high ground. They are holding their positions."

"Keeping us pinned," the lieutenant realized. He worried aloud, "More are coming."

James warned, "Sir, we'll be overrun before we get our vehicles running."

"Yeah, I know." Smith barked, "Everybody grab your gear!"

The squad of Rangers loaded themselves with everything they could carry and ventured into a gorge. They climbed a hillside and secured a position on a rocky ridge.

Lieutenant Smith hailed the base only to learn, "Fort Benjamin is being overrun." He told his troops, "Every base and outpost in the region is under attack."

Corporal Gallagher asked, "Sir, shouldn't we hurry back to Benjamin and join the fight?"

"Negative. They're trying to evacuate. We're to make our way Rocky Alpha."

"Rocky Alpha?!"

Staff Sergeant Liukin mentioned, "Alpha's a hundred clicks due east."

"A hundred and twenty," James corrected, "and on foot."

Gallagher whined, "Every Phantom between here and Alpha is going to pounce on us!"

James smirked, "No, we'll be dead by then." The lieutenant glared at Redriver. The Corporal added, "Unless we keep our cool and stick together." James told Smith, "Sir, we'd getter get moving before we're surrounded."

"Roger that."

The nine Rangers made their way up and down the hills, avoiding any path that could bring them into an ambush. James would scan areas to make sure no hostiles were lying in wait. Gallagher wondered, "What's the range on that thing?"

James answered, "It depends on the settings."

"What do you have it set at?"

"Narrow beam at a thousand meters."

"A full click."

"Yeah: I'd rather see them coming before they're on us."

"No shit."

James detected a party of Phantoms and the Rangers hid. They waited as the enemy crossed their path and moved on. "They're not looking for us," James believed.

Lieutenant Smith asked, "Why do you think that?"

"They're heading due east in tight formation."

"Towards Alpha."

"Yes, sir."

"Let's hope Alpha isn't surrounded or overrun by the time we get to it."

The next two days were uneventful. The Rangers were running out of food and water but hoped a stop at a nearby outpost would replenish their stock. "Do Phantoms eat our food?" Gallagher wondered.

"No," Smith assured.

"What if the outpost is overrun?"

"Then we'll find a lot of bodies that won't be using the food they have stored up."

"Sir, what about the Phantoms?"

"They stay on the move. Once they massacre an outpost they move on."

"Lucky us."

"Not really."

Nights were cold on Crux but not unbearable. Not all the Rangers had coats but a simple blanket wrapped around the shoulders was enough to stay warm. James sat on watch while his buddies slept. His skin crawled and not because of the chill in the air. He activated his bio-scanner and did a sweeping scan. "Oh, crap." James quietly woke Smith and told him, "Incoming hostiles. We're surrounded and they are converging on our location." The two quietly woke everyone else and everyone readied their weapons. "You'll see them," James told his fellows. "We know they're coming so they can't hide in plain sight… easily."

"Easily?" Gallagher worried at the foreboding hint.

"If you glimpse a form, shoot it."

Gallagher noticed what looked like a shadowy silhouette. He squinted… and cringed at the glint of a swiping blade! Gallagher's head popped off its neck with a spray of blood.

Shadows were everywhere! Trios of yellow light glowed in the darkness. The Rangers blazed away, their bullets tearing into the converging forms! Inhuman *shrieks* filled the night and forms collapsed into yellowish white goo. The shadows became yellowish white "ghosts" brandishing swords with broad, curved blades and large, round pommels. The specters washed over the men like a wave, lobbing off heads or smashing skulls as they passed.

The Phantoms disappeared into the night as suddenly as they appeared, leaving dead humans in their wake.

The People of the Third Eye have no use for human technology. They leave it to rot when they have slaughtered the men and women who use it. James awoke to the gentle light of dawn. His head ached. He swooned when he sat up. Apparently he received a glancing blow to the head by a nasty pommel. He still had his weapons and bio-scanner. His friends were dead: their heads smashed or cut clean off. James Redriver sobbed.

It was noon before the sole survivor left his fallen comrades. He would have buried them but he did not have the heart to touch the severed heads. He did take all the food and water he could carry.

Outpost RN-C-1138 was called "Happyville" by its garrison. The troops even posted a sign with a smiley face reading "Welcome to Happyville, the loneliest place on Crux." The garrison was massacred. There was the dried goo and dropped swords of Phantoms so James knew the outpost did not fall without a fight. Sadly, he counted three swords but saw *scores* of human bodies.

The jeeps, trucks and armored personnel carriers still worked. The eight-wheeled reconnaissance vehicle may have been operational but James did not bother to check: all he needed was a ride that could get him as far away as possible. He chose a jeep, fueled it then went about looking for supplies to load into it.

James scoured the buildings. When he opened a door to a storage room he glimpsed the rising muzzle of a rifle. He dove aside just before a stream of rapid fire tore into him! "Whoa!" he shouted. "Stand down! I'm a friendly! Damn it, I'm human!" He heard sobbing and it sounded female. "I'm human!" he assured. "Don't shoot!" The female just continued to sob. James waited.

The female voice eventually uttered, "Sorry. Don't leave."

"I'm not going anywhere."

"Can I have a moment?"

"Sure."

"Thank you." James grinned.

The female was a science officer and the name on her uniform was "Madulin." She told James, "I'm a xenologist."

"An alien expert."

She choked, "I've been to Mystique and Lith. I don't know anything about these... Phantoms? What are they?" She sobbed, "They come out of nowhere! They...

they glare at you with three eyes! Are they eyes? They glow but are so dark." Madulin was having a panic attack when she reminisced, "They *shriek* and you can feel it! You see things. You hear things. Everybody was screaming!"

"It's all right," James assured in as gentle a voice as he could utter. He told the woman, to give her courage, "They can't kill me: they've tried."

Lieutenant Madulin stared up at James. He grinned. She seemed confused. Corporal Redriver told Lieutenant Madulin, "Ma'am, you've been emotionally compromised so I'm going to assume command for a while."

"Okay," Madulin mumbled.

"I'm going to load up a jeep and then we leave, both of us. You'll be safe with me." Madulin nodded.

James loaded the jeep with food, water, weapons and ammunition. He squeezed in blankets and pillows. When he went to get Lt. Madulin, he found her sitting on the floor with her legs folded, her hands pressed together and her eyes closed. Afraid that disturbing her may agitate her mania, he left her to her meditation. He scrounged up a lunch and ate while he waited.

"Cpl. Redriver," the voice of Lt. Madulin addressed. Her demeanor was now collected and her voice calm.

James looked up at the science officer, looking for any hint that she was still crazy. "Ma'am?" he eventually acknowledged her address.

"I shall be resuming command." Cpl. Redriver grinned. Lt. Madulin explained, "I am no longer 'emotionally compromised' so you have nothing to worry about."

"Really? Sitting on the floor for an hour is that therapeutic?"

"It is using a Mystic technique."

James discounted, "Alien mumbo jumbo is the cure for traumatic stress."

"Flow and balance: Our emotions are flow and our thoughts balance. When thoughts are imbalanced it is by feeling channeling into them. Diverting thoughts into the stream restores balance."

"It's that easy?"

"No: that's why I was meditating using the medically proven technique."

"Ma'am, with all due respect, I don't trust you quite yet. Give me a while and if you're good, I'll follow your orders."

"Fair enough. What's your plan?"

"Head to Alpha."

"Alpha is being overrun."

"Is it actually overrun?"

"We lost contact."

James shrugged. He considered, "There's a mining town about fifty clicks to the southwest."

"Calico."

"Yes, ma'am."

The lieutenant surmised, "Even if the town was massacred, we should find more fuel to keep moving on."

"That's the idea."

Madulin nodded. She told James, "We do it your way."

"Yes, ma'am."

Madulin drove while James did scans. The road was dirt and bumpy and the terrain rugged hills. As the jeep neared a rounded corner the bio-scanner lit with signals. "Pull over and kill the engine," James pointed at a spot behind boulders.

The lieutenant did as she was advised. She asked, "An enervator emplacement?"

"Probably: I'm picking up thirteen Phantom signatures and one of them is probably a warlock."

"Thirteen? I watched *one* slaughter an entire squad!"

"Thirteen; probably more but the terrain is getting in the way of my scanning."

Madulin advised, "Let's play this smart."

"Yes, ma'am. Hold this position and I'll take out the emplacement."

"Just you?"

James grinned, "I have the element of surprise." The man's beaming confidence made the woman wonder if *he* was the one who went mad.

A crystal ball sat upon a tripod of crystal. Three crystalline orbs were glowing in orbit of the greater crystal. "Primed and ready," James realized. A warlock's magic was what powered a Phantom enervator. Its thoughts and whispers operated the device.

The People of the Third Eye were barely solid and barely humanoid. Their color was usually yellowish white but changed when their passions tempered. The warlock was bluish in concentration while his dozen swordsmen were glaring yellow in aggressive anticipation.

The Phantoms were hiding "in plain sight" and would normally be "invisible" but James knew to look for them. He aimed at the warlock.

One shot rang out. The warlock's head splattered and its glowing three eyes flashed then went out. The creature's form collapsed into a puddle of goo.

The swordsmen *shrieked* in surprise and rage! They spotted the human and their ghostly forms shot towards him in blind fury! A grenade *blasted* several of them. A stream of fully automatic fire finished others… but the few remaining kept coming.

Alexandra Madulin waited in dreadful anticipation as she heard the shrieks and shooting. When all became silent, she worried.

James waved before coming into view. He ran back, telling the lieutenant, "A warlock doesn't venture out with only a dozen swordsmen. We need to leave before the others get here."

As the jeep rounded the corner James implored, "Stop!"

Madulin stopped. She was surprised when Redriver jumped out and disassembled the enervator. She assumed he was disabling it to protect any other humans coming down the road but he loaded the parts into the jeep. "What are you doing?!" she demanded to know.

"These things work against magic too. We can use it."

"They need a warlock to operate."

James corrected, "Or a human with cables and spare car batteries."

"You said we need to hurry."

"I am hurrying!" James jumped back into his seat. Madulin just stared at him. The man barked, "Let's go!" The jeep sped off.

The Virgin Army controlled the northern third of Region 6 and was mopping up pockets of resistance. The Jingoans were falling back and undoubtedly preparing for a counterattack.

General Wisely-Adamant told General Ilea, "Region 13 shall soon be ours. The enemy is dead or fleeing. We hunt them down as they flee."

"Good," the Virgin Soldier approved. The Concubines of the Great Seen Unseen did not relish the idea of massacres but success was by any means necessary.

Chapter 2
"Wrath of the Queen Mother"

The Hive was a united Great Race and a Galactic Power. Its people were purplish gray and hairless. The form of their kind was a supple torso atop four spindly legs. A hand of three digits was on the end of each of the two arms. The head of the creature was long and narrow and came to a rounded point. Its ears looked somewhat like fish gills. Its face was humanlike but its eyes were vertical black slits within purple irises within purplish white.

Most Hivers were "wenches" as tall and heavy as the average human. The "ladies" were a head and shoulders taller and proportionately heavier. Males were rare but bigger and much stronger.

The Hive was an oviparous species. The Queen was the mother of all but the oldest of her kind. She was the absolute ruler of the race and its realm.

The Concubines of the Great Seen Unseen were an empire of selfless and diligent females: the Queen of the Hive considered them the alien culture most like her own. She was fond of their cheerful manners and flattering curiosity. She deemed them trustworthy. Alas, the Concubines were in league with the Phantoms. The Queen of the Hive was unoffended by war for such was the way that united her race. She hated the Phantoms, however, for they massacred her children wherever they invaded.

Portals opened along the eastern frontier of what the Concubines called Region One. A Hive army poured through: droves of "swarmers" commanded by "ladies" accompanied by heavily armed and armored males. Six-legged beasts, hairless creatures with hides of purple and gray, each had a gyroscope strapped to its back. A wench sat on the neck of such a creature and drove it. A wench sat behind her and operated the gyroscope.

Portals opened midair beyond the horizon. Swarms of dragonfly-type bombers flew through towards the invading forces. Hive gyroscopes started to spin within themselves and colorful crystals set within started to glow. Bolts of lightning connected between some of the gyroscopes and targeted aircraft. Struck bombers burst into flames and exploded. Barely visible distortions were shot by other gyroscopes and the targets lost power and plummeted from the sky.

Bombers shot glowing yellowish missiles with yellow tails. The caseless warheads detonated upon hitting invisible shield barriers. The unseen umbrellas became visible as sparks as they weakened or broke. Streams of white rockets and free-falling bombs that flashed midair fell through gaps or punched through weakened barriers and *blasted* droves of Hivers with explosions of ionized gas. Struck beasts burst into gory and burning chunks.

Portals opened along the horizon as the Virgin Army sent its ground forces into the fray.

General Ilea was with her lieutenant generals standing around a holographic map of Region One. The Phantom General Wisely-Adamant joined them uninvited. "You do not call us to help?" the resonant, androgynous whisper of its race asked the clone women.

Ilea answered, "We need your warriors in Region 13."

The Phantom studied the map. It noted, "Your women are outnumbered."

"Not for long. We're diverting forty legions from the operation to reinforce our defense."

Wisely-Adamant insisted, "You cannot press the offensive in Region 6 without those legions."

"We're securing our positions."

A Phantom's mood was barely discernable in its countenance but one could *feel* it by the stare of those three eyes. Wisely-Adamant was irked but unoffended. It told Ilea, "You say 'secure' with the chill of desperation in your voice."

Ilea confided, "Your ferocity gives you an edge tactically but can be a liability strategically. I'm worried you'll scatter your forces in reactive vengeance."

"Yes," the Phantom seemed to smile. "We are too quick to anger. We value your calm for it tempers us. My warriors shall finish the fight in Region 13 with no thought of elsewhere."

"Thank you."

The stubby cannons of bipedal main battle tanks *blasted* the assailing Hive throngs with sprays of ionized particles. Concentrated bolts punched into Hive war beasts and the creatures erupted into purple gore and grayish bone fragments. Tank commanders manned stormguns and raked the swarms with streams of rapidly fired plasma bolts.

Bolts of lightning connected between gyroscopes and the Virgin Army's mechanical monsters. Though the armor was nonconductive titanium alloy, the unnatural bolts were but a symptom of two points joining. The war machines broke open and erupted into bluish flames and toppled.

Concubine Scouts (the Girls in Green) kept to the cover of rocks and burning vehicles and took potshots with their sharpshooter carbines. The waves of Concubine Sentinels (the Girls in Red) were the cannon-fodder and charged headlong.

Plasma weapons were the small arms of the Virgin Army. The weapons shot glowing bolts of ionized gas that punched and burned into a victim.

Disruptors were the small arms of the Hive Army. The weapons shot bolts of barely visible distortions that stung a victim to death without inflicting wounds.

Hive swarmers were blasted by the volleys of plasma bolts. The onrushing Sentinels winced and dropped when struck by the volleys of disruption bolts. The foot soldiers of the largest armies in the galaxy were expending their vast numbers in what became a grueling battle of attrition.

"We're exhausting our forces on this unexpected front," the Virgin Soldier Lieutenant General Alessa told General Ilea. "We need to fall back and wait for the enemy to meet us in the hills."

"They won't follow us into the hills," Lieutenant General Barbara disagreed. "The regional vortex point is to the northeast."

Ilea stared at the map. She listened to her subordinates in silence and considered their arguments. She eventually decided, "Focus our airstrikes on the enemy center. Punch our ground forces through. They'll secure a position to the enemy rear and establish spatial dominance."

Alessa warned, "The Hive will turn on the forces to their rear and storm their position with reinforcements from Region 2."

Barbara disagreed, "Not necessarily. The enemy can't be cut off if they take the regional vortex point."

Ilea reminded, "We can only guess the enemy's intentions. Let's put them to the test and respond accordingly." The lieutenant generals nodded. Though they remained steadfast in their personal views, the Many of One were always quick to think as one when a superior made her decision.

Swarms of dragonfly-type bombers hammered the Hive center with heavy ordnance. The targets were shielded with kinetic barriers but the enervation and relentless pummeling made gaps. Droves of Hive troops and their war beasts were *blasted* or incinerated.

Locust-type attack entomopters led a swarm of beetle-type entomopters to a mining town that was under enemy occupation. Most of the inhabitants were reportedly still alive, undoubtedly kept to provide slave labor. Now that the Virgin Army was retaking the territory, the enemy was massacring the population.

The locust-types showered positions with caseless rockets. They fired streams of plasma bolts from their chin-mounted stormguns. An aircraft lost power and crashed: the victim of an enemy gyroscope placed atop a building. The victim was avenged by a caseless rocket that streaked towards the device and *blasted* it and its crew into mangled and smoldering bits.

The beetle-types touched down; Girls in Green and droves of Girls in Red hurrying down the tail-ramps. A few had to jump as the aircraft shot back into the air.

Hive strafing gun emplacements mowed the arriving throngs down. Concubine Scouts made headshots with their sharpshooter carbines, silencing as many of the guns as they could.

The fight became a building-to-building struggle as the Virgin Soldiers poured into the town of modular, prefabricated structures.

Saundra Green the Wily was a Concubine Scout. Her weapon was the Carbine Type 11 equipped with a short, telescopic sight. She was perched on a rooftop picking off Hive troops when the voice of a sister hailed, "Saundra Green, is the avenue clear?"

The addressed touched the side of her goggles-communicator and responded, "Negative. I've neutralized the strafing gun but they keep swarming to reach it."

"Shoot the strafing gun."

"Negative: I'm using it as bait."

"Acknowledged. As you were, Saundra Green. Out."

Saundra Green the Wily was killing Jingoans in Region 6 before her legion was called to stay a Hive invasion of Region One. In a fleeting moment of wandering thought, she wondered which enemy she would next fight.

The firearms of the Greater Humanity Empire had excellent range and accuracy. Their troops were generally clever but somewhat cautious. They directed their airstrikes and artillery with devastating precision. Their tracked fighting vehicles were fast and extremely tough but somewhat lumbering on anything other than open terrain.

The disruptors of the Hive had the range and accuracy of plasma weapons but otherwise they were nothing alike. A bolt of ionized gas punches and burns into its target and may burst with gory effect. The distortion shot from the stubby prongs of a disruptor pass through material without causing damage; unless the target is an electronic device. A hit to the arm or leg does little more than inflict a prickly sting. Only a hit to the head or torso was harmful. Though a disruptor bolt was known to pass through helmets and body armor, taking cover did provide protection.

Saundra joined the Girls in Red of what was left of her company. Isabel Red was the company commander and the voice that asked if the "avenue was clear." Isabel commanded Saundra, "Plug your weapon into the charger and eat whether you're hungry or not." Saundra nodded. She would have responded with "yes, ma'am," but that would have embarrassed them both for Isabel was not a Priestess.

Robots bearing loads of supplies on four spindly legs followed Girls in Blue about as the Concubine Keepers provided for the Sentinels and Scouts.

The field ration of the Virgin Army was *synthetic manna*: an ugly but tasty paste of pure nutrients. Flasks of enriched water were passed around.

Isabel told Saundra, "We've confirmed twenty-seven of your kills."

Laura Red snorted, "She probably made at least twice that."

"We don't tally 'probably' but yes, she undoubtedly slew more."

Saundra remarked, "The more of them means less of us."

"Indeed."

Virgin Soldiers prided themselves in their prowess but never as individuals. They were the Many of One and all that they did they did together. Saundra's kills were measured as a success of the Virgin Army and nothing more, even to Saundra.

Only hundreds of the thousands of civilians meant to be rescued were saved. The unfortunate were found as corpses without wounds: gunned down by disruptors.

Concubine Laborers did not wear the elastic one-piece of a Virgin Soldier but rather a pink dress with a miniskirt and hood. The Girls in Pink were tasked with gathering and burying the dead while the troops searched for survivors or lurking enemies.

Saundra was perched above while the Girls in Red scoured below. "Report, Saundra Green," the voice of a sister hailed.

The Girl in Green touched the side of her goggles-communicator and responded, "All clear."

"Acknowledged."

Though danger was everywhere, Saundra Green the Wily felt strangely at peace in this moment of unsettling calm. She was having fun watching over her sisters.

The Many of One were selfless as the Concubines of the Great Seen Unseen. They lived and died serving a will beyond the mortal self. Alas, the cheap and easily mass-produced clone of a human being is as human as its template. Though endowed with the memories of another, the thoughts and feelings of such a creature are its own. Saundra valued her life and dignity. She was glad to have survived and was proud to be part of something undoubtedly important. She savored this moment.

The Hive lured the Concubines into a trap. Its forces converged upon the legions of the Virgin Army trying to press through its middle. The clone women, assailed from all sides, were being slaughtered at disadvantage. The swarms of dragonfly-type bombers coming to their rescue flew into a sky that burst them into flames or caused them to simply lose power and plummet. "We're pulling out of Region 6," it pained General Ilea to declare. "I want every legion rushed to the front in this region." She hesitated before adding, "Inform General Wisely-Adamant that we are in *desperate* need of its *immediate* help."

Lieutenant General Barbara wondered, "Are we pulling the Phantoms out of Region 13?"

Ilea sobbed, "The operation is over: we're being destroyed!"

The Phantoms are called "phantoms" for a reason and reminded their enemies why. The soldiers of the Hive cringed upon hearing the malevolent *shrieks* and their purple blood was shed as their heads were smashed or lobbed clean off. Their war beasts were maddened and trampled them.

The Concubine legions in Region 6 were rushed to the front in Region One and engaged without delay. The airpower that was hammering Jingoan positions was now pummeling the Hive.

General Ilea wept with joy as she said to her colleague General Wisely-Adamant, "Thank you! Thank you so much! You delivered us from destruction!"

The woman could *feel* the smile of the virtually shapeless entity as it told her, "The Hive shall forever rue that it thought to attack us on Crux."

The Greater Humanity Empire already recognized the territorial claims of the Hive. The supreme commander of Imperial forces on Crux was already coordinating a strategy with the commanding general of the Hive forces. The Hive invasion of Concubine Region One was launched earlier than planned but was already planned.

The Greater Humanity Empire swiftly reclaimed what was now being abandoned by the enemy in Drytopia and Rocky Nowhere. It immediately launched a counteroffensive into Concubine Region One: in retaliation, as an opportunity and to relieve a beleaguered ally.

The jet bombers of the Imperial Air Force were faster, could fly higher and carried heavier war loads than the dragonfly-type entomopters of the Virgin Army. Jet fighters were bigger, faster and more heavily armed than dragonfly-type interceptors. The Imperial aircraft could be brought down by electrokinetic pulse cannons. Dragonfly-type interceptors would hover low lying in wait, otherwise the Jingoans enjoyed air superiority.

The Imperial Air Force hammered Concubine positions. When the Phantoms were targeted, sensory manipulation confounded pilots and instruments alike: planes crashed or bombed elsewhere than intended. When the illusions failed, however, Imperial firepower proved devastating.

The tracked main battle tanks of the Imperial Army were heavier and much harder to destroy than the bipedal machines of the Virgin Army. Though useless in the thick of forests the Concubine tanks negotiated easily, all was barren on Crux. The tracked vehicles were twice as fast on open ground than their legged counterparts. Their turrets could fully rotate, unlike the "head" atop the Concubine machines.

Imperial infantry wore helmets and body armor. Though carrying ammunition was cumbersome, their firearms enjoyed superior range and accuracy to that of the Virgin Army's plasma small arms. Imperial infantry were equipped with grenades.

The extensive teleportation capability of the Concubines of the Great Seen Unseen is unrivaled. They can deploy, supply and maneuver their vast forces with fluid ease.

Portals opened midair and along the front, closer to the Imperial forces than any other enemy could open them. Locust-type entomopters and bipedal main battle tanks led the charge, their caseless rockets and ionized bolts *blasting* all before them. The aircraft burned and plummeted and the vehicles burst into flames and stumbled as they were met with great fury. Waves of Girls in Red withered as the Virgin Army pressed its numbers into the rapid-fire of Imperial machineguns.

General Ilea and General Wisely-Adamant were together staring at the holographic map of Region One. The Concubine fretted, "The Jingoans are holding the line. We don't have the weight to shove them back now that we're caught in a two-front struggle."

The Phantom suggested, "Pull your forces from the fight with the Hive and throw them into the fray against the Jingoans."

The Concubine worried, "Your troops will be overwhelmed."

"No. We shall hide and the Hive shall wash over us. We shall catch them unawares and from behind."

"You'll be vastly outnumbered."

The Phantom reminded, "You outnumber the Jingoans already yet need more that your numbers may outweigh their firepower. Our surprise shall outmatch the numbers of the Hive."

"You're taking a dangerous risk."

"Yes. The thrill of war is the slaughter but also the danger."

The Concubines of the Great Seen Unseen did not wage war for the "thrill" of it. They did not relish slaughter and danger. They were appreciative of alien cultures, however, especially that of an ally. Ilea admired the daring of the Phantoms.

The Virgin Army suffered dreadful losses pressing the Imperial Army back. The Hive suffered dreadful losses when thrown into disarray from sudden attacks deep in their formations and from the rear. The Imperial Army fell back and regrouped. The Hive regained its composure and chased the Phantoms into the hills.

The Democratic Plutocracy of Lith was the empire of a united Great Race. Its people were humanoid of a sort; short and stout with thick, stubby legs, broad shoulders and long, powerful arms. The hairless hide of the species was fine scales of orange-beige. The eyes of the race were brown irises amid solid black. Their technology was magical-industrial and their weapons heavy plasma rifles or shotguns. Their war machines were eight-legged monsters of artificial flesh within titanium alloy exoskeletons.

A naked Delver climbed into the cockpit of his Arachnid Type 8 main battle tank. He stuck a tube down his throat, gagging reflexively as he carefully did so. He then nodded to the Delver watching him from above. The hatch then sealed and the cockpit went dark. Warm fluid filled the cockpit as the driver closed his eyes and pressed his hands together. He lost any sense of the fluid as his senses became the sensors of his vehicle. The eight-legged machine walked (the driver felt as if walking) up a ramp and nestled into a spot among like vehicles.

Delver infantry put on their full suits of titanium alloy plate armor and strapped on gear and grenades. They fixed spike bayonets to their rifles or shotguns. They crowded into a chamber and waited for the wall that was a ramp to drop.

Self-shifting edifices of fully armored and heavily armed artillery fortresses appeared across western Region One as swirling flashes of light. Ramps dropped and troops and tanks poured out. The fortresses thundered barrages of heavy plasma bolts beyond the horizon as the Delver forces joined the fight.

Chapter 3
"Galactic Conflict"

In the Age of the Three Empires the humanity of the planet Jingo was primitive tribes and nations, the Hive was many hives and the Phantoms were the feuding barbarians of an uncharted world. The Mystic Confederacy, the Democratic Plutocracy of Lith and the Golgothite Empire claimed the entire galaxy amongst each other.

The humanity of the planet Jingo united. The Hive became one hive. The ghostly inhabitants of an uncharted world became the People of the Third Eye. The new empires devoured the frontiers of old and the age became a new age.

Worlds long claimed by the Democratic Plutocracy of Lith became colonies of the Greater Humanity Empire and the Hive Realm. The Delvers, the citizens and soldiers of the Plutocracy, were taking an opportunity to take them back.

The troops and equipment of the Greater Humanity Empire were *blasted* and ionized by thunderous flashes. The airpower and artillery of the Imperial forces responded with a vengeance: hammering the kinetic shield barriers of Delver artillery fortresses relentlessly. Alas, what little could punch through the shields could do little against the heavy armor. Electrokinetic pulse cannons fried electronics and jet aircraft dipped and crashed. One plane struck a fortress and disabled a shield emitter. "Take that bitch out before they repair the emitter!" an Imperial Air Force general commanded. A "bunker buster" punched into the main reactor and the fortress erupted into bluish flames.

A Delver is very strong. It can endure stress and wounds that would kill one of any other race. It can run and jump in armor of weight that would exhaust anyone else just wearing it. A Delver infantryman was a juggernaut on the battlefield. Alas, gaps necessary to vent body heat and to allow breath and vision were vulnerable to bullets and shrapnel.

Eight-legged war machines led the fully-armored Delver infantry onward. A vehicle not only blasted with its plasma cannon and strafed with glowing streams of rapid fire but it generated a kinetic shield umbrella. Whatever punched through the layers of shielding was usually deflected by armor… but not always.

Imperial troops blazed away and lobbed grenades. They detonated mines. The Delvers closed in, aiming and shooting high-powered plasma bolts. They shot grenades from launchers or lobbed a hand-grenade that was a spiked head atop a metal throwing-handle. They fired caseless rockets from shoulder-mounted launchers at vehicles and helicopters. Though the Delvers were outnumbered, the odds were in their favor.

General Ilea and General Wisely-Adamant were together staring at a holographic map and noting its updates of the battle. The Concubine informed the Phantom, "The Delvers gave their word that they shall relinquish whatever they take of Region One… if we recognize their claim to Region 13. Under the desperate circumstances, I agreed to their terms."

The Phantom realized, "You gave them your word in my name."

Ilea sobbed, "We were losing everything! We need their help!"

"Region 13 was to be a land of my people. It was not yours to give."

"Please!" the woman begged. "We must do this together or we lose everything!"

"Are we to lose that you may gain?"

"No!"

The Phantom's yellowish luminescence dimmed and became bluish. It assured, "The people of the Third

Eye shall honor your terms with the Delvers but under our terms with you."

"What do you want?"

"What do you offer?"

The Concubine thought before offering, "Region 6 was supposed to be ours but we give it to you."

"Pledge your forces to taking Region 6."

Ilea disclaimed, "We're in no position to be taking anything right now. We're pressed just holding what we already have."

"Yes," the shrewd Phantom seemed to be grinning. "Pledge your forces to take Region 6 and we of the Third Eye shall endorse your agreement with the Delvers."

Ilea choked, "As a priestess of the Seen Unseen and a general of its Virgin Army I do solemnly swear that my command shall take Region 6 of the planet Crux."

"You shall do so at my own discretion."

"What? Why?"

"Why not?"

General Ilea huffed before conceding, "We take Region 6 whenever you're ready."

"Yes."

Ilea's lieutenants glared at her, clearly dubious of this new arrangement. Wisely-Adamant assured them all, "We of the Third Eye are not eager to squander our lives on vanity. We merely mean to hold you to your resolve when it is required."

The Mystic Confederacy was a magically advanced civilization. Its race was a very tall and slender humanoid species with black hair, blue or gray eyes and bluish beige skin. It had four digits per extremity and its heart was to the right of the center of its mass. Most of the creatures were left-handed.

The weapons of the Confederate Army were swords, glaives, bows and arrows. Its uniform was black leather boots, bracers and cuirass worn over blue trousers and tunic. A gray and hooded cloak was worn. The infantry were glaivesmen. The cavalry were archers and glaivesmen mounted upon bipedal steeds. The glaive of the cavalry was a short polearm with a long blade.

Portals were opened deep within Region One. Confederate forces marched through and the portals shrank into oblivion behind them.

A crystalline orb with a glowing core was born on a litter carried on poles by eight priests. Such a device was the talisman of every legion of the Confederate Army. The airpower and artillery barrages of alien forces could not touch it or the legion it protected. Machines that flew, rolled or walked into its aura lost power.

The least is the greatest and the greatest least: The legionary talismans were useless against small arms and grenades. Rockets and cannons fired *within* its aura were unaffected. Land mines remained deadly.

The Mystics were a mystical people indeed. Their soldiers wore personal talismans that weakened attacks against them at range or healed grievous wounds nigh instantly. Soldiers could *hide in plain sight* or channel their energies into a *shield of warding*. Intuition and divination made catching a Mystic unawares nigh impossible.

The guns and grenades of the alien powers were deadlier than the blades and arrows of the Confederate Army. Alas, to use a weapon deadly by power other than that of its wielder dispelled the aura of a talisman, breaking its enchantment. The Mystics were bound to their primitive weapons.

The Mystics watched as the Concubines of the Great Seen Unseen and the People of the Third Eye invaded territory claimed by the Greater Humanity Empire. They watched and waited as the Hive readied its forces on Crux. The Hive invaded Region One and the armies of the

Living Darkness withdrew from Imperial territory to stay them. The Greater Humanity Empire then joined the invasion of Region One. The forces of the Living Darkness were beleaguered to the north and east. The Mystics saw an opportunity to march into the west and seize the vortex point of Region One. Alas, the Delvers assailed the Imperial invasion and turned the tide in favor of the Concubines and Phantoms. The Confederate Army took its fleeting opportunity, dreading that its invasion would undoubtedly now prove a grueling fight.

Firepower was the least effective means of dealing with the Confederate Army. Small arms were useful but only at dangerously close range. The Many of One were many indeed: the Virgin Army swarmed the Confederate Army with waves of Girls in Red. The blades of the Mystics hacked and slashed yet more of the clones kept coming.

The Girls in Green skulked about, sniping Mystics while they were distracted by the assailing throngs. Saundra Green the Wily was one of the sharpshooters: she punched a bolt through her target's chest and blue blood sprayed out his back. She crept away to avoid being noticed.

A Mystic cavalryman was shooting arrows into Girls in Red as they surrounded him. As their relentless numbers closed in he switched to his short glaive and cut them down... until a glowing bolt shot him out of his saddle.

General Ilea and her lieutenants were watching the battle via holographic map. "We've brought their advance to a halt," Alessa reported, "but they're not falling back. The Mystics mean to take the vortex point."

Ilea stared at the map in silence before thinking aloud, "The Jingoans are retreating, slowly but surely, and the Hive is digging in."

Alessa reminded, "We can't bring our full strength to bear fighting on three fronts."

"Obviously."

"Let's pull legions from the east and overwhelm the Mystics."

Barbara warned, "The Hive will advance if we pull legions from the east."

"The Hive isn't an imminent threat to the vortex point. We need to secure our readily available connection with Golgoth."

"Agreed," Ilea decided; "but we won't be pulling forces from the east. Contact General Wisely-Adamant."

"Why?"

"Phantoms are the only ones who can sneak attack Mystics."

Reckless Wisdom was a Hero of the Mystic Confederacy. As a captain in the Confederate Army he commanded three other heroes: the renowned swordsman Nefarious Good, the notorious adventurer Dubious Calm and the venerated priestess Moody Serenity. The hair of male and female alike was long and lustrous black. A male of the race also sported a long goatee, but no mustache. "Heroes of the Confederacy," Captain Reckless Wisdom addressed the three of his tetrad, "The malevolent clones are cheap and easy to make: their numbers shall prove endless in a war of attrition. Our few of many must outwit the Many of One or we shall be overwhelmed."

Dubious Calm smirked, "My captain, why is it your habit to tell us the obvious?"

"One cannot keep secrets by telling secrets so I tell you the obvious." Nefarious Good and Moody Serenity chuckled.

Capt. Wisdom resumed, "We must venture into the hills to the northeast. We shall be alone among countless enemies. We must reach a teleportation relay tower and disable it." Everyone understood without explanation that success would allow the Confederate forces to open portals closer to the vortex point of the region.

A small portal opened as close to the relay station as the Mystics dared. The egress point was enchanted to avoid detection but Concubine sensors were unrivaled in their ability to detect spatial anomalies. The tetrad of Reckless Wisdom hurried through and the portal closed immediately. "We must make haste," the captain told his three. "The Virgin Army investigates even the slightest anomaly."

The Mystics were astride the bipedal steed indigenous to Mystique. Dubious Calm was the scout and rode ahead. Reckless Wisdom waved his wand and muttered an incantation as he conjured a swirling breeze to dissipate their scent and cover their tracks. Moody Serenity held her staff and empty hand aloft as she felt for possible danger. "We are alone," she assured her companions.

Her captain warned, "Lest Phantoms are about."

"My captain, the Phantoms are to the north and to the east."

"Let us assume they are near that we may be ready should they be near."

"Yes, sir."

The barren and rocky hills of this land were eerily silent. Capt. Wisdom remarked, "All this fighting for a wasteland of a world."

Rev. Serenity returned, "To you of Mystique a desert is a waste. I am from Numinous and am reminded of home."

"You have my condolences."

Nefarious Good grinned. He assured Moody Serenity, "Take offense knowing you are the favorite of this tetrad."

The priestess smiled. She corrected her gracious companion, "No, Mr. Good, you are the favorite of us all."

"Indeed," Capt. Wisdom concurred. "We need your knack for killing that we may do our part unmolested. As for Mr. Calm, he would be lonely without you."

Vehicles and aircraft are useless against legions shielded by grand talismans. They are exceedingly dangerous to isolated bands of soldiers armed only with swords, daggers, bows and arrows. The Mystics hid as patrolling entomopters *buzzed* overhead or *stomping* bipedal main battle tanks crossed their path. "There shall be more as we get closer," Capt. Wisdom warned his three.

The tetrad made no fire when they made camp for the night. They basked in the moonlight of this alien world. Moody Serenity told her companions, "Our lesser sun lights the night with its gentle glow."

"That sun is red, yes?" asked Dubious Calm.

"Yes."

"Does the light of it redden your night?"

"It does not."

"Your lesser sun is no doubt a lovely sight to behold."

"It is."

"I have seen it," Capt. Wisdom mentioned. He smiled at Rev. Serenity as he told them all, "It is a strange and wondrous sight indeed."

Mystique was the world of origin and the capitol world but it was not every Mystic's home. The eighth and verdant moon of a blue and purple gas giant was but one of thirteen sovereign states in a confederacy of equals.

The teleportation-communications relay station was a tower in the middle of a town of prefabricated structures. Scouts patrolled the surrounding hills. Sentinels guarded the perimeter and the grounds.

The sentries were comely in their skimpy red uniform. They looked so serious behind those black goggles and wielding their little guns. They stood at their posts vigilant and unflinching… until snatched by alien hands. Grunts and groans went unnoticed. The snapping of necks went unheard. The intruders piled the bodies out of sight before slipping into the edifice that was the base of the tower.

Girls in Red guarded the corridors and catwalks while unarmed Girls in Blue went about tending maintenance and operations. Sentinels disappeared from their posts yet the busy Keepers were too busy to notice.

A Girl in Blue was sitting at a console and tapping keys… when grabbed by the head and her face jerked past a shoulder. The *snap* was dramatic but not so loud to attract notice.

Capt. Wisdom plucked the little body from its seat and dropped it to the floor. He sat in its seat and accessed its terminal by waving his wand. He commanded Mr. Good and Rev. Serenity, "Watch over me." Nefarious Good drew the curved blade of his longsword. Moody Serenity closed her eyes and felt for trouble. Dubious Calm was elsewhere guarding the intended avenue of escape.

Reckless Wisdom was familiar with human computers, whether Golgothite or Jingoan. Hacking them was usually easy enough. Alas, he triggered a silent alarm by venturing beyond the dead user's clearance. "Our quest is a failure; as was most likely to begin with. Let us depart in urgent haste."

Throngs of Sentinels flooded the corridors as they converged on the location of the security breach.

A bolt of ionized gas was enervated as it passed through the layers of a talisman's kinetic shield barrier. Shot from beyond forty paces the glowing bolt would burst into a puff of harmless smoke. Concubine Sentinels were trained in how to deal with soldiers of a magically advanced civilization and knew not to waste charges. The

Girls in Red charged headlong intent on blasting the intruders at nigh point blank range.

Nefarious Good raised a hand and the volley of glowing bolts scattered into the walls, floor and ceiling. A swipe of his curved blade disemboweled the nearest two Sentinels. The swordsman hacked, slashed and stabbed as the assailing throng kept coming.

A soldier of the Confederate Army is trained in either channeling his energy into a glamor to hide in plain sight or to focus it into a shield of warding. The temperament of the soldier determined which skill he learned; balance came naturally to the cautious and flow came naturally to the restless. Magic required a magician to be true to his nature.

Nefarious Good was the fighter of his tetrad. He alone mastered the shield of warding. He stayed the throngs of Sentinels while his companions made their escape. "We are out," the silent voice of his captain eventually told him. The swordsman then made good his own departure.

The three awaited their fighter, they already mounted and holding the reigns of their fourth. "Mr. Calm," the captain addressed the scout. "Lead us."

The scout led his tetrad into the rugged hills and found a place for them to hide. The wizard and priestess then combined their skills to hide the spot and bless it with a warding spell.

"You bore the brunt of our escape," Reckless Wisdom told Nefarious Good. "Be rested should you be required to do so again."

"Yes, my captain."

The wizard and fighter were eating rations and drinking from flasks when the wizard mentioned, "The chance was slim but there was a chance. Our success would have saved many lives. Alas, I did fail."

The fighter assured, "To dare the impossible yet fail bears no shame."

Capt. Wisdom shrugged. He uttered, "The Concubines fret minutiae. May they be even somewhat distracted by our failed errand that our guile was not entirely in vain."

Concubine Lieutenant General Barbara reported, "Fifty-four Sentinels and a Keeper were lost, otherwise the incident was uneventful."

Ilea reminded, "They tried to access our primary relay terminus."

"Yes, and they failed miserably."

"Reinforce its security with another battalion."

"We don't need it."

Alessa joined, "We need the troops on the front, not standing idly behind the lines."

Ilea reiterated, "I want another battalion guarding that tower!"

Barbara and Alessa looked at each other before Barbara answered, "Yes, ma'am."

The empires poured their armies into the fight on Crux, turning the battle into a grueling stalemate of murderous attrition. Invasions were launched across the galaxy in the hope of outmaneuvering the strategic deadlock: the Galactic War had begun.

Part 4

THE ADVENTURER

Chapter 1
"The Few of the Many of One"

The Many of One were the Concubines of the Great
Seen Unseen and the inheritors of the Golgothite Empire.
Though they clung to what remained of the empire, their
every invasion failed. Their expeditions to uncharted
worlds went missing. "Why?" the High Priestess asked her
sisters. "Why are we the empire none fear?"

An Elder of the Council answered, "Sexism is
universal, especially towards human females."

The High Priestess reminded, "The Hive is a
matriarchy ruled by a queen they worship."

"They're not human."

"What of it? Why do we hear from Lady Dolorous
that they find us easy to deal with?"

"That is a credit to her diplomacy."

Another Elder corrected, "Lady Dolorous assured
the Hive that we are friendly. Her diplomacy is our good
relations with the Hive."

The High Priestess returned the conversation to her
point, "Why is our only victory the conquest of an already
crumbling empire, our own empire?" No one answered.
"Our bones and artifacts litter worlds across the galaxy as a
testimony of our weakness. Those of us captured flood the
slave markets of our rivals. We hear tell that our Virgin
Soldiers are kept pregnant with monstrous hybrids."

There was a long moment of shamed silence until
the High Priestess told her sisters, "Our faithful ally the
People of the Third Eye are feared as the Scourge of the
Galaxy. The mere threat of them terrifies worlds into
submission."

An elder piped, "The Phantoms massacre civilians and never take prisoners. I hope you're not suggesting we do the same."

"Why not?"

"The People of the Third Eye are a wonderful people but they are inhuman. Their nature is not only alien but monstrous. We're not monsters."

"We respect other cultures," another Elder joined. "We learn from the diversity and use what we learn to broaden our perspectives. The Phantoms see only aliens to be slaughtered."

The High Priestess smirked, "The cultures we respect disrespect us. They totally respect the intolerant and genocidal Scourge of the Galaxy."

"Are you hoping to turn us into a scourge?"

"No."

An Elder reminded, "We are the kept women of the Great Seen Unseen. His Unheard Whisper is our only will and the entirety of our purpose."

"Yes," the High Priestess agreed. "That we may serve him let us do whatever we must to prevail."

"What do you intend?"

"We are more scientists than soldiers. Let our science find a way to make us warriors."

The Many of One dedicated their many keen minds to study and consider possibilities. The young military Priestess Alessandra the Bold had an idea. An Elder of the Council liked her idea and asked the High Priestess to hear it.

Alessandra wore the skimpy elastic one-piece that was the uniform of the Virgin Army. She pulled back her goggles and elastic hood as she entered the office of the High Priestess. The elder sister gestured for Alessandra to be seated. The High Priestess began, "Kay the Astute tells me you have a tried and proven idea."

"Yes, ma'am."

"Tell me."

Alessandra asked, "Did you read my report?"

"Yes."

Alessandra swallowed, excited to be a junior Priestess in private conference with the *High* Priestess—but the moment was also intimidating. "The Adventurer Project." Gwenya White nodded, waiting for Alessandra Purple to continue. "We select a dozen heroines of the Galactic War. We train them to operate outside our sisterhood as bounty hunters and mercenaries. We give them Imperial Credits and assign them jobs through the Penumbrans."

"The Penumbrans?"

"Yes, ma'am."

The High Priestess smirked, "Our venerable Penumbran friends will undoubtedly find this amusing."

Alessandra noted, "The Penumbrans are well connected with every race in the galaxy. Every business, legal and illegal, answers to them."

"True."

"Their influence not only assures our women employment but that our women are treated fairly."

The High Priestess summarized the rest, "Our war heroes become bounty hunters and mercenaries. They are paid as soldiers of fortune and use the money to support themselves." Alessandra nodded. Gwenya White continued, "The idea is that our women learn the ways of the outside and master them."

"They learn the unsavory skills of the galaxy," Alessandra emphasized. "They retire from their adventures and bring what they have learned back to us. They train the next Concubine Adventurers."

"We do this indefinitely?"

"Yes, ma'am. We need practical experience in the field to keep our military and espionage skills sharp."

Gwenya stared. Alessandra squirmed. The High Priestess decided, "We'll do it." A bounce and a giggle escaped the younger Priestess. The elder grinned.

A dozen heroines of the Galactic War were selected for service as the first Concubine Adventurers: seven Scouts, four Sentinels and a Keeper. They were extensively trained in the use of firearms, edged weapons and explosives. They were taught how to operate the vehicles and aircraft of the Greater Humanity Empire. They studied foreign and alien cultures and were conditioned to be ever mindful of their customs.

A Concubine Adventurer would wear the clothes of the Greater Humanity Empire but in her own style. She would favor firearms over the plasma weapons of Golgoth. She would refrain from discussing religion or politics even as friendly conversation. She would ignore rudeness or inflammatory remarks. She was to refuse sexual advances by any means necessary, even to the death. "Report mistreatment to your Penumbran sponsor," she was told. "The lords and ladies of Penumbra shall be watching over you."

The Penumbrans agreed to the idea of the *Concubine Adventurer* quite eagerly. Lord Omen the Waiting of the Twilight, the most prominent merchant in the galaxy, told Gwenya White, "It shall be our pleasure to watch for the endeavor shall undoubtedly prove interesting."

Saundra Green the Wily of the Nineteenth Harvest was a Scout in the Virgin Army before becoming an Adventurer. Her uniform was the elastic, singular green garment with black googles fixed to an elastic hood and nothing more. An olive drab, hooded pullover and black, elastic short shorts were her choice clothes as a "freelance" mercenary. She wore black googles made to look like sunglasses. Her new weapons were a bolt-action sniper rifle, a semiautomatic pistol and a fighting knife, all of it made in the Greater Humanity Empire.

Saundra was riding in the limousine of the Penumbrans Lord Conniving the Ruthless of the Early Light and Lady Presumptuous the Assertive of the Dying Light. The aliens were a married couple and living as honorary citizens of the Greater Humanity Empire. Among the native Jingoans they were "Mr. and Mrs. Early Light." Mrs. Early Light explained to Saundra, "It is gracious to honor the customs of your host."

"Yes, milady," the Concubine of the Seen Unseen answered in the ancient tradition of Golgoth. The Penumbran smiled before telling Saundra, "The Jingoans are not a people of lords and ladies. They are distrustful of any who boast of rank or title."

"Yes, ma'am: understood."

The Penumbrans laughed but their smiles made their mirth reassuring rather than deriding.

Saundra was wearing a green, hooded robe while in Anthropolis. Mr. Early Light wore a three-piece business suit native to the humanity of the planet Jingo. The style was not Penumbran yet such among Penumbrans was worn with pride by the venerable merchant and banker class; on every world where they did business.

Mrs. Early Light wore an elegant gown also of Jingoan make. Though naturally head and shoulders taller than women, the female Penumbran wore high heels.

Mr. Early Light assured Saundra Green, "Your employer was hesitant to consider you until I told him of your military exploits. I assured him that it is the way of your sisterhood to cooperate."

"I will, sir."

"Your companions are sure to give you trouble. Give them trouble back or else their antics shall prove insufferable."

Mrs. Early Light added, "You are under our protection so you need not fear. You may offend your offenders should the need arise."

"Yes, ma'am."

Saundra Green watched out the window as the limousine went with the flow of the busy traffic on the streets of the city of Anthropolis, capitol of the Greater Humanity Empire. Unlike the cities of Golgoth, which were broad edifices of marble and glass, this was one of looming towers of steel and windows. There were few gardens but fountains and abstract art were throughout. The crowds were men and women young or old, and children. "Anthropolis is only forty-eight years old," Mrs. Early Light told Saundra. "It was built by the Jingoans not only to serve as their capitol but to be their very first endeavor as a united people."

Mr. Early Light added, "Ethnic Golgothites also live in this wondrous city. Their children fancy themselves Jingoans."

Saundra mentioned, "I hear tell that Golgothites living in the Greater Humanity Empire are gangsters."

The Penumbrans grinned and looked at each other knowingly. Mrs. Early Light told Saundra, "Merchants legitimate and illegitimate have done business with the humanity of Jingo since before the Greater Humanity Empire."

Mr. Early Light smirked, "They still do."

"Yes. It was the merchants who introduced us of Penumbra to the humanity of Jingo."

Mr. Early Light told Saundra Green, "You shall be inducted into the security forces of the Silverstone Corporation. Mr. Richard Martin shall be your immediate supervisor, your *captain* in what is essentially a paramilitary branch of the business."

"Sir, are you and Mrs. Early Light the owners of this corporation?"

"We do not *own* alien corporations. Our superior practices would antagonize the natives. No, we are in the business of *assisting* indigenous businesses."

Saundra understood, "If they do what you want they get money and the benefit of your connections."

The Penumbran male chuckled. The female smiled. The husband told his wife, "Why is she a Concubine Adventurer when she would make for a shrewd Concubine Merchant?"

His wife cautioned, "Let us not doubt the wisdom of the Unheard Whisper."

"Indeed, we shall not."

Mrs. Early Light told Saundra Green, "We shall be treating you to Jingoan cuisine for lunch. Though there are Golgothite restaurants in this city, and we do patronize their business, we would rather you had the best taste for your first taste of indigenous food."

"Thank you, milord and milady. I would rather try something native."

Mr. Early Light told his wife, "She is a Scout and they are always curious."

"Indeed."

Mr. Richard Martin was a middle-aged Jingoan with his hair as short as if he was still in the Imperial Marines. He had a tattoo of the *Swirl and Anchor* on his left forearm. He shook Saundra Green's hand then gestured for her to follow him. As they walked he told her, "We're going to Far Side on the planet Medley. Bandits have been raiding and looting company property and we're going to do something about that."

The Concubine Adventurer supposed, "We shall quell the banditry by violent means, I presume."

The man laughed, "You're an eager little killer, aren't you?"

"Forgive me, sir, if I have offended you."

"No, I hired you to kill people; if you love your work then so much the better."

"Thank you, sir."

"Three hundred and nine confirmed kills," the man seemed impressed.

Mr. Martin brought Saundra into the presence of a Delver and a young human man. "Gentleman, this is Saundra Green the Wily of the Nineteenth Harvest. She's killed hundreds of people so don't piss her off." Mr. Martin introduced, "This is Danny Danner," the young man smiled and nodded, "and Glint Forge." The short but broad and muscular alien simply nodded. "Dan's our nerd and Glint's our heavy hitter. I'm the boss. You'll be our scout sniper."

Saundra rode with her new companions on their way to the Anthropolis Galactic Teleportation Port. While en route Danny Danner offered his hand. Saundra shook the hand. The man smiled and the woman consciously smiled back. "Welcome to Jingo," Danny greeted.

"Thank you."

"I hope we the natives have been treating you well."

The Concubine of the Great Seen Unseen told the Jingoan, "Your people stare but all are friendly."

"We stare because we hear about you all the time but never see any of you… except in war."

"The war never came to Jingo."

"Exactly: you're an alien novelty here."

"I'm human."

Danny Danner shrugged. He told, "Some of us wonder about that."

"Do you?"

"No. You're human. I have no doubt about that."

Saundra was wearing her black "sunglasses" mindful that her ghostly white eyes would disturb the populace. She thought about the irony that keeping her eyes covered dehumanized her yet in her case, exposing her eyes

114

would make her spooky, thus, equally dehumanize her, if not more so.

"Are you really bald under that hood?" Saundra glared at the man for asking such an insensitive question: the Many of One were ashamed of their baldness. "I don't care if you are," the man seemed to be apologizing.

"Then why did you ask?"

Danny Danner squirmed before turning away in silence.

A portal opened between the city of Anthropolis on the planet Jingo and For Now City of the planet Medley. The ornate cityscape of shining skyscrapers and glistening fountains was replaced with the grungy shantytowns of a frontier settlement on a desert world. The bustling crowds of humanity were mixed with aliens of countless races here. Everyone was openly armed with guns or swords of their respective cultures. Private security seemed to be the only law enforcement.

Saundra was in her pullover and short shorts. Her rifle was slung and she wore her knife and pistol on a belt. She was barefoot, as was the way of the Many of One. Danny asked her, "Aren't your feet burning?"

"No."

Mr. Martin noted to Danny, "A lot of these aliens are barefoot."

"Yeah, but they're not human."

"So? Being human means you've got to have tender feet?"

Saundra told, "Shoes, even sandals, would pain me to wear."

"Okay," Danny accepted, "but I don't smell any sunblock on you. Aren't you worried your exposed skin is going to burn?"

"We neither darken in the light nor pale for lack of it."

"What a what?"

Mr. Martin grinned, "Don't worry about it." He told his people, "I'll treat you all to drinks." He told Saundra, "You'll love the sarsaparilla."

The four entered an established named *the Water Hole*: a bar filled with unsavory types, most of them grungy human males. Those in clean uniforms seemed to be private security on their own time. Jingoan music Saundra knew to be *Country* was playing.

Everyone stared at Saundra. There were whistles and vulgar mumblings. "I heard about the clone coming with you," a bartender told Mr. Martin.

"Don't piss her off," the addressed warned. "She's killed hundreds of people."

"Most of them ours?"

The men stared at Saundra as if expecting an answer. She told them, "Fifty-four Jingoans, two hundred ninety-two Hivers and thirty-seven Mystics confirmed killed by personal action."

"Whoa!" the bartender was taken aback.

Mr. Martin added, "And that's just the *confirmed* count."

"Hell, I'm not messing with her."

Mr. Martin winced as he mentioned, "I'm not happy to hear about those fifty-four... but the war is over, right?"

"Yeah, it's over."

Saundra choked as she assured Mr. Martin, "Sir, I am deeply sorry if our conflicting duties of the past offend you. I was not boasting. I was merely answering your unasked but strongly implied question."

"Conflicting duties," the man chuckled mirthlessly. "I knew people. They didn't come back."

"Here, Top," the bartender handed Mr. Martin a drink. "This one's on me." The bartender raised his own glass and the two made a toast, "To all the bad asses."

Mr. Martin and Danny Danner drank their beer and chatted with the bartender and other patrons. Glint Forge guzzled whatever was poured for him. Saundra sipped her sarsaparilla and delighted in its sweet, bubbly taste. She spilled her drink when someone *slapped* and squeezed her buttock. The culprit snickered as if his discourtesy was somehow clever. Glint Forge suddenly lunged at the man! The Delver grabbed him by the throat and *slammed* him to the floor! One firm squeeze of that large hand and the human's eyes bulged and his tongue shot out. The bulged eyes rolled back as they shrank a little. The man went limp. "He's dead," someone in the crowd stated the obvious.

Another man checked the one on the floor, confirming, "Yeah, he's dead."

The friend of the "victim" shouted at Glint Forge, "Damn digger! What the hell's your problem?!" The Delver snarled and stepped towards him. The indignant human cringed.

Glint Forge roared, for all to hear and take heed, "You men *talk* and do your antics! I *kill* or do not kill. This fool struck my companion."

"Call the Delver office," Mr. Martin told the bartender. "My friend will surrender to the authority of the Delver administrator but he'll kill anybody else."

Feeling responsible, Saundra told Glint Forge, "I'm sorry it came to this."

"Why?"

"It was my problem."

"No!" the Delver stomped his big foot on the dead man's chest and pressed down, "It was *his* problem." The alien smirked, the closest thing Saundra had ever seen of a smile from him.

Medley was a world claimed by the Greater Humanity Empire, the Mystic Confederacy and the Democratic Plutocracy of Lith. The end of the Galactic War brought a treaty that resigned the planet to an administrative triad of equals represented by each of the three.

The Delvers were a fearsome enemy so no one was eager to provoke them. They were honorable to a fault so everyone trusted them. Glint Forge was brought before the Delver magistrate that it could be said that justice was done. He was acquitted of "murder" for among the Delvers a fight was to the death or there was no fight. It was irrefutable that the "victim" initiated hostilities by "striking" a companion of Glint Forge, so he was acquitted in accordance with the law. The dead human's estate was fined for "provocation" as a formality but with the understanding that no effort would be made to collect.

For Now City really was lawless, despite the games pretending to the contrary. Disputes were casually settled with the deadly use of force so one more killing meant nothing to the general population. Richard Martin and his three soldiers of fortune returned to the streets without incident. No one troubled Saundra Green for the rest of their stay.

Chapter 2
"Far Side of Medley"

Saundra and her companions boarded the tail ramp of an awaiting tiltrotor aircraft. Crates strapped down to the deck were also within. "Have a seat," Richard Martin gestured at a row of bucket seats lining the walls.

Saundra took her seat. She was somewhat uncomfortable when Danny Danner sat right next to her. "I won't talk your ear off," he assured her.

Glint Forge brought a battle rifle, a sharpshooter rifle, a grenade launcher and a satchel of grenades and a caseless rocket launcher and ten rockets all loaded on a dolly. He was wearing his full-suit of plate armor and a backpack. He had a spike bayonet and two hand grenades on his web-gear; the grenade was a spiked head on a metal stick. Glint rested his plasma shotgun over a shoulder while he pulled the dolly up the ramp.

Glint Forge was too broad for the bucket seats and in his armor probably too heavy. He secured his dolly loaded with weapons and sat next to it on the floor. "Comfortable?" Mr. Martin asked the Delver. Glint Forge nodded.

Teleportation is a common means of travel but it is not the cheapest. A portal opened midair and a score of planes, tiltrotors and helicopters flew through. The dusk of the one side was the dawn of the other for the link was between opposite sides of the planet. Once through, the swarm of aircraft scattered towards their particular destinations.

"We'll be quartered in the security station of a mining colony," Mr. Richard told his three. "We answer to Mr. Cushing and nobody else. If anyone asks anything about what we're doing, we tell them to mind their own business."

Danny wondered, "They think they have snoops on the inside?"

"Yeah: The bandits always know where and when to make their move."

"What if the insider is Cushing?"

Mr. Martin laughed, "That would be surprising. He's the one who hired us."

"He may want plausible deniability for helping himself to a few things."

"He wouldn't hire a team with a Delver if he wanted it easy."

The mining colony was a grungy town of cinderblock and steel. There was a water tower with the words, "LUKEWARM PISS" spray-painted on it. "Someone had to climb up to do that," Saundra noted aloud.

Danny chuckled, "I guess they weren't afraid of heights."

Mr. Cushing seemed old enough to be Mr. Martin's father. The older man was wearing shorts and had his hairy legs propped up on his desk. His socks were stretched up almost to his knobby knees. His shirt was covered in a colorful floral print. He wore a hat that read "I.H.S. Clover" so Saundra assumed the man was a naval veteran.

The windows were open and the ceiling fan was spinning. A fan on the floor swept the room back and forth, each pass making the little flags on Mr. Cushing's desk flutter. "Have a seat," the host offered. There were only two other chairs. Mr. Martin sat in one. Danny gestured for Saundra to sit in the other but she shook her head. The young man shrugged before sitting.

Mr. Cushing stared at the Concubine Adventurer. "I heard about the clone," he seemed to be speaking to Mr. Martin.

Mr. Martin introduced, "Saundra Green the Wily of the Nineteenth Harvest. She's a war hero."

"Yeah, for killing *our* people."

"So did our Delver friend Mr. Glint Forge. Let's not worry about the past while we've got the here and now to deal with."

"I sent you everything I know. I haven't learned anything knew."

Mr. Martin believed, "You warned that the bandits may have someone on the inside. Do you have your suspects?"

"Nothing I know for sure."

"Anything you tell me is off the record. I just need something to work with."

Mr. Cushing smirked before answering, "I think this is more of an embezzlement ring than anything else. Unfortunately, people are found dead and probably because they heard or saw or otherwise knew whatever's going on."

Mr. Cushing hesitated before stating, "We're probably dealing with employees, and that means Imperial citizens. I can't *legally* hire you to kill our citizens… but you have the right to use deadly force if provoked."

Mr. Martin deduced, "You want us to kill them."

"I'm not saying that."

"I know. I heard it anyway."

Mr. Cushing tittered. He elaborated, "I want you to find them and arrest them. You're officially *security* so you have the authority to make an arrest. I don't think they're going to let you, though."

"I understand."

"I hired a private investigator and we found him shot to pieces."

Mr. Martin grinned, "We brought a Delver."

The four "security officers" were quartered on an observation tower on a hill overlooking the town. The walls were mostly windows with a good view of everything. Saundra stared out at the rolling landscape of rocky desert. A gruff voice uttered, "It is like my home."

"The planet Lith," Saundra knew.

Glint Forge nodded. He told, "The cities are built into the mountains but the hills are like they are here."

Danny told Glint, "Uh, most planets look like Lith: a whole lot of nothing."

The Delver rumbled a chuckle. He snatched Danny and snuggled him, telling him, "Yes: You are blessed with much water and countless trees." Saundra giggled, enjoying the odd comradeship of her mutually alien companions.

Mr. Martin and Danny made plans while Glint sat on the floor stacking little stone blocks of various shapes into various structures. Saundra asked the Delver, "Is this a game?"

The gruff voice of the alien answered, "It is an exercise for the mind."

"Geometry, I suppose."

"Yes. I must be mindful of shape and weight."

Saundra thought the burly alien looked cute playing with his building blocks. "Thank you, Mr. Forge."

"Why?"

"For protecting my honor."

"We are companions. We protect each other."

"I would but I don't think you'll ever need *my* protection."

"Why not?"

"Well, your armor is impervious to most weapons and your species is the heartiest in the galaxy."

"So?"

"So I don't see you being particularly vulnerable."

"No!" the gruff blurt startled everyone. Mr. Martin and Danny resumed their planning. Glint Forge told Saundra Green, "Shrapnel or a bullet or a blade through gaps in my armor may wound me. The wound may prove mortal. An explosion may not damage my armor but may kill me within my armor. I must be careful. You must look out for me."

"I will."

Glint continued playing with his blocks. Saundra dared annoying him with personal questions when she asked, "Why are you a soldier of fortune?"

"One must make his fortune."

"You must make quite a fortune to have that extensive arsenal of yours."

"Yes. My armor and my battle rifle are gifts for my service in the Army of the Plutocracy. All else was purchased by me."

"Your armor and battle rifle were gifts?"

"Yes. They are not in a contract of service. It is the grace of the people that soldiers of the people have a weapon and armor. Our weapons and armor are by private donations."

"Interesting."

"Why?"

"No one else equips their soldiers that way."

The Delver knew, "Your Virgin Soldiers are given everything they have. Is that not the same?"

"Yes, I suppose so."

The Delver's skin was fine scales of orange-beige. His face was broad and looked as solid as rock. His ears were negligible, the lobes being mere bumps with holes. His eyes were close-set and brown within black. Though not particularly beautiful, a Delver was not ugly. It looked fierce even when smiling and though this was intimidating, it made the aspect interesting.

The humans slept on cots while the Delver slept on the hard floor. "Are you comfortable?" Saundra worried about Glint.

"Yes."

"How are you comfortable?"

"The floor is cool and firm."

"The night is chilly."

"Yes," the Delver smiled. "The night is refreshing."

A Concubine of the Great Seen Unseen did not chill for the same reason her skin neither darkened nor grew pale: she was touched by the spirit of Shadow. As a human being she could *feel* the chill, however, though it did not affect her. Saundra snuggled under her blanket. She looked away from her companions when she removed her goggles. She set them on the floor beside her.

It seemed that time had passed when the whisper of Danny Danner called out, "Saundra?"

"I am awake," she whispered back.

"Yeah, I could tell by your fidgeting."

Saundra kept her back to the man. Though it was dark in the room now, she feared the hoariness of her eyes would still show. "Let me fidget in peace that I may settle into slumber."

"Are you having trouble sleeping?"

"I was thinking."

"About what?"

The Virgin Soldier hesitated before confiding, "I am in fellowship with the enemy."

"We're not your enemy anymore."

"For now there is a peace between us."

The man huffed, "The peace won't last with *that* attitude."

"The fate of our empires shall not be decided in this room."

"Maybe it will be."

Saundra turned to face the man. She wanted him to see her eyes, to see his enemy. Much to her dismay, he smiled. He told her, "I didn't expect those eyes to be lovely." The Concubine of the Great Seen Unseen turned back around. "I didn't mean it the way that sounded," the man assured. The woman remained silent. The man told her, "I don't think you're as freaky as you think you are: that's all I meant."

"Good night, Mr. Danner."

"Yeah, you too: Good night."

Morning: Mr. Martin offered Saundra Green operation of a four-wheeler. He asked, "Can you handle one of these?" She answered him, "Sir, I was trained on one just like it before setting out on this adventure."

"Good. You're our scout. Keep ahead and stay vigilant."

"Yes, sir."

"Just so you know: I was a first sergeant, and from what I was told, you were the equivalent."

"Yes, sir, but you are my superior on this team. Your authority exceeds that of a non-commissioned officer."

"Hardly."

"Would you rather I call you *Mr. Martin*, sir?"

Mr. Martin shrugged. "Let's go," he dropped the issue. "Rev her up and take point."

"Yes, sir."

As Saundra mounted her vehicle the voice of Danny warned her, "Those peddles are going to hurt your feet."

She looked over her shoulder to tell him, "We walk on hot coals and broken glass."

"Why?" The Concubine of the Great Seen Unseen ignored the silly Jingoan. She instead revved her engine.

Saundra rode ahead while the others followed in a small, all-terrain truck. She followed the numbers and arrow that lit within her goggles until coming to a hill. She dismounted and her companions stepped out of their truck.

Mr. Martin led everyone to the top of the hill. He pointed at an isolated facility across the valley. He had everyone take a closer look through his binoculars. "This one's going to be looted, sooner or later," Mr. Martin believed.

As Saundra was looking through the binoculars she asked, "For the silver?"

"Some of it maybe, but the machinery is worth more than a truckload of silver."

Danny Danner mentioned, "Silver's useful but hardly rare."

"Exactly."

Saundra noted, "The machinery is big. Would the thieves not prove easily caught possessing it?"

"Not if it finds its way to some other far-flung mining colony. Hell, they may be stealing and selling it back and forth to the same people."

Glint Forge snarled. Danny asked him, "You people have these problems too?"

"No."

"Then why do you sound pissed?"

"We do not like thieves."

"Yet you conquer the worlds of weaker races."

"Conquest is honorable."

"Whatever."

Saundra rode about planting motion sensors and bio-scanners. She hid whenever she heard vehicles or glimpsed workers. She was concealing a sensor when the *crack* of a rifle echoed. Saundra listened. Another *crack* then another sounded. The *boom* of the *crack* sounded as if the shot of an anti-materiel rifle. "Saundra Green!" Mr. Martin's voice hailed. "Saundra Green, respond!"

The Concubine Adventurer touched the side of her goggles-communicator and responded, "This is Saundra Green."

"We're under fire and pinned down! Take a position overlooking us and return fire!"

"Yes, sir." The veteran Scout crawled in among boulders. She kept her head low as she surveyed the hills overlooking her companions. She was on the same hill as the shooter: a man in desert camouflage was just below and aiming an anti-materiel rifle.

Another shot sounded, but from elsewhere. This one was undoubtedly a high-powered rifle but not of the power of an anti-materiel rifle. Yet another shot sounded and it too from elsewhere. "Triangular crossfire from above," Saundra deduced. She sought the other shooters. When she spotted them, she aimed at the one below with the anti-materiel rifle... and shot him. She then crawled away and took up another position. "Damn it, girl, we are pinned!" Mr. Martin fumed, "Take those shooters out!"

Saundra touched the side of her goggles-communicator and responded, "This is Saundra Green reporting, over. The anti-materiel rifle is silenced."

"What?"

"Stand by."

"Yeah, right."

Saundra was amused that the shooters never relocated. She aimed at another and sprayed his brains out of his head. She relocated before aiming and shooting the remaining gunman. All became silent but for the desert breeze. Saundra reported, "Saundra Green reporting."

"Report!"

"Three shooters located and terminated. No sign of others detected."

Saundra returned to her companions. There was a dent in the helm of Glint Forge. "Anti-materiel rifle," Mr. Martin explained, "The only small arm that can actually penetrate that armor. They knew what they were dealing with." The man grinned before amending, "Well, they didn't take *you* seriously enough."

Glint fretted, "A glancing shot. I felt the blow to my head and it stunned me."

Danny patted Glint on the back and joked, "I think your skull would have stopped the bullet."

Mr. Martin told Saundra, "They shot out our engine and we've lost contact with Cushing. We've got a long walk back or we risk moving in."

The Delver roared, "We attack!"

Mr. Martin cautioned the Delver, "If Cushing's dead then there's no money in this anymore. We don't risk our lives for free." Glint grunted.

Saundra implored, "We acquire a vehicle for your transportation and depart."

"There are probably a lot of bad guys where the trucks are."

"Yes, but the barren wilderness hinders the option of a long walk back."

"We'd better hurry," Danny warned. He was watching the camp through binoculars. "They're loading every truck."

Mr. Martin took a look. "A lot of guys," he noted. "It looks like they're holding the workers prisoner and using them to load the trucks." He told his three soldiers of fortune, "The enemy outnumbers us and is heavily armed. Take no prisoners: we're not at liberty to do so. We fight for a truck then get the hell out of here."

Saundra took up a position on the high ground and watched over her companions as they moved in. She sniped perched snipers. The enemies below became frantic and their "involuntary labor" scattered. A man pointed up at Saundra. She put a round through the center of his mass.

Glint Forge charged, the *blast* of his shotgun ripping and burning men apart with glowing sprays of ionized particles. Danny and Mr. Martin covered him with grenades and suppressive fire. A score of men were slaughtered before the bandits lost their nerve and fled.

Danny climbed behind the steering wheel of a truck. "Glint!" Mr. Martin called. "Get in the back!" Mr. Martin then joined Danny in the cab.

The voice of Mr. Martin sounded, "Saundra Green, return to your wheels. We're out of here."

The sniper touched the side of her goggles-communicator and responded, "Acknowledged."

The truck sped along the winding dirt road. Glint Forge was in the back with his shotgun at the ready. His low center of gravity enabled him to keep his balance in the swerving and bouncing vehicle quite easily.

Saundra sped towards the truck from above. She rolled down a hillside and took the lead, so as to not be smothered in the dust kicked up by the truck. Unbeknownst to the woman, the men were awarded a favorable view of her posterior. Danny remarked, "Now that is a nice ass."

Mr. Martin grinned. "Keep your eyes ahead and about."

"I'll try."

Chapter 3
"No Killing For Free"

Saundra glimpsed a glint up on a ridge. She veered her vehicle behind a rise and gestured for the truck to follow her. She came to a halt and hurried to cover. Her companions exited the truck and also hurried to cover. Saundra Green reported, "I glimpsed a reflection up ahead. I believe it was a spotter or sniper perched on a ridge."

Mr. Martin commanded, "Whatever he is, take him out."

"Yes, sir." Saundra scurried up the rise. She kept low atop. Saundra's back was to the sun so she felt comfortable peering through her scope. After a while of searching, she touched the side of the goggles-communicator and reported, "This is Saundra Green. The threat seems to have relocated."

"Stay to the high ground and keep looking."

"Yes, sir."

Saundra noticed a helicopter approaching. In the distance she could barely hear it. She peered at it through her scope and acknowledged that it was indeed civilian. A door was open and legs and a rifle barrel were poking out. Saundra reported, via goggles-communicator, "A civilian helicopter is approaching. An armed passenger is aboard and seems intent to shoot."

"Can you make out any markings?" Mr. Martin hoped.

"Negative. My angle only gives me a clear view of the front."

There was a moment of silence before the voice of Mr. Martin told his scout, "Corporate security is not supposed to be here. Assume the helicopter and its occupants to be unfriendly."

"Sir, are you clearing me to fire upon it?"

131

"Let's not pick a fight with an aircraft if we can avoid it. Stay hidden."

"Yes, sir."

Saundra heard the sounds of ground vehicle engines. Dust was kicked up. The scout reported, "Sir, vehicles are flanking us off road."

"Yeah, I hear them," Mr. Martin responded. "Can you see them?"

"Only the dust they kick up."

"We're holding our position. Keep to the high ground and cover us."

"Acknowledged." Saundra watched from above as her companions took cover behind boulders and under shade. Flint Gorge readied his rocket launcher.

The gunman in the helicopter took a shot at Saundra's companions. She aimed at the center of his mass, compensating as her target moved with his perch. She let out a breath, squeezed the trigger—and blood sprayed out the man's back. He dropped his rifle to the ground below but his body remained aboard, his legs dangling. A caseless rocket streaked from below and *blasted* the helicopter into a burning, spiraling wreck. The aircraft exploded behind a hill into a pillar of smoke and flame.

"Damn, that was nice shooting!" Danny Delver cheered. He meant Saundra but his thought compensated to mean Glint as well as he said it.

The Delver reloaded his launcher. The caseless rocket was a thick rod bulbous at the tip and pointy at the tail. The material was both the fuel *and* the explosive. It would either burn itself into smoke in flight or hit something hard enough to trigger its detonator.

The enemy vehicles poured into view, one of them a jeep with a mounted machinegun. The gunner blazed away… until Saundra shot him.

A truck loaded with shooters drove by. Danny Danner timed his throw before lobbing a grenade into its back. Men bailed out or were blow out. Mr. Martin shot the driver and the vehicle crashed.

A man on a motorcycle sped up a hill. A sniper rifle was slung over his back so he was undoubtedly taking a position on the high ground. Saundra shot him off the bike.

Attackers swarmed on foot. Glint ran one through with the spike fixed to his shotgun. The Delver then charged the nearest group, the men blazing away but to no avail. Blasts of ionized particles tore and burned their red meat, shattered and charred their bones and spilt their organs. Glint plunged his bayonet into the last of them, his upward thrust lifting its victims up off the ground.

The shooting stopped. Wreckage burned. There was groaning. The voice of Mr. Martin hailed, "Saundra, do you have a clear visual on our situation?"

"Yes, sir."

"Report."

"Sir, all enemy combatants down."

"Keep an eye on us while we confirm."

"Acknowledged."

The team captured three hostiles, two of them wounded. Danny Danner treated the wounded. Mr. Martin questioned the unscathed prisoner, "Who are you?"

"Gilbert Tatum."

"Who hired you?"

"Some guy in For Now City."

"Who?"

"We call him 'boss man' and that's the only name we know. He always wears a hat and sunglasses so don't expect a vivid description of him."

Mr. Martin supposed aloud, "I doubt your 'boss man' is really the boss man."

"Hey, we're paid in cash and all we have to do is what we're told."

"Of course."

"Man, you won and we *totally* lost. Let us go and you'll *never* see us again."

"Make it worth my while and I will."

"What do you want?"

"Tell me *everything*, even if you think it's unimportant."

"Okay."

Mr. Martin smirked. He warned his prisoner, "I have a way of knowing when someone's lying to me. Make anything up and my Delver rapes your ass." Glint Forge growled. The prisoner gulped. Mr. Martin added, "They're a very well-endowed species." The Delver grinned.

Saundra Green watched over her companions from above. She would also look about to ensure new arrivals were not closing in. The voice of Mr. Martin eventually hailed, "Saundra Green, we're letting our prisoners go. Watch them closely. One has his arm bandaged otherwise they are to keep their hands on their head. They are to stay together. If any one of them breaks the rules, kill them all with extreme prejudice."

"Understood, sir."

Saundra watched the released prisoners while her companions looted the battlefield of supplies and ammunition. The voice of Mr. Martin soon called, "Saundra Green, meet me below."

"Yes, sir."

The scout met her leader below. He told her, "The road should be clear. Take point and we'll follow you back to base." The woman nodded. The man warned, "The goons didn't know anything but there may be actual professionals in this mix. Be ready for anything."

"Yes, sir."

Saundra's four-wheeler took point while the lumbering truck followed. Danny Danner was driving the truck and enjoying the view. "Stop ogling and keep your head on the swivel," Mr. Martin scolded.

"Sorry."

A man wearing a hat and sunglasses was armed with a knife, pistol, grenades and assault rifle. He led six other dangerous men into the hills just outside of the Silvertown Mining headquarters, planet Medley. They took up opposite sides of the dirt road leading into the town. They readied their weapons, which included a rocket launcher and an anti-materiel rifle. Richard Martin and his team would be rolling into ambush.

Mr. Martin asked Danny, "How far out are we from camp?"

"Nearly a click."

Mr. Martin touched his communicator and called, "Saundra Green, pull over behind concealment. We'll be joining you."

"Yes, sir," the voice of the Concubine Adventurer responded.

Danny wondered, "Why are we stopping?"

"We're not."

"We're pulling over."

"Yeah, we're going in on foot."

"Why?"

Mr. Martin answered, "If I was 'boss man' I'd be waiting for us to roll right into a kill zone."

Saundra kept to the high ground. Glint took point. Top and Danny kept close but not too close. Danny asked Top, "Do you think Cushing's dead?"

"I hope not: all we'll get is the down payment."

"He seemed like an okay guy."

Top reminded, "We didn't really get a chance to know him."

"Yeah, I know, but I don't want to turn into a bastard who only cares about the money."

"Little Danny, I'm going to let you in on a little secret everybody in the real world already knows: if you don't watch your butt, somebody's going to poke it. I'll risk my butt when I should but I'll bend my knees, not my back."

"Top, you are totally weird." Mr. Martin chuckled, unoffended.

Danny asked, "What do you think of Saundra?"

Richard Martin reminded, "Saundra Green the Wily of the Nineteenth Harvest is a Concubine of the Great Seen Unseen. Do you know what that means?"

"She's a clone."

"Uh, she's a nun. You can look but look away when she looks back. Don't touch. You respect her or you're disrespecting me. I'll take it personally." Top added, "Glint will take it personally… and you know what *he* does when he takes things personally."

Danny tittered. He explained, "I was asking if you're glad she's on the team."

"Oh, totally. I don't think that girl's missed a shot yet."

Danny added, "I know what it means to be a Concubine of the Great Seen Unseen. I know why they call their military the *Virgin* Army. I never even considered making her uncomfortable."

"Then don't. Do your job and let her do hers."

"I will."

"Good."

One of the managers watched out the window of his office as Richard Martin, Danny Danner, Glint Forge and Saundra Green snuck into town. The manager touched the communicator he wore on his lapel and called, "Boss Man, we've got a problem."

"Make it quick," the voice of "Boss Man" responded. "I'm lying in ambush."

"That's why I'm calling: Your targets won't be coming."

"They're dead?"

"No, they're already here."

Danny Danner had rigged the latch to the door of the observation tower to electrocute anyone who thought to open it. He now had to take the time to undo his handiwork. "Make it quick," Top Martin hurried him.

"I don't want to fry if you don't mind!" Danny returned his tools to his belt and opened the door.

Saundra was not with her three. She was perched atop a building keeping watch. She noticed the armed men sneaking towards the tower. She touched the side of her goggles-communicator and hailed, "This is Saundra Green reporting, over."

Mr. Martin's voice responded. "Tell me all about it."

"Armed men are sneaking their way towards your location. Am I clear to fire at will?"

"Are they wearing security uniforms?"

"Negative."

"Do they look itchy for a fight?"

"Yes."

"Cover our escape."

"Understood."

Saundra glimpsed one man carrying a rocket launcher. She aimed... and fired. The man dropped. His companions took cover. Saundra leapt from one roof to another.

Top Martin and Danny Danner hurried down the stairs of the tower. Glint Forge readied his high-powered sharpshooter rifle and covered them from above. When the humans reached the bottom they took up positions. Top hailed, "Big Boy, we're in position. Get your ass down here." The nickname "Big Boy" was the Delver's call sign. Richard Martin's was "Top" and Danny's "Little Boy" and Saundra's "Girl." When the woman complained about her call sign Mr. Martin warned, "I won't remember anything fancy. Let's keep it simple so we have a better chance of staying alive." Saundra was a veteran and could not argue with the Jingoan's sound logic.

Glint's dolly was heavily loaded. It sounded like a fully automatic weapon as he hurriedly pulled it down the steps. Unbeknownst to him, the enemy did take cover upon hearing it.

An enemy was concealed behind a corner and in shadows. He readied his anti-materiel rifle. He watched as the Delver descended the steps. The man waited for a clear shot. Saundra Green already had one. A round punched into the man's back and blood sprayed the ground underneath him.

The rapid fire of assault rifles and the *blast* of a shotgun made everyone in every building duck for cover. The foolhardy risked peeking outside.

Glint Forge had already switched to his shotgun. A *blast* of ionized particles had already burst one of his attackers into red gore. The Delver charged, bullets ricocheting off of his impervious armor. As the men scattered away from their cover Glint *blasted* them. His bayonet skewered the one who did not run away quickly enough.

The enemy "Boss Man" lobbed a grenade. The blast knocked Glint to the ground. Saundra traced the arc of the throw back to its point of origin. "Boss Man" ducked out of sight before she could shoot him. The shooting stopped.

Glint Forge writhed on the ground, orange blood gushing out of a gap in his armor. The undergarment was torn and the plates scored, otherwise the suit seemed

138

undamaged. The Delver rolled back onto his feet and ran after the enemy who had thrown the grenade.

Blasts alerted Boss Man that the stubborn Delver was in hot pursuit. The human darted around corners and hopped over a vehicle. The Delver kept coming. The human hurried over a fence. The Delver plowed into the fence and his weight and momentum brought it down. Boss Man drew his pistol and fired. The shots ricocheted off the indestructible helm... but just one round in the eye or mouth would put the raging brute down. Boss Man's head exploded and his shoulders burst apart from the high-powered blast of ionized particles.

Top Martin and Danny Danner found Glint standing over the sprawled and beheaded mess that was once the notorious Boss Man. "Damn," Mr. Martin was aghast. "So much for identifying him by his dental records."

Saundra Green watched over her companions from above. Her first battle alongside the enemy proved an interesting experience. Then again, the Delvers were an ally during the Galactic War. Still, the Concubine of the Great Seen Unseen had grown fond of her Jingoan associates.

Mr. Cushing had been away on business. Apparently he was called to meet with the reputed gangster Simon Fink. "The bastard offered me a cut if I worked for him," Mr. Cushing told Mr. Martin. "He warned that I'd be out of business with nothing to show for it if I didn't."

"Do you think he's the real 'boss man' behind the whole thing?"

"Yeah, but I can't prove it. He's too well connected to accuse without proof."

"Report it," Top implored. "Just having it on record will make killing you more of an inconvenience."

"Yeah." Cushing explained, "Fink owns half the Jingoan mining operations on the planet. He wants the other half: that's all this is about."

Mr. Martin reminded, "We slaughtered his men and downed a helicopter. Maybe he'll think twice about this little frontier terrorism of his."

Cushing smirked, "Oh, he'll just get sneakier about it."

Martin offered, "Make it worth my while and I'll make it miserable for him."

"Maybe you already have."

Mr. Martin and his team were paid to stay as "security" for a while but no more banditry plagued Mr. Cushing's operation. The four soldiers of fortune returned to For Now City. "We're still on call," Mr. Martin told his soldiers, "and we don't stay on call for free. Consider yourselves on salary for the time being."

Saundra rented an apartment while in For Now City. Her room was between Mr. Martin's and Danny Danner's. Mr. Danner would periodically pester her with a visit but the pestering became board games, video games and watching Jingoan movies. "I hope you're having fun," Danny asked as Saundra played a video game totally deadpan.

"I don't have the reflexes for this one," she told him.

"You chose it. You said you wanted a challenge."

"The impossible is not a challenge. A challenge is an opportunity." Danny shrugged. The stoic Concubine of the Great Seen Unseen bounced and giggled when she bested the game.

Saundra treated Danny to dinner after the game. She wondered, "What does Glint do for his leisure?"

"I think he visits old war buddies in the Delver district. They probably sit around drinking stoically." Danny asked, "What do you girls do when you're not busy being busy?"

"We socialize."

"You prattle. You girls are just like our girls."

Saundra smiled. She added, "We sing and dance both for amusement and in solemn ritual."

"You don't play games or watch movies?"

"We do but we prefer team sports to video games and musicals to the violent pornography of Jingoan cinema."

"Musicals? The Concubines of the Great Seen Unseen actually make movies?"

"Yes, but mostly documentaries. Most of our fiction is of old."

"You like old movies?"

"Some of them."

Danny told, "I was hoping you'd like what I share with you."

"I do."

"Really?"

Saundra elaborated, "Your video games do challenge thought and reflexes. Your movies are… amusing… and there is sometimes an actual plot."

"I just want you to have fun."

Saundra smiled, "I am having much fun."

"Good."

Mr. Martin and company held weekly "meetings" at the Water Hole. It was to assure that everyone was all right and if there was any news, everyone would be updated. Saundra and Danny were playing darts while Top Martin sat and drank with Glint Forge. Mr. Martin watched Saundra and Danny. He remarked, "Those two have become quite a couple."

Glint looked. He reminded, "Concubines of the Great Seen Unseen are chaste."

"Yeah, I know."

"There can be no coupling."

"They're friends."

The gruff Delver snorted, "Danny would mate with her if she was agreeable."

"Wow! That sounded crude."

The Delver stated, "One should not mate without a lasting commitment. Children need a father."

Mr. Martin knew the Delvers were a strictly monogamous race. They viewed fornication as an alien vice unworthy of their respect. Top chuckled at remembering he threatened to have the Delver rape a man. Glint played along… but would he have actually gone through with it? Top would never ask.

When Saundra went to the bar she ordered a sarsaparilla. "No charge," the bartender refused payment.

Saundra insisted, "I have money."

"Yeah, I know: you always leave a fifty in the tip jar."

The Concubine of the Great Seen Unseen assured the Jingoan, "My sisterhood provides. I want for nothing. Please accept what you need more than I."

Barty "the Bear" Hill was a veteran who had fought against Virgin Soldiers in unsung conflicts and eventually the Galactic War. Never before had the Many of One been anything more to him than a cheap and easily mass-produced army of fake humans… until now. He told Saundra Green the Wily of the Nineteenth Harvest, "Sweetie, I love you coming here. Consider it my payment for your company."

Not wanting to be rude, Saundra honored Barty's gracious insistence. She enjoyed her sarsaparilla.

Part 5

MYSTERIOUS BOSKY

Chapter 1
"Witch of Legacy"

A private expedition was under attack.
Machineguns blazed away. Girls in Red were slaughtered in droves as they stormed the site. "We're surrounded!" a defender shouted.

The assailing throngs were stealthy Concubine Scouts and swarms of Concubine Sentinels. The Scouts took cover and aim. The Sentinels charged headlong.

A woman, a Vexite and a Tetran were the three resisting this attack by hundreds. "Fall back to the mansion!" Jane Westmore, the woman and leader of the three barked via the communicator she wore in her left ear.

The voice of Fancy Indulgence, the Vexite, warned, "We will be trapped."

"I think we already are."

Jane was heavily armed but manned a heavy machinegun emplaced behind stacked supplies. The Vexite was bigger and stronger than humans and wielded his general purpose machinegun as easily as if brandishing a rifle. The Tetran was bigger and stronger than even the Vexite and carried a heavy machinegun. The three blazed away as they backed into the crumbling mansion behind them. The converging throngs did not follow them in. Fancy wondered, "What are they waiting for?"

Jane supposed, "They don't want to walk into whatever we may have waiting for them."

Jane was a human female somewhat bigger and stronger than most human females. Her skills and intuition made her deadlier than most males of her kind.

Fancy was a Vexite male, humanoid but head-and-shoulders taller than most humans. His was a hairless hide of fine, grayish green scales. His eyes were yellow with slits for pupils. His fangs could be glimpsed when he spoke.

Fancy Indulgence was an alien yet he favored the clothes and weapons fashioned by the humanity of the Greater Humanity Empire. He was bare-chested and wearing military web-gear. His trousers were olive drab and had pockets on the thighs. He wore black and green combat boots.

Strong-Hearts was a Tetran, a hermaphrodite creature with four arms and two hearts. A Tetran's stature towered over that of most humans and was over a head taller than a Vexite's. The Tetran's skin was course and bluish gray. Its eyes were silver and the pupils were shiny rather than black dots.

Strong-Hearts was both male and female yet he identified as masculine. Among his monogamous people he was expected to court and marry one who identified as feminine, though even as the husband he may bear a child from the loins of his mate.

Strong-Hearts wore a silken loincloth of his culture but other than his dagger and hatchet, his weapons were of human make. He wielded a heavy machinegun and was laden with its ammunition. He carried explosives in his backpack.

The Scouts and Sentinels of the Virgin Army took up positions. The Girls in Green perched in trees or went prone behind bushes or rubble. They peered through the scopes of their sharpshooter carbines. The innumerable Girls in Red merely surrounded the mansion and waited.

A woman with black hair, brown eyes and an olive complexion stepped out from among the surrounding ranks. Concubines of the Seen Unseen were bald under their elastic hoods and their irises were faded white. This woman wore a white blouse and black, elastic trousers. She also wore boots and it pained the Concubines to wear anything on their feet. This woman wore a holstered pistol on a utility belt. She walked with a swagger. She stopped and stood akimbo, her head held high. "This is not one of the clones," Jane stated the obvious.

Fancy asked, "Should I shoot her?"

"No. I want to know who she is first. Besides: we're surrounded with no way out so I think we should oblige."

"I am Elzora!" the strange woman introduced. "I am in command of this battalion of Virgin Soldiers. You shall answer to me as they do."

Jane challenged, "By what authority do you make demands on a world claimed by the Greater Humanity Empire?"

"Your empire relinquished its claim to this region when it signed the Treaty of Bosky. As a priestess of the Living Darkness I am the authority here."

Jane asked outright, "What do you want?"

Elzora smirked before answering, "You are undoubtedly here for an interesting reason. Interest me and I may not have you slain. I may even pay you for your services."

"We killed a lot of your girls. Do you forgive us?"

"They live beyond their mortality as the Many of One. Provide that their deaths were not in vain and your lives shall be spared."

"This is a lot to think about," Jane was actually stalling. "I'm the leader but we all get a say in what we do. I need to discuss all this with my team."

"You may sleep on this matter," Elzora allowed. "I shall have your answer by noon tomorrow."

"Thank you."

Elzora stared at the mansion for a moment before disappearing behind her wall of Girls in Red. A Girl in Purple followed beside her and they made their way back to their nearby compound. The Concubine Priestess asked Elzora, "Why did you give them until noon?"

"I didn't. Have your Scouts find ways in. When they are in position the Sentinels will storm the mansion. The Scouts will shoot the enemy from behind within the mansion."

"You lied to them."

The Concubines of the Great Seen Unseen were selfless, loyal and obedient dupes. The fools lived and died for agendas that did nothing for them. They were chaste and hopelessly honest. They were pathetic and expendable. Elzora assured this one, "I never promised we would not attack. If they surrender before noon they will be spared." The clone nodded, seemingly persuaded by the argument of the sophistry. Elzora grinned.

"We don't have until noon tomorrow," Jane Westmore warned her fellows.

"The Concubines of the Great Seen Unseen never tell lies," Fancy reminded.

"She's not one of them."

"She commands them."

"So? Maybe she got the job because she can do what they can't. Make sure nobody gets in here."

Tammy was a human female and the fourth member of Jane's party. Though not a fighter like the others she was the very reason they were all here. Tammy asked Jane, "Why are they attacking us?"

"Because we're here."

"Why are *they* here?"

Jane shrugged, "For the same reason we're here, I'd suppose."

"They know about the tetrahedron?"

"I don't know what they know. I need you to hide for now. I'll get you when we're ready to sneak out of here."

Tammy shivered, "Sneak out of here? How are we going to sneak out of here when we're surrounded?"

"I have no idea."

Concubines Scouts slipped through cracks in the walls or dropped in from holes in the ceiling. They tiptoed or crawled as they moved into position. One of these Girls in Green was staring down at Jane and Tammy. The Scout touched the side of her goggles-communicator and whispered, "This is Teeya Green. I am in position overlooking the targets."

A voice like Teeya's responded, "Acknowledged, Teeya Green."

Teeya readied her Carbine Type 11 and peered through its scope. She did not notice the four very large hands reaching for her.

Fancy told Jane, "Strong-Hearts found a way out."

"No." The Tetran corrected, "A Concubine Scout found a way in. We may use the way to escape."

Structures were built into the ruins using as much of the original architecture as possible. What was once an overgrown ghost town was transformed into a bustling compound.

Elzora and her entourage of Virgin Soldiers made their way up an exposed winding staircase of stone. They crossed a tunnel of windows.

Two Sentinels guarded Elzora's office. The Girls in Red snapped to attention as she passed between them. The office had a balcony and Elzora went out onto it. She stared down at the vigilant Sentinels and stormgun emplacement below.

Cloris Purple was with Lady Elzora. The Concubine Priestess touched the side of her goggles-communicator and uttered, "Acknowledged." She reported, "Our Scouts are tracking the enemy northward."

"They have no idea."

Cloris corrected, "They undoubtedly know we're tracking them."

Elzora rolled her eyes. She explained, "They were searching the Longfinger mansion like we did. We probably know more than they do. That they know to even look is worrisome, however."

Cloris received on update. She reported, "Eighty-seven Sentinels and three Scouts confirmed dead."

Elzora ignored the report, "A Golgothite must have told them. How else would a Jingoan know anything about Cyrus Longfinger?"

Cloris reminded, "The Greater Humanity Empire did grant amnesty to many Golgothites. They were accepting defectors and immigrants a generation before that."

Elzora laughed. She dismissed, "No one privy to our mysteries would leave the realm of Golgoth to live among those barbarians. Someone within our realm is whispering to Jingo."

Cloris was one of the Many of One, the selfless, loyal and obedient Concubines of the Great Seen Unseen. She stated confidently, "If there is a traitor, it is not one of my sisters."

"No, of course not. You clones do nothing for yourselves. I believe one in my own coven is to blame."

"Why?"

Elzora explained, "There are those who would rather we fail that I may fail."

Cloris loathed these witches and their conniving ways. They heard the Unheard Whisper but only when it suited them. They worshipped the Great Seen Unseen but as harlots.

Elzora sneered at the Virgin Soldier as if knowing her thoughts. She told the clone, "Your lives are cheap and easily mass-produced. We sacrifice you in droves whenever it suits us. Why not? It is cheap and easy enough to make more of you."

Tammy led her friends into a chamber of the ruins. Computers, monitors and other modern technology lined the walls or were in the middle of the floor. Cots and footlockers could be seen in the next room. "Our home away from home," Tammy told the others. "We were cozy and never bored but we had to leave."

Jane asked, "You were recalled?"

"No. Some of us wanted to stay. Most of us didn't want to be trapped behind enemy lines. We had a vote and 'leave' won by one vote."

"What did *you* vote to do?"

"I wanted to stay."

Tammy was not really a coward but she was not particularly bold either. Jane disbelieved, "You wanted to hide out behind enemy lines in a time of war? Was the tetrahedron really that promising?"

"It wasn't really a 'war' yet," Tammy explained. "We found Bosky and claimed the whole thing. The Mystics, Delvers and Concubines heard about it and sent people to lay claims. We tussled with them but nobody declared war until the Galactic War, and that wasn't until the Battle of the Six Armies on Crux."

Tammy was a graduate of the Imperial Science Academy. She was a student when originally on Bosky. Jane wondered, "What happened to your professor and the other students?"

Tammy reminded, "You aren't supposed to ask me anything confidential."

"Why is that confidential?"

"Bosky is a weird planet. Weird things happen."

"Like what?"

Tammy answered, "Bosky may seem like a paradise but it wreaks havoc with technology and magic. People think they know where they're going but they end up somewhere else or back where they started. Things are glimpsed but never found. People hear weird sounds and indistinct voices but never discover the source."

"You're telling me what we already know."

"Jane, I really don't know much more than you do."

"You know something 'confidential' that may make all the difference in me being able to help you."

Cloris Purple was in the command-and-control room when one of the seated Girls in Blue called, "Ma'am, a vortex is forming."

"Call everyone into the circle."

"Yes, ma'am."

Kay Red, the chief Sentinel, reminded the Priestess, "Our Scouts are hot on the trail of the enemy."

"They won't be if either they or their quarry disappear on us. Call them back."

"Yes, ma'am."

The sunny and calm day turned dark and windy suddenly. Lightning flashed and thunder rumbled. As the Concubine Scouts hurried back to base they glimpsed ghostly forms lurking in the forest. One of the Girls in Green stopped and stared. Another stepped into her view and snapped, "Ignore it!" The addressed nodded and the two continued on in greater haste.

Jane was surprised by the sudden tempest. "It's a symptom of an anomaly," Tammy told her. "These rooms are within a protective field. If we stay here we should be all right."

Jane realized, "You're not worried about the wind and lightning."

"No. Well, yes, but not as much as the weirdness."

"Like what?"

Tammy told, "Ghosts haunt these woods. Well, we call them 'ghosts' but we don't really know what they are. People and things disappear."

"Taken by the ghosts?"

Tammy shrugged. She explained, "We were here studying the anomalies."

"Why here?"

"For some reason this region suffers the worst of it."

"Why?"

Tammy snickered, "That's why we were here: to find out."

Strong-Hearts stood just outside, his four arms outstretched. "You'd better get inside," Jane implored.

Fancy shook his head. He told Jane, "Our friend knew the storm was coming. He must feel it that he may see into it and hear its whispering."

"Really?"

Fancy nodded. He explained, "There are such storms on Tetra."

"Did he say what causes them?"

"No."

Jane stared at her Tetran friend, wondering if she should disturb his reverie and get him safely inside. Trusting his discretion, she decided to leave him be.

Elzora was one of the thirteen Witches of the Legacy, the inheritors of the knowledge of Cyrus Longfinger. They were in the grace of the Penumbrans when the Penumbrans whispered to the Concubines that the Many of One should become the Golgothite Empire. The coven of the Legacy became ladies in this new empire. They were made officers in the Virgin Army and commanded expeditions that explored the mysteries of yore.

The Concubines of the Great Seen Unseen were more women of thought than of feeling. Their intellects were keen but their intuition weak. They make for excellent scientists but lousy witches. Their Many of One was not magically inclined. They needed the Witches of the Legacy to fully utilize the mysteries they studied.

Cloris despised Elzora for being a necessary evil. Elzora was contemptuous of Cloris for being selfless, loyal and obedient.

Elzora was out on her balcony enjoying the gusts, flashing and rumbling. She felt, watched and listened as the energy washed over her. She could hear the many voices and feel their many passions. The experience was exhilarating… but overwhelming.

Elzora awoke on her couch. She found herself being tended by a Concubine Keeper. "You fainted," the Girl in Blue told her.

A voice like that of the Keeper asked, "Is she all right?" It was a Concubine Priestess who inquired.

"Yes."

Elzora finally remembered that the Girl in Purple was Cloris the Thorough. The Concubine Priestess scolded, "You shouldn't be outside during a storm."

Elzora reminded, "We are within the protective circle."

"The wind and lightning can still hurt you."

"My dear Priestess, we cannot do great things by caution."

"What were you doing?"

"Do you want me to teach you magic?"

The clone thought about the question. "Would you?" she wondered.

"No," Elzora laughed. "Your narrow thoughts serve my purposes better than they would your understanding the mysteries."

"I am a mystical physicist."

"My dear, you cannot understand magic by analysis any better than you can know a person by dissecting her. You must *feel* to understand the mysteries."

Common bigotry dismissed the humanity of human clones. Cloris assured, "My feelings run deeper than you may realize."

For all the grief, Elzora was ultimately fond of this cheap and easily mass-produced woman. Though superficially identical to any other of the Many of One she was different... and the most interesting.

Cloris stared at Elzora through those black goggles. Elzora stared back into the eyes behind the goggles. The clone flinched. The witch smiled.

Elzora invited, "Would you join me for dinner this evening? I would very much like to discuss things with you on a deeper level."

"Yes, ma'am."

"Come as my quest," Elzora insisted, "not as my underling. I will find you more interesting if you come interested."

"I will join you for dinner."

"Good. I'll call you when dinner is ready. You are dismissed." The Girl in Purple bowed and departed.

The Girl in Blue stayed, not knowing if she should or depart. "I need a bath, to relax," Elzora told her. "I want you to scrub me."

"Yes."

Chapter 2
"Apparitions"

A forest on Bosky was as green and lush as any on Tetra but the leaves differed and the browns were yellowish on Tetra. Beasts had arms and hands as well as feet and legs. It looked and *felt* as if Strong-Hearts was on Tetra. A creature with four legs used the hands of its two arms to lower a branch and pluck a fruit. The animal noticed Strong-Hearts and ran off with its prize. Everything swirled and Strong-Hearts felt is if pulled back.

"Is he all right?" the voice of Jane Westmore asked.

"I think he fainted," the voice of Tammy answered.

The reverberating voice of the Vexite Fancy Indulgence wondered, "Why did he faint?"

"I don't know."

Strong-Hearts found himself on the floor surrounded by his alien friends. "All is well," he assured them. "My spirit was on Tetra. My flesh swooned here on Bosky for lack of spirit. I returned to my flesh or else I would have perished."

"You were a ghost on Tetra?" Tammy asked.

"Yes." The woman surprised the Tetran by giggling. "My near-death amuses you?"

Tammy explained, "Your experience answered a question because you lived to tell about it." Tammy told Jane, "The 'ghosts' really are ghosts. Strong-Hearts was a ghost on Tetra."

Jane wondered, "Are the ghosts on Bosky alive on other worlds?"

"Maybe. Some of them may be alive on Bosky but are disembodied by the same phenomenon."

Strong-Hearts corrected, "I was not disembodied. My spirit was pulled but not severed from my flesh."

"I know. I understand everything you told me. Well, I understood everything you meant and it enlightened me."

Jane enquired, "Is this what you were studying?"

Tammy laughed before saying, "There is a *lot* of weirdness on Bosky and we are smack dab in the middle of it."

"I was on another world," Elzora told the Girl in Blue scrubbing her. The skimpy uniform of a Virgin Soldier was not unlike a swimsuit: Elzora did not ask her nor did the Concubine Keeper bother to undress. "It was forested and the moon of a blue and violet gas giant."

Molly Blue, the Keeper, asked, "Was it inhabited?"

"I don't know. I was in the middle of a forest."

"Were you remembering somewhere?"

Knowing Molly's thoughts Elzora explained, "My experience was not a vision. I was actually on another world."

Molly washed Elzora's long, lustrous black hair. The witch could feel the pang of envy suffered by the bald clone. "Hair is a bother," Elzora told Molly. "We only care about it because it is a means of attracting males. Our instincts vex us to compel us to do what propagates our naturally prolific species."

"You don't like having hair?"

"Oh, I am quite proud of my beautiful hair. I oblige my instincts that I may enjoy peace of mind and body." The Concubines of the Great Seen Unseen were chaste as a matter of devotion to a will beyond their own. They yearned for sexual intercourse as was natural but denied the yearning. Elzora was free to indulge and this was yet another blessing one of the Many of One was never to enjoy.

The witch told Molly, "Tell me about your Priestess."

"Milady?"

"What is Cloris Purple the Thorough to you?"

"She's my sister and my commanding officer."

"Is she just another sister and one of many superior officers? Would you miss her if she went missing?"

Molly shrugged before answering, "We are not peers. We are not at liberty to fraternize."

"Fraternize?" Elzora grinned. "I know you girls kiss and fondle. Your frolic is both lesbian and incestuous." Molly cringed. Elzora assured, "Your perversions are among the few things that make your prudish sisterhood interesting."

Privacy was not the way of the Concubines of the Great Seen Unseen. Their Many of One was proud of its utopia of true and absolute communism. Doors were not factored into their architecture save for entirely practical function. Though the Bosky Research Station 13 was built into the ruins of an old Golgothite colony, missing doors were not replaced. Cloris could smell the food cooking in Elzora's quarters before entering. Elzora was the one actually cooking. "We have culinary specialists ready to serve you," the Concubine Priestess reminded.

Elzora smiled. She told Cloris, "I invited you to be my guest. I wanted to treat you myself."

Elzora gestured. Cloris sat on the floor at the table. As Elzora poured her guest a cup of tea the hostess told, "I wanted to include the cooked worms of Phantom cuisine. Alas, I have neither the worms nor the skills to cook them."

"I have eaten such worms on Erythro," Cloris mentioned.

"I know. You liked them very much." Cloris did not remember telling Elzora about the worms. As if hearing her thought, Elzora mentioned, "Anjesca Red and Nazneen Blue were with you when you dined with Lord Earnestly-Seeking."

"Yes," Cloris assumed her officers told Elzora about their memorable visit to Erythro.

159

The women ate in silence until Elzora began, "We are camped in what was a secret in the Age of The Three Empires. The Jingoans believe they 'discovered' this world but Golgothites lived here long before. A colony from Earth dwelt here before even then. The older ruins were being studied." Elzora was telling what Cloris already knew. Elzora continued, "Cyrus Longfinger and his disciples and a staff of slaves and golems hid away on this uncharted world of mystery. Cyrus would return to Golgoth to mind his financial and political affairs but Bosky had become his permanent residence."

Cloris was hoping for new information. She told Elzora, "I am already privy to all you are telling me."

"Yes, I know. You have read the books and letters available and reviewed the evidence. You know nothing."

Cloris fumed, "You tell me what we shared with you only to tell me I know nothing?"

Elzora smirked. She leaned forward to claim, "I am a disciple of Cyrus Longfinger."

The Concubine Priestess corrected, "You've heard a legend and read the supposed writings of a dead man."

"No. He is alive and he calls to me. I heard him in the wind. I glimpsed him in the darkness."

"What are you rambling about?"

Elzora grinned, "I knew what I came here for. I know why you are with me. You think to make use of me."

Cloris assured, "We all have a job to do."

Elzora knew, "You were told to learn from me what you can. You were advised to respect my supposed authority that my selfishness would get the best out of me. You are authorized to rescind my supposed authority at your own discretion."

Elzora's claims were true. How the witch was privy to secret orders was worrisome. Cloris would interrogate Elzora through conversation, as was already her way with her. "Are you paranoid?" the calm Concubine Priestess asked. "Practice of the dark arts is notorious for inducing a negative emotional state."

Elzora laughed. She knew, "Your Sentinels follow my orders without question... but if you command them to arrest me, they will obey *you* without question."

"You are not our prisoner. As a Priestess of the Unheard Whisper..."

"I am a priestess of subliminal suggestion?" Elzora interrupted. "Your 'Seen Unseen' is *darkness* by definition."

The kept woman of the Living Darkness squirmed: unsettled by the heresy that rang true. Elzora asked her, "Why do you fear to acknowledge your deity for what it truly is?"

"We shall not profane what is beyond us."

"No, we shall not. You shall worship an ideal and I shall pay homage to the reality."

The darkness flashed. Wind howled and thunder rumbled. "Is this storm ever going to end?" Jane worried. She wondered if the "weirdness" was going to take them all.

Tammy answered her, "Entropy assures that nothing in the universe is truly perpetual."

"Oh. Thanks for the reassurance."

Strong-Hearts was gazing outside. He told Jane, "This is a storm or possibilities."

"Good or bad?"

"Possibilities are decided by actions."

"Am I the only one who stayed sane?" Jane chided her companions. "Seriously, people: we need to keep our thoughts on the clear and present dangers."

Fancy hoped, "The storm may be what is keeping the enemy from finding us."

Jane patted the Vexite on the arm, telling him, "Thank you for being the first voice of optimistic realism this evening."

Tammy corrected, "It isn't late. The darkness is the storm."

Jane looked at her watch and was surprised to see the digital numerals blinking. She asked Tammy, "Is your watch working?"

"I don't wear one."

"How do you know it isn't evening?"

"Because it was early afternoon when the storm started and it doesn't seem to have been that long."

"It seems long to me."

Tammy considered, "There may be some sort of temporal distortions in this storming anomaly."

"Yeah, whatever."

Fancy showed Jane his deck of cards. "Let us play a game while we otherwise do nothing."

"Not for money."

"We never play for money."

Jane and Fancy sat at a table and played cards. Tammy brought them warm plastic-bottled drinks. Jane asked, "Are you sure this is still good?"

"Spit it out if it isn't."

Jane removed the cap to her bottle. She sniffed before sipping. She smiled and declared, "It tastes good enough."

Tammy giggled, "It should be. Nothing in it is real juice."

Jane held her bottle aloft and toasted, "To fake!"

Tammy held her own bottle aloft and echoed the toast, "To fake."

The Vexite read the label of his before drinking. Jane asked him, "Are you worried there may be something harmful to your kind in it?"

"No. Some ingredients are distasteful."

"Like what?"

"Alcohol."

Jane laughed, "We don't put alcohol in plastic bottles, silly!"

The raging storm suddenly and eerily... went silent. The darkness flashed but there was no howling wind or rumbling thunder. "Is it passing?" Jane hoped. As if in answer, a whistling sounded as if the wind with an almost human voice. Though soft and melodic, the noise made Jane's skin crawl. The whistling became a guttural moaning and she swooned. Fancy caught her as she fainted.

Jane found herself lying on a cot. The bright and silvery eyes of Strong-Hearts were staring down at her. "What happened?" she asked him.

"Your spirit was caught in the wind."

"There was no wind."

"There is wind. It swirls about us silently but I feel it. You felt it."

"You have these storms on Tetra?"

"Yes."

"What are they?"

"They are a storm as any storm. All is imbalanced and the disturbance intensifies."

Jane realized, "This is beyond some meteorological phenomenon."

"Yes. It is the flow of living energy swirling into a vortex. Let us brace ourselves that our energy shall not be swept from us."

"Is that what happened? Your spirit was caught in a whirlpool?"

The Tetran smiled. He told his human friend, "The mysteries are a mystery even to me."

Jane assured him, "Your guesses are more credible to me than most people's facts."

"My guess is that an evil is beckoning."

Tammy was in the other room sipping from a plastic bottle. Jane stormed in and demanded, "You tell me what's happening or we're leaving right now."

"We can't leave. The storm may be silent but it's still raging."

"How do you know?"

"We've weathered this before."

Jane sneered, "You know something you're not telling. Spit it out or I'll have Strong-Hearts squeeze it out of you."

Tammy looked up at the towering, monstrous alien. He grinned and she cringed. "I don't know," she insisted.

Jane *slammed* a fist on the table! She noted, "You wanted to stay even when you knew hostile troops were moving into the area. You risked your life coming back. Nobody goes that far without a clear and damn good reason."

Tammy told, "We were studying anomalies. We left without answers and it's driving me crazy."

"And?" Tammy shrugged. Jane told Fancy and Strong-Hearts, "Grab your gear and let's go."

Tammy whined, "It's not safe out there yet!"

"I'm not afraid of ghosts."

"Not just ghosts! Weird things happen... and there are monsters."

"What monsters?"

"Shapeless things that lurk in the darkness."

"Really? Why didn't you warn us before we set out on this little adventure?"

"They come with the storm and leave with the darkness."

"They have an aversion to light?"

"I don't know.

Jane looked up at Strong-Hearts. The Tetran was the mystic of her trio and she hoped he had an insight to share. The resonant voice of the Tetran answered the unasked question, "We are being watched and not by a human gaze."

"Can you hear their thoughts?"

"I would risk their hearing mine."

"Risk it."

Strong-Hearts nodded. He went into the room with the cots for privacy. He sat on the floor and folded his legs. His lower hands pressed together and his upper hands pressed together. He closed his eyes and slowed his breathing. Jane whispered to the others, "We need to be quiet. They could hear anything Strong-Hearts hears."

Girls in Blue were monitoring the storm and its strange effects. "Thirteen entities detected," a Keeper reported.

The senior Girl in Blue came over and looked at the readings. She questioned, "Where are they?"

"Their mystical signatures spiked and they disappeared."

"Magic?"

"Probably. There's too much interference to get a clear reading. Whatever they are, we scanned enough to know they are not a race we have on record."

The senior Keeper touched the side of her goggles-communicator and reported, "Security, this is Nazneen Blue reporting."

A voice like Nazneen Blue's but that of Anjesca Red responded, "Report, Nazneen Blue."

"We may have a problem."

"How do they know we're here?" Tammy wondered.

Jane answered, "Aliens of the Great Races are typically psychic. They sense us whether they see or hear us or not."

Fancy joined, "Humans are psychic. You sense danger without seeing or hearing the danger."

"That's intuition," Jane corrected. "We still need to actually see or hear to ever know for sure."

Strong-Hearts opened his silvery eyes. Jane was standing in the doorway watching him. He told her, "They knew I was listening. I dared show them who we are. They did not reciprocate but they did assure that they would avoid us if we avoid them."

"What if we happen upon them?"

The Tetran shrugged his four shoulders. "I cannot hear their thought or feel their feelings. I do not know them or know their ways."

"This situation keeps getting more and more interesting."

Strong-Hearts reminded, "We are adventurers. It is our way to venture where things are... interesting."

Jane smiled. She admired the Tetran's calm, reassuring and eloquent way of confirming that a situation was indeed worrisome.

Elzora called the Concubine Keeper Molly Blue the Caring to her quarters. The Girl in Blue watched as the witch stood out on the balcony with arms stretched. When Elzora swooned, Molly caught her and gently lowered her. "I hear him," the witch smiled. "Even in the silence I hear him." Molly already knew Elzora meant Cyrus Longfinger.

Elzora called Cloris. The Witch of the Legacy and the Concubine Priestess stared at a holographic map of the area overlaid with a fainter image of what the ruins of the Longfinger colony were before they too were ruins. "Here," Elzora pointed, "is where Cyrus Longfinger secreted his tetrahedron."

Cloris disbelieved, "Placing it atop the tower of the gathering hall would be foolish."

"Yes. He knew his untrustworthy disciples would believe it to be hidden within his mansion as we supposed. The shrine sanctum would be another logical possibility."

Cloris insisted, "Hiding a coveted item where everyone had access is unlikely."

The witch explained, "Hiding in plain sight is 'invisibility' to the uninitiated. Longfinger hid his treasure in plain sight to assure it could not be discovered."

Cloris was a science officer. She knew better than to believe nonsense. She dismissed, "Your claim is improbable to say the least."

"I was shown by the wraith of Cyrus Longfinger himself."

"Supposing your 'vision' was more than a hallucination, why would he show you what he hid from his disciples?"

"I am tasked to revive him from his slumber."

"He tasked you?"

"I am sworn to him as a witch of the Coven of the Legacy."

The Concubine Priestess interrogated, "Where does his body rest?"

"He is interned on Acteeno. His colony here on Bosky spanned three worlds."

"The other world is Tetra?"

"Yes. This region is linked to the region zero vortex point of Bosky, Acteeno and Tetra. In the days of forgotten yore, when all was in perfect flow and balance, this place was a natural gateway."

"What do we do now?"

"Shamans of Acteeno have come to Bosky. They remember Cyrus Longfinger and were his enemies. They may have discovered his secret while he was probing theirs. They may be seeking the tetrahedron."

"They may or may not?"

"There is the possibility for better or worse."

The Concubine Priestess confided what was classified, "We've sent expeditions to Acteeno and they've all gone missing. Do you know anything about its natives?"

"Yes. Longfinger called them the 'Shapeless Males' and they were one of few things he feared. Their magic and prowess undoubtedly made short work of your expeditionary forces."

"Will our weapons be effective against them?"

"They are shapeless and master illusionists but overcome their stealth and cunning and your weapons may kill them."

Cloris had dozens of Scouts and hundreds of Sentinels to deal with these dozen "Shapeless Males" yet... she worried.

Chapter 3
"Atop the Broken Tower"

A dozen Girls in Green ventured into the wooded ruins. Only two of them reached the broken tower and crumbling walls of what was once a gathering hall. The two found each other and waited... but the others never showed. The one Scout touched the side of her goggles-communicator and reported, "This is Danielle Green reporting, over."

"Report, Danielle Green."

"Wanda Green and I are at the gathering hall. Our squad mates did not arrive and are not responding to hails."

"Danielle Green, your squad mates are not a priority. Proceed."

"Acknowledged." Danielle and Wanda knew what to look for and where to look. They ascended the winding steps of the broken tower. Though Concubine Scouts were conditioned not to be afraid of heights, the gaps in the walls and steps did give them pause.

The top of the tower was a small observatory with a domed roof lined with openings. The top of the roof was a round skylight. Glyphs marked the spot under the skylight where a removable tile was to be found... but the floor was solid. The Girl in Green squatting over the spot touched the side of her goggles-communicator and reported, "This is Danielle Green."

"Report, Danielle Green."

"The situation is not as supposed. There is no removable tile under the skylight."

"Note the patterns marking the floor."

"The patterns are confirmed as supposed but the floor is solid."

Cloris Purple and Lady Elzora were in the command-and-control room directing the operation. Cloris looked at the witch and questioned, "Are you sure your information is accurate?"

"She found the patterns on the floor," Elzora noted, "and is entranced by their enchantment. Her mind is too weak to see beyond the illusion. Her grasping hand shall always reach around and never touch the tile."

Cloris leaned over the shoulder of a Girl in Blue who was sitting at a console and monitor. The Girl in Purple told the distant Girl in Green, "The tile is within your grasp. Ignore the illusion that hides it in plain sight."

"Acknowledged."

Elzora laughed. Cloris scowled at the witch. After a while Danielle Green reported, "I've been straining my eyes and groping the floor. Ma'am, there is no section of removable tile here."

"Let Wanda try."

"Yes, ma'am."

Elzora knew these witless clones would fail to see what was hidden in plain sight. She wanted them to fail or else they would no longer need her. These clones were useless unless they needed her. "I will go," Elzora volunteered.

Cloris reminded, "Our Scouts are on location and still searching."

"They are too stupid to dispel an enchantment that was beyond the observations of Lord Longfinger's very disciples."

Cloris Purple the Thorough was too dutiful to fret a petty insult when there was work to be done. She instead fretted, "It's too dangerous. We need your expertise. We can't have you disappearing or worse."

Elzora had already decided, "A company of Sentinels shall accompany me. The gathering hall is not so far away. We shall make a mad dash, snatch the tetrahedron and hurry back." The Concubine Priestess hesitated. Though Elzora was supposedly in command, Cloris could override her authority at a whim. Elzora reminded her, "The Shapeless Males or Jane Westmore and her party may snatch it from us if we don't hurry."

The wraiths of naked bald women haunted the forested ruins. Their eyes were ghostly white but so were the eyes of living Concubines of the Great Seen Unseen. "Are these the women we killed?" Jane wondered. She was looking outside but staying inside.

"No," Strong-Hearts answered.

"How do you know?"

"These are ghosts of the living."

"There's a difference?"

"The dead are cold. These ghosts are warm."

"When I fainted earlier, was it happening to me? Would I be haunting the area as a ghost?"

"Your spirit would be here or elsewhere. Mine was pulled to Tetra."

"Maybe that's because you're Tetran. You're spiritually linked to that world, right?"

"Yes."

Jane chuckled. She realized, "The weirdness is starting to make sense in a weird sort of way… or I'm just going crazy."

"You are of sound mind," Strong-Hearts assured.

"Really? I think I'm having a conversation with a big blue hermaphrodite who has four arms and silvery eyes. I might be sitting in a corner in a padded cell talking to myself."

Strong-Hearts laughed. Though he did not understand the meaning of the specifics of the joke, he *felt* the humor and was amused.

A full company of ninety-six Concubine Sentinels stood in ranks at attention. Elzora stood before them. She told them in her lovely but loud voice, "I shall reach the gathering hall and return with an item. Your survival is inconsequential. Some of you may stumble, disappear or be snatched but we keep onward. We never look back." The Girls in Red were thoroughly conditioned to disregard their own safety in the defense of essential assets and personnel. They were not being asked to do anything they were not prepared to do. "Let us make us haste."

The Sentinels surrounded Elzora and the throng ventured into the forested ruins. The Virgin Soldiers were athletic and could run fast and far but were mindful not to outpace Lady Elzora. "I can match your stride!" the witch assured them. "Do not slacken your pace on my behalf! Make haste!" The throng quickened its pace as if Elzora was one of them.

Women dropped as if dead but those behind them leapt over them and kept onward. Shadows lurked and snatched women into the darkness. The others kept running. Tentacles lashed out and plucked women into the bushes or up into the trees. The throng kept running. Screams, grunts and groans were ignored. Desperate haste gave everyone vigor.

Virgin Soldiers ran through the ghost of a naked sister and it followed after them… until they reached the crumbling and overgrown ruins of the gathering hall. "This is hallowed ground," Elzora told the remaining Sentinels. "Remain within what is left of the walls and you should be safe from all but the Shapeless Males."

As Elzora made her first step onto the winding steps of the tower a Girl in Red asked, "Milady, should we follow you up?"

"No. I need you to keep anything else from doing so."

"Acknowledged."

Two Girls in Green were already at the top of the tower. They snapped to attention as Lady Elzora joined them. They watched as the witch leaned down and lifted the tile they could not find. She snatched up a crystalline tetrahedron and slipped it into a pouch on her utility belt. "Come," she then gestured for the Scouts to follow her down.

Elzora and the two Girls in Green met up with the crowd of Girls in Red below. One of the Sentinels reported, "Milady, thirty-two of our number is missing."

"I have enough of you left to assure I make it back."

"Yes, milady."

The dark sky swirled upward. "What did you get us into?" Jane asked Tammy.

"It never got this weird before," Tammy assured.

"You have no idea what may happen next?"

"I have no idea."

"Why did we bring you along?"

Tammy whined, "It's *my* mission!"

"Oh, yeah."

Jane looked up at Strong-Hearts but he was too busy staring up at the vortex to notice. Fancy was not as tall as a Tetran but he was more than tall enough to wave a hand in front of a Tetran's face. "No," Jane stopped him from doing so. "Let him see whatever he's seeing because it won't be anything we'd notice."

Tammy prepared a cold meal from canned goods and plastic packages. "Come and get it!" she called everyone to the table. Jane and Fancy joined her to eat.

As Jane ate she told Tammy, "I love your lukewarm soup and stale crackers."

"Thank you. I opened them myself."

Fancy mentioned, "I like the stale crackers."

Tammy told Jane "I've been monitoring something I've never seen in the anomalies before."

"What?"

"Well, I've been *hearing* it, not *seeing* it. Actually, it does register visually as a frequency display."

Jane *slammed* her hands on the table, making Tammy *squeak* and bounce. Jane smiled a threatening smile and her "calm" was clearly threatening when she asked, "What did you see, hear or whatever? Just get to the point and tell me what you noticed?"

"A human voice."

"A voice?"

"A man's voice."

"You're hearing voices?"

"Just one."

"Do you recognize the voice?"

"No."

"What does the voice say?"

"I don't know but whatever it's whispering it makes my skin crawl."

"It whispers?" Tammy nodded. Jane told her, "Normal people on a normal day hear 'voices' in the wind, rain, animal calls and anything else that makes a noise."

"Oh, this was a man's voice! I hear it when it's quiet especially."

"How do you *hear* a *voice* when it's quiet?"

"I don't know. I just… feel it… and feeling it is like hearing it."

The resonant voice of Strong-Hearts vouched, "The Unheard Whisper is the voice of the Living Darkness. She does not understand its utterance for its meaning is a Seen Unseen."

Jane worried, "The Seen Unseen the Concubines worship is the voice?"

"No, for it is a human voice, but the voice of one who is touched by the spirit of the Living Darkness."

"Cyrus Longfinger!" Tammy blurted the revelation. "The ghosts, of course: Cyrus Longfinger haunts this place."

Jane glared at Tammy and asked, "Who is Cyrus Longfinger?"

Tammy cringed as if she blurted what she never meant to mention. She eventually told, "Cyrus Longfinger was a Golgothite sorcerer in the Age of the Three Empires. His cult built the town that is the newer ruins."

"He was here for something."

"Yes."

"You were looking for the same thing."

Tammy nodded. She confided, "The Concubines and Elzora are here for it too, probably. We have to find it first."

"What are we looking for?"

"The Book of the Dead."

Jane mentioned, "They have the Book of the Dead in museums on Jingo."

Tammy laughed. She told, "Those are *not* the Book of the Dead. The Codex of Legacy is the real thing."

"Why is this Codex important?"

"Cyrus Longfinger was rich and powerful but mortal and only human. He wanted to be immortal."

Jane disbelieved, "This Book of the Dead would not save him from the inevitable. I think you're all after an inevitable disappointment."

Tammy countered, "You don't understand: Cyrus Longfinger is still alive."

"And you know this because?"

"He's been whispering to me."

Elzora made it back to the Bosky Research Station 13. Two Scouts and fifty-six of the Sentinels made it back with her. No effort would be made to find the missing.

Elzora held the crystalline tetrahedron aloft to show to Cloris Purple the Thorough. The Concubine Priestess asked, "What does it do?"

"Nothing."

"Why did we bother finding it?"

"It's a map."

The Girl in Purple fumed, "Why didn't you mention this detail earlier?"

"My dear Concubine of the Great Seen Unseen, your own women are expendable. I don't want to be sacrificed because I outlived my usefulness."

Cloris assured, "We have no intention of betraying you."

"Yes, but I want it to be in your best interest to assure my survival."

Tammy was in the shade of forest under a sunny sky. The colorful birds of Bosky were singing. All seemed lovely… until she happened upon a sprawled Concubine Scout. Tammy approached the form. She snatched up its dropped carbine and pointed the weapon at the body. The mouth of the Scout was gaped and its tongue hung out. Tammy dared to touch the body's leg… and found it cold to the touch. "She's dead," Tammy concluded aloud. There were no wounds to be seen. "Your soul lost its link to your body." Tammy merely thought what she said and was sure she did not actually speak… yet she heard the thought as if she had actually uttered it. "You're a victim of the phenomenon," Tammy told the dead Scout. Tammy feared being the phenomenon's next victim. She heard a chuckle.

A man's voice, the one Tammy had heard without hearing, told her, "Only the weak succumb. The strong have the strength to weather the storm."

Tammy followed the voice. Did she want to follow? She held her captured weapon ready and ventured into the overgrown ruins. "Who are you?" she thought as if actually calling out.

"You doubt your own insight?"

"Humans don't live two hundred years."

"My dear, we once lived for centuries."

"Why are you calling to me?"

"You are beautiful, insightful and eager to learn. You would be perfect."

"Perfect for what?"

"For me."

Tammy felt as if she was prey being stalked by a hungry predator. She stopped. She looked about, thinking she was ready to shoot the first thing she saw. The unseen man chuckled. He told her, "Yours is a gentle power. Killing is not your way."

Tammy lowered the weapon. She asked, "What do you want?"

"I want you to do nasty things with your gentle power."

"Why?"

"An evil gentleness can best aggression. Alas, the primal can best the intellectual. We shall see."

"See what?"

"You or Elzora. There can be only one."

Tammy awoke. She was still on her cot… but she was holding the scoped carbine she had picked up from the dead Concubine Scout. The voice of Longfinger whispered, "She has an army. You have an army. Fight it out."

"What do you mean?"

Jane wondered, "Who are you talking to?"

"I think it was Cyrus Longfinger."

"Or you were dreaming." Tammy held up the carbine. Jane admitted, "Or not."

Everyone sat at the table having breakfast as Tammy told them, "We have to find the Codex before the Concubines find it."

Fancy wondered, "Do you know where we should look?"

"You'll have to follow me."

Jane insisted, "Just tell us."

"I can't."

"You said you know where it is."

177

"I *feel* where it is. You'll have to follow me."

"Where is your *feeling* telling it is?"

"It's not. I just have to follow its lead."

After breakfast, everyone readied their gear. Fancy loaded a fresh belt into his machinegun before strapping on his web-gear. Strong-Hearts put on a heavy pack and slung a large satchel before picking up his bigger machinegun. Jane told Tammy, "Bring your carbine.

Tammy tittered, "That may not be a good idea."

"If you're going with us then you need to be ready to join the fight."

"I don't know how to shoot and I'd probably shoot one of you with my bad aim."

Jane nodded. She asked her team, "Are we ready?"

"Yes," Fancy answered. Strong-Hearts nodded. Tammy nodded.

Jane told Tammy, "Lead the way."

The four ventured out into the forested ruins under the gloomy, swirling sky. Tammy was in the lead but Jane was right behind her. Fancy was off to the left and Strong-Hearts to the right, ready to spray a stream of bullets to protect their respective flanks.

A Concubine Keeper was monitoring bio-scans. She reported, "Ma'am, four entities are approaching, two of them human and one a Vexite."

The senior Girl in Blue looked at the monitor and surmised, "The fourth entity must be the Tetran." She touched the side of her goggles-communicator and reported, "Security, we found the Jingoans and their associates." Tammy did not mean to lead her friends towards the Concubine basecamp: she was merely following her feeling. Jane, Fancy and Strong-Hearts were wary for they knew they were getting closer to somewhere they would rather not go, but they went along with Tammy's lead.

Girls in Green armed with scoped sharpshooter carbines ran ahead of a throng of hundreds of Girls in Red. Cloris was in the command-and-control room monitoring her troops when Elzora arrived. The Girl in Purple asked the witch, "Why are they coming to us?"

"How would I know?"

"You seem to know everything."

Elzora grinned. She told the Concubine Priestess, "They need the tetrahedron as much as we do."

"They are four against nearly a thousand."

"Oh, they would rather not fight, I'm sure."

"They are about to whether they'd rather or not."

Bluish white plasma bolts *zipped* at Tammy and her companions. "Where are they?" Fancy could not find their attackers.

Jane barked, "We follow me now!" and led her companions into the cover of ruins. She hurried up broken steps, mindful not to trip over vines. Tammy did trip but a hand from Strong-Hearts caught her.

Jane leapt across a gap in the broken floor. Fancy followed her across easily. Tammy hesitated. "Jump!" Jane implored.

"I can't!"

"Yes, you can!"

Tammy shook her head. Strong-Hearts suggested, "Continue on. I shall be with her and we shall meet up with you."

"Can you hold her and make the jump?"

"I bear the burden of our heaviest gear already. I doubt I could do as you ask." Jane hesitated. "You must go, my friend," Strong-Hearts insisted. Jane nodded but still hesitated. Strong-Hearts again implored, "Hurry onward that we may all escape."

Jane waved her hand and Fancy followed after her.

"Come," Strong-Hearts told Tammy. He dropped down through the gap. He outstretched his upper arms and assured, "I shall catch you."

Tammy dropped down to the awaiting arms. "Halt!" a voice barked. Girls in Red surrounded the Tetran and the woman he held.

Chapter 4
"Captivity"

Tammy and Strong-Hearts were captured. They were brought to the Concubine basecamp and interrogated separately. The Tetran was sat on a floor under a heavy guard of Girls in Red. A Girl in Purple and a Girl in Blue entered the chamber. The Girl in Blue waved a device over Strong-Hearts and walked around him doing so. She then nodded at the Girl in Purple, who nodded in return. The Girl in Blue left the room.

The Girl in Purple stared at Strong-Hearts through those black goggles that covered the eyes of every Virgin Soldier. The Tetran could see the eyes behind the blackness and he gazed into them. "Are you a Tetran?" the Girl in Purple interrogated.

"I am Strong-Hearts of the Insight-Calm nation."

"Are you a Tetran?"

"I am of the People of the World."

"Are you Tetran?"

"The nations are united against you. In our unity we are the Tetrans."

"Why are you a mercenary?"

"I am a warrior. Why not be paid for my skills?"

"Are your people now an ally of the Greater Humanity Empire?"

"I do as I do of my own accord."

The Concubine Priestess pressed, "You say your people are united against us."

The Tetran explained, "We resist your invasions."

Cloris told, "Our expeditions to your world go missing. What happens to them?"

"Your invading armies are destroyed."

"You kill us?"

"We slaughter the many but keep the few of our choosing."

"What few and for what purpose?"

"A warrior may take a wife of his choosing. The others are kept or sold into slavery." The Concubine Priestess shivered. She steeled herself and glared at her prisoner before storming out of the chamber.

The heavy machinegun and load of gear was left behind by the captors. The Scouts and Sentinels were antsy to get back to the safety of their basecamp. The load was too heavy for human females, anyhow, and was only a weapon and supplies they neither needed nor wanted. Jane and Fancy ate and drank from what their companion left behind. "Why did they hurry back?" Fancy wondered.

"They had prisoners and any excuse not to stay out here was good enough."

"Virgin Soldiers are selfless."

"They're human and any human being of sound mind would not stay our here in all this deadly weirdness."

The Vexite was also of sound mind. He suggested, "We should not stay out here. We should return to the safety of our secret place."

"I'm not abandoning our friends."

The Vexite was insulted. In defense of his honor he explained, "We cannot save our friends if we disappear or worse."

"Yeah," Jane ignored Fancy by agreeing with him. The Vexite huffed. He ate beyond his fill so as not to fidget.

The woman and Vexite were on the ground floor of a broken building. The roof was virtually gone and if they looked up they could peer into the swirling gloom that dominated the sky. Jane wondered if the vortex of the upward whirlpool went anywhere.

Fancy remarked, "The silence is loud. I can feel what I cannot hear and the feeling is like hearing."

Jane *felt* it too as if *hearing* the very silence. She wondered if she was going insane… or awakening.

Concubine Keepers turned a room into a holding cell. They fixed a thick, translucent door with small holes into the threshold. Tammy was already in the cell when she was startled by the loud *click* of the heavy-duty mechanism that sealed the door unlatch. Strong-Hearts ducked into the chamber, a full squad of Concubine Sentinels behind him. The door sealed with the same loud *click* and the Sentinels in view departed. "Tammy," the Tetran smiled.

The woman embraced the alien and sobbed. The four long, mighty arms of the alien gently embraced her in kind. Three long and articulate digits were the hand of a Tetran and two of these fingers tapped the woman's back to comfort her.

Tammy worried, "What are they going to do with us?"

"They listen," Strong-Hearts whispered. "Let us perk their curiosity that we may not outlive their interest."

"What?"

Elzora and Cloris were together watching, via monitor, as their prisoners embraced. "Strong-Hearts is not so strong at heart," Elzora smirked. "Tammy is his weakness."

The Tetran blurted, as if speaking to Tammy, "I may need to cooperate if the Concubines are to allow me to resume my quest."

"Your quest?"

"My solemn quest."

"Oh! Yeah, I wish you luck. Your quest is… very important."

Cloris Purple the Thorough listened with peaked interest. Elzora grinned, thoroughly amused.

Jane and Fancy agreed to camp where they were for the night. Actually, Jane insisted on staying and Fancy would not leave without her. They knew it was getting late: though the sky was as dark as it was, the land got darker and they were getting tired. Fancy volunteered, "I shall take first watch." The Vexite always took first watch. He slept better when he was bored to drowsiness.

Jane nodded. She curled up on the ground and closed her eyes. Fancy knew when she was actually asleep by the sound of her breathing.

Fancy Indulgence was enjoying this misadventure. Though he feared for Tammy and Strong-Hearts, he figured if the clones wanted them dead then he and Jane would have found Tammy and Strong-Hearts dead with the gear. Tammy was a citizen of the Greater Humanity Empire and Strong-Hearts was an official Friend of the Mystic Confederacy: surely the Imperial and Confederate governments would secure their release.

Fancy liked Jane Westmore. She was his boss when they worked for Blue Water Security Incorporated. "Are you a veteran?" he remembered asking her.

"I was with the resistance on Farrago," she told him. The human colony on the planet Farrago resisted a Delver invasion before and during the Galactic War. Farrago was liberated by the Treaty of Penumbra. The humans claimed to have "won" their guerilla war. The Delvers insisted otherwise. Regardless, the humanity of Farrago outlasted the invasion and their world was now safely within the Greater Humanity Empire.

Strong-Hearts was a mercenary serving the Mystic Confederacy during the Galactic War. "My swords of Tetra were my weapons in the Confederate Army," Fancy remembered the Tetran telling him. "The war ended and I was unemployed. Humans offered me a job if I would provide myself as a 'self-propelled machinegun emplacement' as they termed it. I fretted abandoning the protection of my talismans but needed employ. I grew fond of my new weapon and have held to its use since."

Tammy was assigned to Fancy and his team by an anonymous employer. Fancy assumed Jane knew who had hired them but trusted her judgment regardless.

Elzora invited Cloris to dinner. As they ate, the Concubine Priestess mentioned, "We're having trouble accessing the map."

"Fill the crystal with light and it shall shine the map on a wall."

"We understand such artifices. We've been pouring light into it and all the crystal does is separate the white into its colorful spectrums."

"Do you note the patterns?"

"We've analyzed every pattern."

Elzora mused, "You may be blind to what you are indeed seeing."

"Enlighten us."

Elzora chuckled.

The Virgin Soldier warned, "We are the Golgothite Empire. As a Golgothite, if you are withholding information, you are committing treason."

Elzora uttered, "I answer to the High Priestess."

"Yes. Playing games with her expedition is showing contempt for her authority."

Elzora suggested, "I shall make a fire and light the tetrahedron myself."

"Why?"

"I alone on this expedition am qualified to perform the proper rite."

"What rite?"

"You may watch me and note what you will."

"Tell me about the ritual."

Elzora claimed, "You wouldn't understand even if I explained it to you."

"I am a mystical physicist."

"Yes, I know."

Cloris insisted, "No more secrets."

Elzora insisted, "I must honor the will of Cyrus Longfinger."

"We're not here for Cyrus Longfinger."

The women glared at each other. Elzora conceded, "After supper, call your science officers and I'll explain everything to them."

"Everything."

"Yes." Elzora smiled. Cloris could not read the witch's countenance whatsoever. She remembered the mystical notion of "hiding in plain sight" and believed such was that ambiguous smile.

The dark sky rumbled and the upward whirlpool seemed to glow. Fancy considered waking Jane but was at a loss as to why he should bother. He was unsettled by the sudden cacophony of whispers. He glimpsed ghosts through the holes and cracks in the walls. He was glad he had his machinegun… though such a weapon was useless against ghosts. "Fancy," he heard his name whispered. "Fancy," the voice sounded like Tammy.

The upward whirlpool lost its sudden glow and the rumbling stopped. The whispers faded into silence and the ghosts disappeared. Fancy wanted to waken Jane, just to have someone with him… but he let her sleep.

Elzora told a dozen Girls in Blue about how to perform a particular ritual and the results to expect. "Why do you say such a thing?" one of the Keepers wondered.

Elzora answered without answering, "The proper incantation is necessary for spiritual reasons." The witch did not explain that the words of themselves were meaningless. It was the thought and feeling channeled through the words that cast the spell.

Cloris watched as the witch told the ritual to the dozen Keepers. The Girl in Purple asked Elzora, "Is there anything else we should know?"

"Yes. I am not to be disturbed while performing the rite."

Cloris and her science officers watched as the witch set up a tripod over a small pile of kindling. Elzora insisted that she burn wood for a fire that would light up the tetrahedron. In actuality, the lamps offered by the Concubines were entirely adequate. The witch was distracting the clones with extraneous particulars so as to hide the reality of the ritual in plain sight. Elzora rambled in gibberish knowing the fools would hang on her every utterance. Only the first one word and the last one word were the actual enchantment.

The Concubines worried when the same mishmash of color lit on the wall. The fools were mindful of every detail and in so doing they were blind to the obvious: the only true pattern was the white light. Elzora followed the arrows and saw them pointing at a shape she recognized. She told the Concubines, "The Codex is under the Arch of Dusk."

Cloris noted, "That's on the far side of the ruins."

"Yes."

"Are you sure that's where it is?"

"Yes."

"How do you know? What are you seeing in these patterns?"

"I see the Arch of Dusk."

Cloris Purple and her officers reviewed and discussed their situation. They did not invite Elzora to their meeting. "We lost fifty women just running to the gathering hall and back," Anjesca Red mentioned. "The Arch of Dusk is three times farther away *and* our people will be outside longer *and* that is where we first detected the

187

Shapeless Males. We should wait for this… 'storm' of weirdness… to pass."

"I agree," Nazneen Blue voiced. "The phenomenon disrupts communication and scanning."

The Priestess reminded her Sentinel and Keeper, "The Shapeless Males and soldiers of fortune are already out there vying for the same prize. We may not have time to wait."

Anjesca blurted, "Let *them* get lost in the storm. If they disappear, we won't have to bother killing them." Nazneen nodded.

The Codex of Legacy was not buried under the Arch of Dusk. It was within the protective field that surrounded the Bosky Research Station 13. Elzora was out on her balcony staring down at the courtyard below. The Codex was underneath the courtyard. The Concubines would dig it up but not to give it to Cloris. Elzora would not allow the prize to slip from her into the hands of the clone High Priestess.

A full squad of Sentinels marched to the cell of the prisoners. "Step away from the door!" one of the Girls in Red commanded. The Tetran and Jingoan complied. A Sentinel opened the cell door. The one who spoke pointed her weapon at Strong-Hearts and demanded, "Rise with your arms folded behind your back." The alien obeyed. The Sentinel stepped back before barking, "Step out of the cell. You will follow me."

The squad of little Girls in Red escorted the giant alien to wherever they meant to take him.

Tammy was sitting in a corner lost in thought when a sweet voice uttered, "You must be lonely without your friend." The prisoner looked up and saw Lady Elzora standing at the translucent cell door. "You must join me for lunch."

"Huh?"

Elzora commanded the one Sentinel guarding the cell, "Open it."

The Girl in Red obeyed. Elzora stepped into the cell and offered her hand. Tammy hesitated before taking the hand. "Come," Elzora smiled. "We have things to discuss."

Strong-Hearts was made to lay on his back spread-eagle. The squad of Sentinels watched over him as a Keeper squatted next to him. The Girl in Blue pricked him with a device and the bottle fixed to it filled with his blue blood. She then handed the device to the Keeper standing next to her in exchange for another device.

Strong-Hearts was already made to remove his loincloth for these examinations. The Girl in Blue squatting next to him asked, "Is your race exclusively hermaphrodite?"

"Molly Blue the Caring," the Tetran somehow knew her name.

"Is your race telepathic?"

"Yes."

"Is your species exclusively hermaphrodite?"

"We assumed all creatures were male and female. You females were strange to us."

Lady Elzora instructed Molly to record the Tetran's palm and finger prints. Elzora wanted a copy of the optical scans as well. "She is not one of you," Molly knew the Tetran meant Elzora.

"We are human and Golgothite and so is she."

"Yes, she is your race and nationality but she is not one of your Many of One."

"We ask the questions," the Virgin Soldier snapped. There was no insult meant in her tone so Strong-Hearts was unoffended.

"Molly Blue the Caring, you are not the woman you remember."

"I know who I am."

"Yes. Your Many of One is indeed many."

The clones were in the likeness of their template and endowed with her memories but they were not her. She was athletic and studious whereas the Sentinels made from her favored athleticism and the Keepers preferred study. A Girl in Blue was notoriously curious. Molly asked the alien, "We're strange to you?"

"Yes. You are small, beige and only female. You have only two arms and your hands are many fingers. Your feet are many toes."

"Do you find us interesting?"

"Yes."

"Strange is always interesting, I suppose."

The Tetran corrected, "Only a passing fancy is interesting for being strange. You are truly interesting." Molly smiled.

Tammy was brought into what looked like private quarters. Elzora gestured for her to sit on the floor at the table laden with bread, fruit and a pitcher. The "hostess" poured her "guest" a cup of the red liquid from the pitcher before filling her own cup. As she did so she wondered, "Why were you leading your companions here?"

"I was following a feeling."

"Are you a witch?"

"No."

Elzora smiled, "I think you are. Would you like to learn how to use your powers at will?"

Tammy tittered, "I don't have any powers."

"Oh, you do. I can feel the warmth of your power. I can see it sparkling in your eyes." Elzora stared at Tammy, making her squirm. "Would you like me to teach you?"

"What do you mean?"

Elzora explained, "Talent cannot be learned. Magic, unlike technology, is from the inside out. Witchcraft is the art of channeling feelings at will into effect shaped by thought. I am willing to teach you my craft."

"Why?"

"A left hand needs a right hand. Will you be my right hand?"

Tammy wanted to learn magic. She was also a moral person. She pondered for a long while before choking, "I am a loyal citizen of the Greater Humanity Empire. I will not collaborate with the enemy."

Elzora laughed. She explained, "These Concubines of the Great Seen Unseen are not my people. They are the slaves of my people. Their uprising supplanted the Golgothite Empire."

"You're acting against them?"

"My people are the ghost of a dead civilization. The Concubines of the Great Seen Unseen are an undead empire."

Tammy asked again, "Are you acting against them?"

"I am acting in my own best interest. I ask only that you do whatever suits you."

Tammy insisted, "I don't want to hurt anyone. I don't think I could even if I thought I wanted to."

"Yes, I know."

"What? Uh, okay. I thought you were going to teach me the dark arts."

"The feelings must be dark if the magic is to be black. Your thoughts must be wicked if you are to be a *wicked* witch."

Tammy stared at Elzora, wanting to ask her many questions but not having even one to ask. The Golgothite witch smiled a sweet smile. She assured, "You are gentle and I want you to be gentle. May I teach you my craft that you may learn to use your powers for good?"

"Uh, I don't know." Tammy grinned, "I'll really learn how to cast spells and everything?"

"Yes."

"Wow! Seriously?"

"Oh, I am always serious."

A Sentinel was charged to return Tammy to her cell. Strong-Hearts was already back. "Move to the far corner!" the Sentinel commanded the Tetran. Strong-Hearts complied. The door opened and Tammy was nudged inside. The door sealed shut behind her. "Are you okay?" Tammy asked Strong-Hearts.

"I am all right."

"What did they do?"

"I was examined. My race is a mystery to their science." Strong-Hearts knew, "You were with Elzora."

"Yeah."

"She offered to teach you her craft."

Tammy huffed. She wondered, "Do I have any privacy around you?"

"I do not hear your thoughts. I feel what I know and know without knowing."

"Uh, what?"

"You must refuse."

"What do you mean?"

"Elzora is not your friend. She will enchant you from within. Refuse her or she shall use you to your death." Tammy gulped.

Chapter 5
"Shapeless"

Fancy told Jane, "I must relieve myself."

"Bring your gun."

"Yes," the Vexite stood holding his machinegun. "I can wiggle myself with one hand."

"I really didn't need to hear that."

The woman and Vexite were still encamped in the crumbling building where Strong-Hearts dropped his gear when captured. There was a room that was once a lavatory that Jane and Fancy used as such.

Jane sat on fallen masonry… when snatched over the mouth and a tentacle whipped around her body! The assailant plucked the woman from her seat and dragged her across the floor. Her one arm was bound to her side but the other was free. She drew her knife and slashed the tentacle, shedding its green blood. The monster *shrieked* and reflexively released her. Jane drew her pistol and shot rounds into the shapeless horror's vagueness of a face.

Fancy hurried back, his machinegun held at the ready. "What is that thing?" he wondered about the writhing cluster of tentacles.

Jane shot it once more, answering, "Dead." The tentacles did stop twitching.

The woman and Vexite took a position back-to-back and waited. They looked above worrying that tentacles may drop down to snatch them. They were mindful of the holes in the floor lest things creep from below. Anything could come around the corners. All was eerily silent but the woman and Vexite could feel being stared at. They cringed when they heard the slithering.

Jane snatched up her assault rifle before holstering her pistol. She whispered, "They are a race of people."

"How do you know?"

"It had a face."

Jane had fought Delvers, the toughest soldiers in the galaxy. A Delver's armor was virtually impenetrable. A Delver could fight even when shot and blasted into a gory mess. A Delver's weapons tore its victims apart. A Delver could crush a human skull with his bare hands. Jane feared this shapeless enemy more than she had ever feared the Delvers.

Tammy awoke in a dark room. A man was in the room. His aspect was merely a shadowy silhouette. "You're the voice in the forest," Tammy recognized.

"Yes." The man seemed to be smiling, though Tammy could not actually *see* his face.

"Cyrus Longfinger."

"You know a name but you do not who I am. We should know each other."

Tammy told the shadow, "You're spooky."

"I am a living darkness. My voice is an unheard whisper."

The room lit up and the shadowy form disappeared. Tammy found herself still in her cell. Strong-Hearts was still curled up in his corner sleeping.

Nazneen Blue was the chief science officer of her battalion. She was also in charge of operations. She was visited by Marlene Blue, who reported, "A spike of interference scrambled our eavesdropping on the prisoners."

"Storm related?"

"We should be insulated from the effects of the storm."

"Show me."

Marlene sat at Nazneen's personal computer and accessed the recordings with her own clearance. Concubine Keepers are thorough and Nazneen would examine everything thoroughly.

Elzora sat alone and naked out on her balcony with her legs folded and her hands in her lap. She stared up at the swirling gloom. Lightning flashed but all remained still and silent. The witch closed her eyes and felt the stillness and listened to the silence.

Jane ate lunch while Fancy watched over her. She would return the favor when she was done eating. As she ate, Fancy hoped, "You bested one of them. We may have scared them off."

"No," Jane disbelieved. "These creatures are people of a sort: not mindless animals. We slew someone they know personally: they're bent on revenge."

Fancy looked over at the sprawled mass of greenish brown tentacles. Its blood was green, like a Vexite's. Fancy was disgusted to have something in common with the hideous thing.

The Vexite asked his human companion, "What shall we do?"

"I don't know."

"Our supplies may not outlast their patience."

"Probably not."

Fancy wondered, "Do you mean to rescue our friends?"

"Will you accompany me if I do?"

"Yes."

Jane warned, "A rescue is harder than a fight. We'll be vastly outnumbered and where the enemy is strongest."

"Jane, my friend, you are clever. If there is a way to rescue our friends you shall find it."

"I hope so."

"Jane, my friend, I follow you because I believe in you."

The woman smiled. She told Fancy, "We need to escape these monsters if we're to rescue our friends."

"Why did the creature attack you?"

"Monsters are monstrous."

"What?"

Jane explained, "If something looks monstrous, it's probably a monster and that means being monstrous."

Fancy mentioned, "My people raided and pillaged the colonies of the old Golgothite Empire. We destroyed and looted their armies. They were human like you and they called us 'monsters' though we fought them warrior-to-warrior."

Jane told the Vexite, "You look like a giant humanoid lizard and you have fangs. You're a monster." The woman was smiling and the smile seemed friendly so the Vexite was unoffended. He smiled back at her, inadvertently showing his fangs.

Cloris Purple was in her quarters tending to a potted plant native to Bosky when she was visited by Nazneen Blue. "We realized something we should have already noticed, it was so obvious," the Keeper told her Priestess.

"What?"

"The ghosts do emit a signature no different than those of corporeal specimens. The emission is faint but otherwise indistinguishable."

"Interesting."

Nazneen Blue reported, "A human male visited our prisoners."

"A human male?"

"Yes."

Cloris reminded, "There was no human male among the band of mercenaries."

"Yes, I know."

The Priestess wondered, "Do we know who this human male is?"

"He was a ghost but one able to breach our warding field."

"How?"

"I don't know."

"Cyrus Longfinger," Cloris considered aloud. "Elzora claims to have been seeing him. Why would Cyrus Longfinger visit our prisoners?"

Nazneen suggested, "Perhaps we should ask Lady Elzora."

The Priestess snickered. She told the Keeper, "The witch will tell us everything but anything. Keep her in the dark and investigate this matter yourself."

"Yes, ma'am."

Jane and Fancy were still under siege. "It won't help us to wait," Jane concluded. "I think we need to get to killing."

Fancy warned, "They may be too many."

"Then why aren't they attacking?" The Vexite shrugged. The woman told him, "We need to take the initiative before they do."

"Search and destroy?"

"Yes."

Fancy had a machinegun. Jane had an assault rifle. The machinegun took point.

The crumbling building was useful as a fortress for the same reason it could prove a trap: there was plenty of room to move and plenty of places to hide.

"Let's get upstairs," Jane urged. Fancy nodded. The Vexite and human made their way up a winding staircase to the third and top floor. They took up a position that gave them a panoramic view around the building and an overhead view of its interior. "I still feel them staring at us," Jane told Fancy.

"Yes. I too still feel their gaze. We may not be able to find them until they make their move."

"Yeah, they're holding the initiative as tightly as they can." The resistance on Farrago was sneaky against an enemy that preferred the direct approach. Jane now had an idea of what the war on Farrago was like for a Delver.

Elzora led a squad of Sentinels past the one Sentinel guarding the corridor to the prisoners. She glared at the Tetran through the translucency of the cell door and told him, "You should have minded your own business."

Strong-Hearts countered, "Tammy is my friend."

"You may be *her* friend but she is not *your* friend. She came for a purpose and you dissuade her from that purpose."

Elzora obviously knew that Strong-Hearts discouraged Tammy from accepting Elzora's offer to teach her witchcraft. Tammy offered, "I'll cooperate fully if you leave him alone."

"Him? The alien is both and neither a 'he' and or a 'she.' It is a freak even among aliens."

"He's not a freak."

Elzora laughed. She told the Tetran, "My master knows where you live. We're going to snatch your people and turn them into the monsters they really are."

"Your master?"

"Cyrus Longfinger," Tammy already knew.

Elzora ignored Tammy and instead kept glaring at Strong-Hearts. The witch smirked. She told the Tetran, "Your people have a weakness within your strength. Your duality gives you balance but it can be imbalanced by enticing suggestion. Your thoughts can be collapsed into a singularity. The something can be reduced to a powerful nothing to be filled with living darkness."

The Tetran lunged at Elzora and *slammed* into the door! Tammy *squeaked* and the Sentinels cringed. Elzora did not even flinch. The witch and Tetran glared at each other face-to-face through that translucent door.

Another squad of Sentinels arrived. "There is nothing to fret," Elzora assured them. "We don't need more of you here. Let the Tetran have its tantrum. It can't escape."

The one Sentinel of the arrivals addressed, "Lady Elzora, you are under arrest."

"I command this battalion."

"Your authority is rescinded."

"What is the meaning of this insolence?"

The Sentinels already with Elzora pointed their weapons at her. The one told her, "Your authority is rescinded and you are under arrest." This one looked to the other and awaited her lead.

The Sentinels escorted Elzora to wherever she was being taken. The one Girl in Red already posted to guard the prisoners was the only Sentinel who remained.

"What was that all about?" Tammy wondered.

Strong-Hearts sat in his corner and closed his eyes. He calmed his two hearts before answering Tammy's question, "It is a fortunate mystery for I believe Elzora meant to take me outside to have me executed."

"Why?"

"Did you not listen to what she told me?"

The door was slightly ajar. "Uh, Strong-Hearts?"

The Tetran raised his bowed head and followed the pointing of Tammy's finger. He noted, "It was not my rage that broke it open for it is not broken. The door is unlocked."

"How?"

"Let us not squander our opportunity to ponder it."

The one Sentinel guarding the prisoners was not posted to watch them but rather to prevent unauthorized access to them. Her back was to the corridor to their cell. Feeling herself being stared at, she looked over a shoulder. Monstrous hands were reaching for her! The woman cringed and screamed.

A Sentinel was on the floor below the cell block. She stood erect and with both hands on the grips of her minicarbine… clueless that three of four alien hands were reaching for her… until they gripped her shoulders and *snapped* her face past a shoulder. "Come," Strong-Hearts beckoned Tammy. "Let us make haste before an alarm is sounded."

Elzora was brought before Nazneen Blue, Anjesca Red and Cloris Purple. The Priestess asked the prisoner, "Lady Elzora, do you understand why you are under arrest?"

"I have not been charged."

"You are charged with treason."

"I am? What is the basis for your accusation?"

Anjesca Red snapped, "Tell us *everything* you know or we'll squeeze it out of you."

"Torture?" Elzora grinned. "No, you clones are too sophisticated for such barbarity. Mind probes? You'll have me drugged first, to make me more agreeable with your questioning."

"We are willing to commit torture should the need arise."

Elzora looked at Cloris and asked, "What did I not tell you that you now know?"

Nazneen answered rather than Cloris, "A wraith entered the cell of the prisoners. Why did you not tell us the wraith of Cyrus Longfinger was within our warding field?"

"How do you know the wraith was Cyrus Longfinger?"

"Who else could it be?"

The witch grinned, "Oh, it was indeed my master. I told you I heard his unheard whisper. I could see what is unseen. You witless clones have neither eyes to see nor ears to hear. You blame me for yourselves being blind and deaf. You did not hear what I told, or see what I showed you. Is that my treason?"

Nazneen added, "The luminary map is encrypted. You would not be able to use it to avail without decrypting it. Why did you not share the secret of its encryption?"

"Bring me before the High Priestess and I shall tell her."

Anjesca countered, "Cloris Purple the Thorough is the commanding Priestess here. The authority of the High Priestess is the very authority of the Priestess."

Elzora knew, "You have yet to tell me what you know. You think to play with me as I play with you, telling me only enough to keep me interested." The clones did not respond. The witch grinned, "I am flattered that you would imitate me."

The clones looked at each other in silence, as if having a silent conversion. Nazneen Blue nodded. Cloris Purple then told Elzora, "The luminary map was encrypted. We overlooked its sheer simplicity. A mystical signature was in a pattern and we found the pattern in the map. The Codex is in the old library."

Elzora reminded with a smirk, "Our base of operations was built into the library."

"No, I said the *old* library. Cyrus Longfinger built his colony over ancient ruins. The original library is *beneath* his."

"Interesting."

Nazneen Blue added, "You claim to see the wraith of Cyrus Longfinger. You say he guides you to where we search. Are we to believe he 'forgot' to mention this little detail?"

"You doubted my claim."

Anjesca Red mentioned, "What may have been the wraith of Cyrus Longfinger visited our prisoners within their cell. Our eavesdropping went offline and stays offline. Why?"

"Ask Cyrus Longfinger."

"Did he not already confide his intentions with you?"

"Will you believe whatever I tell you?"

"We will after you've been conditioned to be… cooperative."

Cloris Purple ordered the Sentinels guarding the witch, "Take her to medical and watch over her as she is prepared."

Strong-Hearts used his power to hide in plain sight but such a power was useless if an enemy knew when and where to look. The insightful would see through such a trick of the senses anyhow. The giant alien made a point to crawl, tiptoe and hide behind cover. Though Tammy was much smaller than the Tetran, she had more trouble being stealthy. "I will not leave without you," Strong-Hearts assured the human, "but neither of us shall leave if you alert the guards."

"I'm sorry."

"Let me do the peeking."

"Okay."

"Say nothing lest it is urgent that you do so." Tammy nodded. "Come."

A squad of Sentinels blocked a gap between fortified ruins. Strong-Hearts pointed a long finger in the opposite direction. Tammy whispered, "We'll be moving *deeper* into the enemy basecamp."

A long finger raised before the Tetran's lips as a sign for the human to be silent. She nodded then repeated what she said but silently. Strong-Hearts knew the direction was *deeper* into the enemy basecamp but moving out *towards* the guards would be nonsense. He waved a hand for Tammy to follow him. She huffed, the noise of which made him cringe, but he kept onward.

The forest within the basecamp was cleared wherever necessary but was otherwise left thick and wild. Strong-Hearts led Tammy into a patch of trees and bushes. He heard her *squeak* as she fell through the ground behind him.

Elzora was strapped to a table and the table erected so that she was suspended upright. Sentinels watched her while Keepers were busy preparing for the interrogation. "My dear Elzora," the voice of Cyrus Longfinger sounded as if actually spoken in the room. "I need you clever if you are to be of any use to me. How were you outwitted by witless clones?"

"They mind every detail as a matter of course," she blurted.

"What?" a Girl in Blue was curious.

Elzora told the Keeper, "You are treating your rightful superior officer most disrespectfully." The Girl in Blue shrugged and resumed her task.

Though the room was brightly lit, the shadowy silhouette of a man in the dark strolled into the room. The clones clearly did not notice him. The entity stood before Elzora and stared into her eyes. Though she could not see the face, Elzora could *feel* its hard gaze. "You may speak," the voice of Cyrus Longfinger issued from the shadowy face. "The fools shall not hear what they hear. They do not see what they see."

"Milord," Elzora shivered even in her restraints. "Forgive me."

"You are beautiful. Beauty alone would decide but in aspect you are equals."

"Milord?"

"Beauty is a form of power," the rich and melodious voice of the inhuman man explained. "A beautiful voice gives credence to its words. A beautiful face gives radiance to its countenance. A beautiful lie is believable because the listener *wants* to believe."

"Yes, milord. I have read your books."

"You have read what I wanted found. You have seen what I wanted seen. You are as I want you to be."

"Milord?"

The shadowy form outstretched its arms. The shadowy face seemed to be smiling. The cold yet lovely voice uttered, "You shall be with me as you are now… or you shall be as the ghosts who haunt this world."

"Milord, release me and I shall do all that you ask."

"Oh, a good servant does not wait to hear the will of her master. She knows his will and is commanded by its unheard whisper."

"Milord, shape me with your teachings. Bind me with your wisdom. By your instruction I may know what to do."

"Perhaps."

"Milord, please."

"Oh, to grovel is not to serve. Be selfish, entirely and you may serve me well. Alas, there can be only one, always."

Chapter 6
"Under It All"

Tammy had fallen into a wide, long and vaulted corridor of fitted stone. Plants grew thick in the countless spots where light poured in. The giant alien that was Strong-Hearts dropped into the corridor. "We are not underground," he realized. "The ruins above are upon an overgrown edifice."

"Yeah, I noticed," Tammy agreed.

"Are you all right?"

"I know how to take a fall."

"Come," the Tetran waved an upper hand. "The Concubines surely know of this place beneath them and are sure to scour its halls and corridors."

The lower hands of the Tetran each held a minicarbine taken from a dead Sentinel. Though the weapon was designed to be gripped by a pair of five digits each, the three long digits of a Tetran held the artifice as if it was a mere pistol.

"Come with me," the voice of a clone echoed down the corridor. A like voice answered, "It isn't heavy. You can carry it by yourself."

Strong-Hearts and Tammy ducked into a shadowed alcove.

"Yes, but this place is scary."

"It was a library."

"Come with me!" the one clone whined.

"You're a Virgin Soldier. You shouldn't be afraid of the dark."

"I'm not a Sentinel. It's not my job to be fearless."

There was a loud and exaggerated *sigh* before the one clone obliged, "Let's hurry so our task won't take all day."

Two Girls in Blue strolled past where Strong-Hearts and Tammy were hiding. The one Concubine Keeper scolded the other, "You're acting like a child."

"This planet is dangerous. Let's not take undo risks."

"You make your cowardice sound so sensible." The "coward" giggled shamelessly.

Strong-Hearts and Tammy continued on as the Concubine Keepers passed them. "Did you hear that?" the Tetran and Jingoan happened upon a pair of armed Girls in Red.

"Hear what?"

The Sentinels moved to investigate until they heard and recognized squabbling voices. "It's Elsa and Jolene," the one Sentinel concluded.

The other Girl in Red snickered. She remarked, "Those two bicker as if a married couple."

When the Sentinels looked away, Strong-Hearts and Tammy snuck past them.

Cloris was in her quarters, her goggles and elastic hood pulled back, exposing her bald head and white-within-white eyes. She was sitting on the floor with her legs folded and reading a book via tablet. Anjesca Red entered the room but said nothing. She just stood there staring down at her Priestess. Cloris looked up at her but the Sentinel still said nothing. The Priestess shrugged. The Sentinel reported, "She's dead."

"Who?"

"Elzora."

"How?!"

"We don't know."

Cloris considered aloud, "Was she slain by the will of Cyrus Longfinger? Was she a liability because we were about to probe her memories?"

"I don't know and I don't know. Our Girls in Blue are already investigating."

The voice of a sister hailed, "Anjesca Red."

The chief Sentinel touched the side of her goggles-communicator and responded, "Report."

"The Tetran and Jingoan escaped. We are already tracking them."

"Full alert. Scour the base. No one is to leave the warding field even in pursuit."

"Acknowledged."

Elzora was alone with a Concubine Keeper. The witch's body was unbound and naked as it was prepared for autopsy. The Keeper's back was to the "body" as it sat up and quietly stepped off the table.

The Girl in Blue was startled when an arm wrapped around her neck. She struggled... but soon went limp.

Elzora kept squeezing even as she lowered her victim to the floor. She stripped the body of its skimpy uniform. Elzora could not disguise herself as a Virgin Soldier. Though she could tuck her hair under the elastic hood and cover her eyes with the black goggles, her mouth was not identical to the mouth of a clone of Persis Mulberry. Her stature and physique were similar but similar was not the same. Elzora was proud that her breasts were somewhat larger.

Elzora did not cover her head with the elastic hood. She would if she needed the goggles for night-vision, otherwise there was no point: the communicator function would not respond without the confirmation of a retinal scan. She was barefoot but a witch of Golgoth dwelt in the forest naked and barefoot regularly.

Sentinels hurried past the medical wing. They were not searching for Elzora, not yet, but having them on alert made her escape doubtful. "You must be clever, my dear," she heard the silent voice of Lord Longfinger. "You are doing quite well so far. Be proud and you shall find your courage."

A Concubine Sentinel did not leave her post. When an alarm was sounded it was the job of the response teams to respond. The secured areas still needed guarding. A Sentinel would investigate if she heard or glimpsed anything of interest, but she was not to wander far. She was not to report unless there was cause for concern.

A Sentinel was standing guard… when she heard sobbing… then giggling… then silence. The weirdness was not unusual on this planet of weirdness. The ghosts that haunted the forested ruins did such things. Though the warding field was supposed to keep apparitions out, those already in were glimpsed wandering and to no one's harm. The Sentinel went around the corner to confirm what she suspected… only to be snatched and wrestled to the floor by a woman of flesh and blood!

Elzora squeezed with both hands… and the Sentinel went limp. The witch was excited, not only from the violence but from the thrill of killing. She told her victim, "You were in my way and I need your weapon." Elzora grinned when she heard Cyrus Longfinger laughing.

Cloris was in the command-and-control room when the voice of Anjesca Red reported, "The body of Lady Elzora is missing."

"What?"

"It killed two of our sisters and acquired a minicarbine."

"How is that even possible?"

"Elzora is either undead or she faked her death. We did confirm that she was the one who killed our sisters."

Cloris thought for a moment before deciding, "No more prisoners. Anyone and anything not one of us is to be terminated with extreme prejudice."

"Acknowledged."

Nazneen Blue was with Cloris Purple. The Keeper said unto the Priestess, "These mysterious happenings may be troublesome but they are opportunities to examine the occult." When the Priestess said nothing the Keeper reminded, "We are here to study the unknown."

Cloris nodded. She told Nazneen, "We will not ask Anjesca to compromise security."

"I won't."

"Take these opportunities as you see fit."

"Yes, ma'am."

Concubine Scouts were expert trackers. Concubine Sentinels, though not as proficient, were capable trackers in their own right. Elzora needed to be clever if she hoped to escape. She leapt from a roof to a section of broken wall. She then ran and jumped to other sections of wall. She then dropped down behind the cover of overgrown rubble. She set down her weapon, folded her legs, rested her hands in her lap and closed her eyes.

Strong-Hearts and Tammy were negotiating the halls, corridors and rubble of the ancient library. They avoided the Sentinels standing guard and the busy Keepers doing whatever.

The Tetran stopped when Tammy pulled on one of his lower shoulders. The woman pointed at a group of Girls in Blue operating devices. Not understanding what Tammy meant, the Tetran shrugged his four shoulders. The woman whispered, "We need what they're standing on."

"Why would we need the floor?"

Tammy rolled her eyes. She explained, "Not the floor, silly! The book! It's right there!"

"What book and why do I not see it?"

"The book! The book!" The Tetran raised a finger to lips. Tammy said quieter, "The book is right there."

It is the human tendency to assume one is mad if that one rambles emphatically. A Tetran has no such inclination. Strong-Hearts could hear the urgency in the woman's voice and see it in her face. He could feel the truth in her words though he did not know what they meant. Whatever this "book" was, it was important. Though he could not see it, Strong-Hearts believed it was where Tammy pointed. He was convinced the "book" was worth the risk of getting it.

Elzora knew what Tammy felt like. She could feel the soft warmth of the girl and see its glow. Elzora found Tammy and Strong-Hearts. The Jingoan and her Tetran found the book and meant to get it.

Elzora opened her eyes. She picked up her gun and searched the area. Finding a gaping hole in the ground, she dropped down into it and into the stone chamber below.

Two Sentinels guarded a corridor of the ancient library. "Did you hear that?" the one asked the other.

"Hear what?"

Bluish white plasma bolts lit the gloom and *zipped* into the Sentinels! There was a *smack* as each bolt struck and a sickening *sizzle* as the victims fell. Elzora strolled past the sprawled bodies. She could smell the mild, burning stench of their smoking wounds.

Elzora turned a corner. She startled and blasted two more Sentinels.

Strong-Hearts and Tammy heard the report of plasma fire. They hid fearing they were the ones being shot at, though no glowing bolt zipped past them.

The nearby Sentinels and Keepers responded immediately, the Girls in Blue gathering their things and the Girls in Red quick to escort them out of the area. Tammy hoped, "This may be our chance."

Strong-Hearts reminded her, "There is shooting and perhaps at us."

"Did you see a bolt? Those things glow, you know." Tammy ran to where the Keepers had been working. "Here!" she pointed at the floor.

"That is solid floor."

"Yeah, we have to dig it up."

"There is no 'digging' through a stone floor."

"We need the book!"

"Our need may be beyond our power."

Tammy pouted. She glared at the Tetran as if he was being unreasonable. Strong-Hearts shrugged his four shoulders.

The Tetran snatched the woman off her feet and ran with her. Glowing bolts *zipped* past him as he dove into a patch of bushes. Shots kept being fired but no more towards Strong-Hearts or Tammy. "Come out," the voice of Elzora called. Half a dozen Sentinels lay at her feet.

The witch was armed but she did not point her weapon at Strong-Hearts or Tammy. "They want me dead," the witch explained. "They were shooting at you with no call for your surrender so I doubt they'll bother taking you alive."

Strong-Hearts did not trust the witch, but he lowered his own weapons. He asked, "Are you wishing to accompany us?"

"I need you."

"We do not need you."

Elzora looked at Tammy as she told Strong-Hearts, "You need me if you want that book."

The witch and Tammy stared at each other. It was as if the Tetran had left them alone together. Elzora told the two, "I'm not asking you to trust me. I'm asking you to act in your own best interest. Help me and I'll help you… for now." Tammy hesitated. Elzora mentioned, "More

211

Sentinels will be coming; many more to be sure. We must hurry."

"Without the book?"

"For now. We'll be back for it."

Tammy looked up at Strong-Hearts. The Tetran answered her unasked question, "An enemy is most dangerous when near."

Elzora countered, "There is a human saying: keep your friends close and your enemies closer."

"You are indeed an enemy."

"So keep me close."

Tammy asked, "Why are you wearing a Concubine Keeper uniform?"

"I did not want to make my escape nude."

"Yeah, but that uniform is so skimpy, you almost are."

"My body is covered."

"Not your arms and legs. You're barefoot... and the crotch is a thong."

Elzora rolled her eyes. She looked up at Strong-Hearts and told him, "We must hurry."

The Tetran waved one his lower hands, one holding a weapon, as a gesture for Elzora to take point. She snickered, knowing he would never turn his back to her. She admired him for his good sense but also hated him all the more for it.

It took Fancy two trips to bring up all the weapons, supplies and gear Strong-Hearts had dropped. Jane watched over him from above as he made each venture. As the Vexite set down the last load he remarked, "We were cruel to have our friend carry so much."

"He volunteered."

"Strong-Hearts is gracious but we were not."

"Fancy Pants," Jane used her nickname for the Vexite, "I can't carry all that. I'd be struggling just carrying his weapon without its ammo! He knew what he was doing. He didn't do it because he's gullible."

Fancy worried, "Have we delayed too long? May we yet rescue our friends?"

Jane sighed. She admitted, "We have wasted too much time… but I don't know what to do. Those things crawling around are sneaky and there are plenty of places to hide down there."

Fancy whined, "We are cowering from unarmed aliens."

"Yeah, we are."

"We should not cower."

"No, we should not." Jane was not one to cower. She would do whatever was necessary… when she knew what to do. Having no idea how she would *find* her friends somewhere in an enemy base much less deal with its *hundreds* of troops and *if* her friends were still alive or still in the basecamp—any of it was daunting and all of it was overwhelming. Jane was willing to die to do right but she would never get herself killed being stupid.

The dark, swirling sky flashed and rumbled. "It's as beautiful as it is scary," Jane commented.

Fancy looked up at the ominous sky. Its swirl seemed to be glowing. "The sky of Vex has no clouds," the Vexite mentioned.

"How does it ever rain?"

"It never rains. A mist at night waters what few forests we have."

Jane's homeworld Farrago was considered a "desert" world by most Jingoans, though it had rivers, lakes and seas. The settlements grew along the rivers and around the lakes and seas. The barren hills and open deserts were most of the planet and desolate. "We have rain on Farrago," Jane told Fancy. "Not often but we do." She was startled when droplets pelted her. "Did someone up there hear me?"

she was amused by the irony. She took shelter under what was left of roof as the sprinkling became a downpour. The lightning *flashed* brighter and the thunder *cracked* and *rumbled* louder.

Fancy stayed out in the rain still staring up at the stormy sky. Jane warned him, "We're on the high ground and you're sticking out like a lightning rod. Get under cover before you get zapped." He ignored her. Jane's skin crawled. "Fancy?" Her friend still "ignored" her. "Fancy, are you all right?"

Elzora used vines to climb up a wall towards the storm above. The minicarbine of a Concubine Sentinel did not have a shoulder strap so Elzora slipped it into her elastic garment behind the neck.

Tammy clung to the neck and rode on the back of Strong-Hearts. The Tetran held his weapons with his lower hands while his feet and upper hands did the climbing. Tammy *squeaked* when he slipped. "All is well," he assured her.

Elzora and her wary associates climbed up to a spot of growth and ruins. "The rain is refreshing," the witch basked in the downpour. "The storm is invigorating."

Elzora led the Tetran and Jingoan to a spot behind an overgrown wall. The witch sat down and folded her legs. She set her weapon aside to put her new companions of convenience at ease.

Tammy doubted, "We're going to sit out here in the rain?"

"Yes."

"During a storm?"

"Yes."

The Tetran was armed with two minicarbines. The Jingoan was unarmed. Elzora asked what she already knew, "Why are you unarmed? There were six weapons at my feet and you were close enough to snatch one up."

"You killed those women."

"Yes. I needed you and they were going to kill you."

"You ambushed them."

"I did."

"Everything you do is sneaky."

Elzora laughed. "We all have our powers."

"Power?"

The witch explained, "Whatever gives you an edge is a power."

"I see them," Fancy told Jane. "I hear them."

"Who? In the sky?" Fancy keep gazing upward. Jane asked him, "Are you talking about Tammy and Strong-Hearts?" The Vexite would not answer.

Elzora told Strong-Hearts and Tammy, "My people became the slaves of our slaves. We were exiled to the barren colonies to toil for them as if a conquered people."

Tammy reminded, "They are clones of one of you."

"Yes. Persis Mulberry was a daughter of Golgoth. She was taken by the Living Darkness and made its concubine. She was the favorite of its one thousand kept women. The Darkness devoured her to death but not to her destruction. It consumed the others and made a thousand in the likeness of the favorite by the dust and water of them all. The one and many became the Many of One."

"The Concubines were actually concubines? Well, their template was, you mean?"

Elzora snickered, "They are still the kept women of the Great Seen Unseen. They are still his Concubines."

"Why were the clones your slaves?"

"The cult of the Living Darkness was the mystery religion that became the official religion of the Golgothite Empire. Our lowly were gathered and consumed. Their dust and water became the flesh and blood of the Concubines of the Great Seen Unseen. The women were bound to the authority of our priests and priestesses."

"The clones rebelled."

"Yes."

Strong-Hearts said unto Elzora, "Your rulers used the new religion to enslave the people. It used the people to make slaves."

Elzora explained, "We cleansed our blood of the stupid and ugly and replenished their numbers with selfless, loyal and obedient women made from one of our better daughters."

The Tetran shrugged his four shoulders. He claimed, "Before the World was 'Tetra' and the People 'Tetrans' the nations of the world did fight. Never did a nation conquer its own. Never again shall our nations fight each other. The humanity of Golgoth was and is desperately wicked."

Elzora sneered, "Oh, the Concubines of the Great Seen Unseen are never wicked. They are selfless fools."

Tammy asked, "Then why do you hate them?"

"I hate when it suits me and I love when it suits me. The clones have become an inconvenience and you have become an opportunity."

"You want to use us."

"Yes. I want you to use me in turn."

"How can you help us?"

Elzora looked up at Strong-Hearts as she told Tammy, "First I will teach you the simplest techniques for making the most of your powers."

Tammy looked up at Strong-Hearts, hoping for his approval. The Tetran glared at Elzora. The Golgothite witch stared back at him and was smirking. Strong-Hearts looked at Tammy… and nodded.

Chapter 7
"The Legacy"

Elzora's teachings were amazingly simple and entirely forthright. She told Tammy, "Let your every thought flow freely. Never stifle your feelings. You may watch your words and mind your behavior but never shall you do so within. Take advantage, always."

"Take advantage... of people." Tammy hesitated.

"Inhibition is what hobbles you."

"I'm not going to hurt people."

"We can only be true to ourselves. Should we deny ourselves, we do so as ourselves."

"What does that mean?"

"The fearful cower. Deny yourself and you cower within."

Strong-Hearts grinned. Tammy asked him, "What?" The Tetran pointed at Elzora as a gesture for Tammy to ignore him.

The witch explained, "The truth always manifests, even as lies."

"Even lies are true?"

"The truth behind the lie is the design of the liar. To see the design of all that is said and done is to know the truth."

"I thought you were going to teach me magic."

"A science is a philosophy. To grasp the cause is to mind the effect."

"How do I use my powers?"

"Be swift to hear and slow to speak or you shall neither see nor hear." Strong-Hearts nodded.

Tammy sighed. She imitated the way Elzora sat, even resting her hands in her own lap. "I'll shut up and listen," Tammy promised.

Cloris was taking a bath in the bathhouse when Anjesca and Nazneen joined her. The Priestess told her officers, "One of us should be in the command-and-control room."

Nazneen told her, "We've come to report."

Cloris nodded her approval. The Keeper stepped into the water and sat to the Priestess's right and the Sentinel did so to her left: their battalion was a *research* battalion and the chief science officer was the de facto executive officer. Nazneen told Cloris, "The prisoners and Elzora met in the great hall of the ancient library. Ten of our sisters were murdered and by the same weapon."

"Elzora," Anjesca mentioned.

"Yes," Nazneen confirmed.

Cloris wondered, "Are they conspirators?"

Anjesca told, "They met in the great hall and departed together. They made a point to cover their tracks by giving us an obstacle course to follow."

Cloris elaborated on her thought, "Was Elzora in collusion with these people from the beginning?"

"Probably not."

"How do we know?"

Anjesca told, "Our Sentinels witnessed an altercation. Elzora provoked the Tetran to anger."

"Their altercation may have been an act."

Cloris Purple was a Keeper-type Priestess. Like the Girls in Blue she was prone to obsess over every detail. Anjesca Red was a Sentinel. The Girls in Red had the keener instincts. As the chief security officer Anjesca insisted, "Whether they were in collusion from the beginning is irrelevant. They are together now and roaming within our perimeter. When we find them, we'll find them all—and kill them."

"Yes, please do."

Tammy could feel the rain pelting her and washing over her. She was Jane... and she was with Fancy Indulgence... on what remained of the top floor of the crumbling ruin... where Strong-Hearts and Tammy were captured. The Shapeless Males were lurking below.

Tammy opened her eyes, surprised to see Strong-Hearts... and the witch. "Oh," Tammy remembered everything. "I thought I was Jane. Well, not entirely but I felt like her... or whatever."

Elzora asked, "What did you see?"

"I know where my friends are." Tammy told Strong-Hearts, "They're on the top floor of that building where we were captured. They're sort of trapped."

"Trapped?" Strong-Hearts worried.

"The Shapeless Males are lying in wait. Well, Jane thinks they may be lying in wait. She can't see or hear them but she feels they're down there waiting."

"We must go to our friends and deliver them."

Elzora interjected, "Let us get the book first; we're so close and the Concubines are soon to find it."

The Tetran shook his head. He told Tammy, "We do nothing lest we help our friends."

Elzora glared up at the Strong-Hearts. The Tetran glared back. He told the witch, "Unlike you, we do not forsake those with us. We shall not forsake you."

Elzora smiled. She assured, "I need you people not only to get the book, but to escape this planet. For my own sake I'll lead you out of this basecamp. Tammy must lead us to your friends."

Elzora crept ahead and Tammy followed after her. Strong-Hearts kept to the rear. The Tetran remained vigilant, not only watching for the Concubines but to watch out for treachery.

Elzora seized a Sentinel in a choke-hold. Strong-Hearts grabbed a pair of others and *snapped* their faces past each other. The escapees then disappeared into the forest beyond the basecamp perimeter.

"We found it," Nazneen Blue reported.

Cloris Purple reminded, "We're here for many things."

"The Book of the Dead," Nazneen specified. "A preserved copy of the original manuscript was kept by Cyrus Longfinger. He buried it within the foundation of the original library from whence he found it."

"Are you certain it's still there or that he actually put it back?"

"Longfinger marked the site with a seal and the seal is unbroken."

"Excavate it."

"We will. We're doing scans to ensure we can extract the Codex without damaging it. We're also mindful of traps. We've suffered the misfortune of losing artifacts by activating devices meant to destroy them should they be uncovered."

"Cloris Purple," the Priestess was hailed by Anjesca Red.

Cloris touched the side of her goggles-communicator and responded, "Report."

"Elzora, the Jingoan and the Tetran escaped the grounds."

"Together?"

"Yes."

The Priestess stated, "We don't have a reason to risk women chasing after them."

"I agree."

"Let them go."

"Acknowledged."

Elzora, Tammy and Strong-Hearts could *feel* themselves being watched. They glimpsed a form slithering in the bushes. The three went far around those bushes. They saw "vines" creeping up into the branches of a tree. The companions went around that tree, mindful not to be under its branches. They looked up into the other trees fearful that "vines" would drop down and snatch them.

"There," Tammy pointed at particular ruins. Elzora moved to take the lead but Tammy warned her, "Let me take point so my friends don't shoot you."

"Yes, please be between us. Show them we are coming."

"Show them?"

"Yes."

"How?"

Elzora told, "You feel them because there is already a connection. Use the connection to share your thoughts."

"I'm not telepathic."

"You are, actually."

"Really?"

"How else do you know where to find them?"

Tammy warned, "I may be wrong."

"No, I feel that you right."

"So what do I do?"

"Sublimate your feelings into thoughts and direct them along the lines of your connections."

Tammy fumed, "Oh, thanks for making that as clear as mud!"

"My dear, did you expect to learn my craft from a secret?"

"Yeah."

"Do you not have eyes to see? Do you not have ears to hear?"

"You know, this is exactly why my people prefer technology."

"Technology is easier, of course. I make plenty use of it myself." Elzora brandished her minicarbine with a sly grin.

Strong-Hearts told Elzora, "They know we are coming. They are watching us from above."

"I know. I was hoping Tammy would use her powers regardless."

Jane and Fancy watched as Tammy led Elzora and Strong-Hearts up to the top floor. Fancy wondered, "Why is that Golgothite witch with them?"

Jane wondered, "How do they know we're up here." She grinned, "Why is Elzora wearing that skimpy uniform?"

Jane hugged and kissed Strong-Hearts. She smiled at Tammy and sneered at the Golgothite. Strong-Hearts explained, "The Concubines arrested her and she escaped. She helped us escape. Tammy found a book and I believe it is the Book of the Dead we seek."

Jane wondered, "Do you have it."

"It is under the floor of the ruins under the Virgin Army basecamp."

"Under the floor? In a chamber?"

"Under the stone of the floor."

"Buried?"

"It would seem the book is within the very foundation of an ancient ruin."

Elzora interjected, "The Concubines decrypted the map. They'll decipher the glyphs if they haven't already. They'll be excavating the Codex quite soon."

Jane snubbed, "I really don't care."

Elzora claimed, "The Book of the Dead is a record of mysteries, not the least of which is the means for turning the living into undead slaves." Jane laughed. Elzora continued, "The Concubines of the Great Seen Unseen hope to use the secrets of the book to ease the production of their own. They also hope to negate the effects that render them hairless and their eyes ghostly white. It is in the best interest of your Greater Humanity Empire to thwart them."

"What do you care, Golgothite?"

"The book is written in such a manner that the reader shall read other than what is truly written lest the reader has eyes to see. You're people will be misled rather than enlightened. I would be of use to you."

"What's in it for you?"

"As I decipher the book for you I may learn the secret to extending my youth, if not my life."

Jane looked up at Strong-Hearts. She told him, "You didn't kill this bitch so that's got to count for something."

The resonant voice of the Tetran told Jane, "She is treacherous but she is selfish and wise. We must trust her to do what is best for her."

"I don't like watching my back."

"My friend, we may need her if we are to snatch to the Book of the Dead from the enemies of your people and my people."

"Our people may not be threatened. Seriously: I don't believe in all that mumbo jumbo."

"You know magic is real."

"Yes, and I know even magic always has a rational explanation. Zombies and eternal youth are flights of fancy, irrational fantasy."

Strong-Hearts told, "I served as a mercenary in the Confederate Army. The Mystics told me how your people were fools who discounted their army with swords, bows and arrows. You believed your guns and bombs would make short work of them. Your guns and bombs failed. In your desperation you believed your poison gas and nuclear weapons would avail you. They did not avail you. To your dismay, your greatest weapons were the least effective."

Jane explained, "We had never encountered a magically advanced civilization before. We know better now."

223

"Know better to know that there are things unknown to you." Jane nodded. She did not believe in zombies or eternal youth but she did believe in her friend Strong-Hearts. That he was adamant was good enough for her.

"You tripped motion sensors then walked into the crossing waves of bio-scanners," Elzora told. "You should have used the terrain and its ruins to your advantage."

Jane explained, "We were following Tammy's intuition and didn't want her to lose her connection."

"Yes, and it got her and Strong-Hearts captured." Elzora told the Tetran, "You were not detected until a Scout spotted you. Her scan revealed your nature."

Strong-Hearts admitted, "I did not notice the Scout."

"She was sent to investigate your friends."

Jane reminded, "You said we're in a hurry."

"Yes."

Elzora led her companions the "long way" to the Concubine basecamp. Two Sentinels guarded a hole in the ground… until the *pop pop* of Jane's silenced pistol silenced them.

The companions used a rope to climb down into the hole. Jane removed the silencer from her pistol and holstered the weapon before doing so.

Elzora led the way alongside Fancy and his machinegun. Jane and Tammy followed close behind. Strong-Hearts and his heavy machinegun kept to the rear. The Tetran kept on eye on Elzora more than he watched for Virgin Soldiers.

Half a dozen Girls in Blue were operating devices over the section of floor where the Book of the Dead was buried. A dozen Girls in Red stood around them with their backs to them. Elzora told Jane, "There's no way we can do this sneakily."

"I'd rather not have hundreds of Sentinels converging on our location."

Elzora advised, "We kill the women quickly, use their equipment to uncover the book and we leave the way we came."

"That simple, huh?"

"These clones overthink. The direct approach is not what they're prepared for."

"Yeah, that sounds about right." Jane looked at Strong-Hearts. When he nodded she told him and Fancy, "We take out the girls without damaging their equipment. No grenades and mind your shots." Tammy covered her ears.

Two machineguns and Jane's assault rifle blazed away. Blood sprayed out of the clones and they dropped en masse. "Let's get that book," Jane hurried her team to the spot. She asked Elzora, "Do you know how to use the equipment?"

The witch smirked, "Not as well as I know how to use Tammy."

"What?"

The witch laughed and all became pitch dark!

Tammy was alone with Cyrus Longfinger. She could neither see nor hear him but she could *feel* his unsettling presence. She *felt* his unheard whisper tell her, "Your untrained potential was tapped into by Elzora with your blessing. She channeled what you gave her to cast a spell beyond her own power."

"I did this?"

"Yes."

"Elzora is attacking my friends!"

"She cannot use your power to attack your friends. To even try would break the spell and they would surely kill her."

"I don't understand any of this!"

"Potential cannot be taught but it cannot be realized without learning. Come to me and I will teach you."

"So you can tap into my power too?"

"Oh, yes."

Tammy felt like a little girl alone with a child molester. She snapped, "No way!" Whatever she did, it broke the spell. She "awoke" from the "darkness" and found herself with her friends. There was a hole in the floor and Elzora was gone. "She has the book!"

Jane insisted, "Then we need to get her."

"Not that way!" Tammy stopped her friends from chasing after Elzora the way they came. "Follow me."

"You know where she is?"

"Follow me!"

Strong-Hearts vouched, "Her eye to see has opened. Let us follow her gaze."

Tammy led everyone down a corridor. As they rounded a corner they happened upon two sprawled Sentinels with smoking wounds.

There was light at the end of the corridor. Tammy led her friends outside. They happened upon crowds of Concubine Sentinels. Everyone raised their weapons. Minicarbines, machineguns and an assault rifle blazed away. The crowds of Girls in Red withered but throngs more were coming.

Strong-Hearts implored Jane, "Follow Tammy and get the book! Fancy and I shall stay the Concubines." Jane hesitated. The Tetran smiled, "My friend, forsake us if you must. For all whom we love, leave us behind."

Jane nodded. Tammy led the way. Jane gunned down any Sentinels who got in their way.

Elzora could hear all shooting. She hid as groups of Sentinels passed, knowing they were hurrying to the fight and not searching for her. When beyond the perimeter of the basecamp she ran as fast as she could.

The sky was dark and swirling but the land was as bright as it would be on an overcast day. The forest and its ruins were shadowy and the witch knew to fear these shadows. Ghosts haunted, horrors lurked and a spot was not always in the same place. Chilling winds could pull a woman's soul right out of her and carry it to wherever.

Elzora held her weapon in one hand and carried the Book of the Dead under an arm with the other. She ran up the steps of a ruin and perched where she would see her pursuers coming… if they were coming. "Bold and wily," a chilling breeze sounded as if a whisper.

"Milord?" Elzora wondered if it was the voice of Cyrus Longfinger. "Milord, I have the book and mean to bring it to you."

Tammy hid. She pointed up at a ruin and told Jane, "She's up there waiting for us."

"You see her?"

"No, I *feel* her."

Jane looked up through the optical sights of her rifle. She spotted the face of Elzora… but it ducked behind the wall it was hiding behind. "She didn't see you," Tammy told Jane. "She felt you staring at her."

"She felt me?"

"Don't we all *feel* it when someone's staring at us?"

"Not always. I've shot people who didn't see… *feel* it coming."

Tammy told, "Well, you're not going to get the drop on Elzora."

"So what do we do?"

"I don't know."

"Figure it out."

Tammy grinned. She decided, "I'll use what Elzora taught me."

"Milord, help me," Elzora pled.
"There can be only one, always," the voice of Cyrus Longfinger whispered. It chilled the woman to hear it. "Be the one and I shall be with you."
"Milord, I bested her!"
"We shall see."
Tammy could *feel* Elzora's heart pounding within her own bosom. She could see through the witch's eyes as if they were her own. Her thoughts told Elzora as if Elzora's thoughts, "You taught her by using her. She knew what she did not know and used you to teach her." Cyrus Longfinger chuckled.
Elzora could see Tammy ascending the steps as if she was Tammy. She beheld herself through the eyes of Tammy. She watched herself cringe before her. All went dark. Elzora may have been screaming but she could only *feel* her cries. Her wailing broke the spell… but her weapon and the Book of the Dead were missing.
Tammy returned with a tome and a minicarbine. "Let's get out of here," she implored. "The Shapeless Males are coming."
"What about Elzora?"
"Like I said, the Shapeless Males are coming. They've been watching us the whole time."

Strong-Hearts and Fancy Indulgence made their escape *away* from where Tammy and Jane had gone. "We're not following them into the storm," Cloris Purple decided.
Anjesca Red commanded her women, "Disengage. Return to the warding field."

The Virgin Army lost two hundred more women from the unexpected raid. They had many hundreds more but preferred not to squander their many.

Tammy and Jane found Strong-Hears and Fancy Indulgence on what remained of the third floor of the overgrown ruin that had become their abode. The bulk of their supplies were on that floor. "The storm is breaking," Tammy told her friends. "We need to leave the area before the Concubines come after us."

Jane reminded, "We could be lost in this storm of weirdness."

"Yeah, or we can wait to be surrounded and overrun."

"Good point."

Strong-Hearts carried most of the gear, as usual. He mentioned, "Spending so much ammunition lightened my load."

Jane responded, "That's kind of good *and* bad. We might need that ammunition."

Tammy asked the Tetran, "Did you know Elzora was enchanting me with her lessons?"

"Yes."

"Why did you let her?"

"Tammy, my friend, do you understand why my people name our people as we do?"

"No."

"She roused you and in doing so, she opened your eye to see."

"I see," Tammy giggled.

The shadowy form of a man watched as Tammy and her friends departed. The young witch would read the book and when she read what was hidden within the obvious, she would return... and he would be waiting for her.

Part 6

THE RELUCTANT GANGSTER

Chapter 1
"The Wrong Place at the Right Time"

Noburg was a Jingoan city on the planet Vex. Most of the inhabitants were humanity from the planet Jingo or its colonies. The mayor and city council were exclusively Vexite. Penumbrans were the only alien race allowed citizenship. They alone were allowed to participate directly in Vexite politics. These privileges were exercised discreetly, however, for it was the way of the Penumbrans to live among natives as a seen unseen.

All was well between the natives and their resident visitors. The Penumbrans and Jingoans brought business and technology to the otherwise poor and primitive world. Jingoans provided labor and skills the naturally barbaric Vexites were uninterested in providing.

Noburg was a center for trade both legitimate and illicit. The empires of the galaxy and their slaves lived in the city as plentiful minorities. The Mystics, Delvers, Hive and Golgothites all had their enclaves. The Lunks, Piddlings and other slave races had their ghettoes.

Lester Freeman was on his way home after a hard day of work. He went into a tavern for no other reason than he was thirsty and did not want to wait. He did not drink alcohol but was sure the establishment served non-alcoholic beverages.

The tavern was operated by humans and most of its clientele was human but aliens were also customers. Delvers were ate a table drinking what looked like beer. Though there were several of these creatures together, they enjoyed their beverages without conversation. The Vexites were intermingled with the humans and just as rowdy.

A Vexite was what Jingoan science classified as *pseudo-reptilian*: scaly but warm-blooded. A Vexite was greenish gray and its negligible ears looked somewhat as if fish gills. Its eyes were yellow with elliptical pupils. The creature had fangs and its countenance was scary when it smiled. A Vexite was humanoid but its stature head-and-shoulders taller than most humans. Its females had breasts and firm buttocks and many humans actually found them comely. Lester was embarrassed being one such human.

Lester went to the bar and ordered a sarsaparilla. The bartender laughed but poured him a glass. A grungy human male wearing a sleeveless shirt snatched up the glass. He gestured as if making a toast then started gulping the drink down. His associates, equally grungy human males, laughed as if this outrage was somehow clever. The thief kept drinking until the glass was empty. He then belched in Lester's face and told him, "I hate sarsaparilla. It tastes like piss." The bully's friends laughed all the more.

The Mystics were a humanoid race of creatures as tall as Vexites but otherwise very unlike them. Mystics were slender and their every feature long and narrow. Their irises were large and either deep blue or silvery gray. The hair of a Mystic was long and lustrous black. A long goatee dangled from the chin of a male.

A Mystic sitting alone glared at the bully. One of the bully's friends pointed the alien out. The bully asked the Mystic, "What are you looking at, lefty?" Most Mystics were left-handed and "lefty" was a racial slur. The Mystic smirked. "I'm going to slap that smile off your face," the bully threatened... but the Mystic kept smirking. The bully shrugged as if challenging the silent alien. The human raised a middle finger at the Mystic before leading his friends out of the tavern.

The Mystic waved for a waitress to come to his table. When she came to him he whispered in her ear. She nodded. The waitress told the bartender, "Give this gentleman anything he asks for. Mr. Merit is paying."

"Another sarsaparilla?" the bartender asked Lester. When Lester failed to answer right away the bartender poured him another sarsaparilla anyhow. "Enjoy."

"Thank you." Lester raised the glass for the Mystic to see and told him, "Thank you." The Mystic smiled and nodded. Encouraged by the smile, Lester went over and asked, "May I join you, sir?" The Mystic gestured for the man to sit with him. "Lester Freeman," the human offered his hand. The Mystic nodded but would not take the offered hand. Lester took the hint.

"I am Dubious Merit," the melodious voice of the Mystic spoke. He said nothing more and the silence made Lester squirm.

"I hope I'm not bothering you." The Mystic shook his head. "Dubious Merit," Lester repeated the name. "What brings you here all the way from Mystique?"

"I am not from Mystique nor have I ever been there."

"Oh, yes, I'm sorry. Your empire is a confederacy. I didn't mean to imply all Mystics are from Mystique. I just can't tell the difference… I mean, I don't know what to look for to tell the difference between Mystics from one state or another."

The Mystic grinned and Lester could not tell if the grin was a smile or a smirk. "A nature is what it is," Dubious Merit stated. "Nothing else truly matters."

"What? I'm sorry but I don't know what you mean."

"The man who bullied you is a mindless brute. His animosity is impersonal and his aggression pointless. I shall not suffer such a restless fool."

"Yeah," Lester agreed.

233

"You are timid… but such is not your nature. You must become what you truly are."

"I'm sorry: what?"

"Lester Freeman, why did you come to this dangerous place?"

"What, to the tavern, the city, the planet?"

"Yes."

"Which place?" The Mystic grinned and would not answer. His eerie calm unsettled the human. Lester tried to answer what the Mystic asked, "I came to the planet and this city because that's where my job sent me. I came into the tavern because I was thirsty."

"All these places are dangerous… yet you came."

"Well, I need the money so I don't really have a choice."

"Your need is to venture into danger."

Lester tittered. He reminded, "You just watched me shake like a leaf while some guy stole my drink and guzzled it right in front of me."

"Yes. You should kill him."

"What?"

Dubious Merit reconsidered, "You are not yet ready. I shall kill him."

"What? No!"

"Why not?"

"You can't just *kill* people because you feel like it."

"Why not?"

"You're not talking about self-defense. You're talking about murder."

"Yes," the Mystic grinned, his inhuman countenance as cold as it was enthusiastic. He asked, "Did you fight for your people?"

"What?"

"Are you a veteran?"

"No."

Dubious Merit told, "I was a scout in the Confederate Army. I slew many of your people on Bosky. I fought alongside your people on Crux." Lester nodded. Dubious Merit explained, "We were enemies when it suited us. We were friends when it suited us. Never did our natures change, only the circumstances."

Lester again nodded, but he asked, "What are you getting at?"

"My friend, our circumstances favor you." The Mystic stood, his towering stature looming over the insignificant human as if a shadow of death. "Be here tomorrow at noon."

"I can't. I have work tomorrow. I'll be on the other side of the city."

"I shall be waiting." Dubious Merit passed Lester Freeman. When the human turned, he noticed the Mystic had completely disappeared.

Lester took the bus to his apartment complex. He made his way up the flight of stairs to the top floor. As he fiddled with his keys to open the door, his neighbor and co-worker Annie Smith greeted, "Hello, Lester!" Annie was a cute girl who was usually shy but never when alone with Lester. He believed she was flirting but was too shy himself to ever respond in kind. "You're getting home late."

"Yeah," Lester agreed. "Anton had me on the other side of town."

"Doing what?"

"The usual."

"Why so late?"

"He waited until the last minute to get it done."

"For *you* to get it done, you mean."

"Yeah." Annie smiled at Lester in silence. He squirmed before telling her, "You have a good night."

"You too."

Lester was on the other side of the door and locking it when he realized he may have lost an opportunity to invite Annie inside… but would she be offended if her smiles were not meaning anything? Lester never knew what to do, even after the fact.

Lester took his *lizard hamster* out of its cage and petted the little thing. He sat and laid the thing in his lap. He giggled as it crawled up his shirt. It perched on his shoulder and licked his neck. Lester chuckled when it licked his earlobe.

The *lizard hamster* was indigenous to the planet Vex. The creature was called a "feisty morsel" by the Vexites because the Vexites ate the poor things. Lester purchased his from a meat shop that catered to Vexites. He named his *feisty morsel* "Spunky" and pampered the little thing.

A *lizard hamster* was neither a *lizard* nor a *hamster* yet it looked as if a hybrid of the two. Its greenish gray, scaly body was warm unlike a reptile. It had large, yellow eyes with large, almost elliptical, black-dot pupils. The thing was always fidgeting and sniffing. Its little tongue shot out to lick anything it happened upon.

There was a knock at the door. Spunky's frills popped out. "It's all right," Lester patted his little pet. He kept Spunky on his shoulder while answering the door. Anton was the one on the other side. "Not tonight," Lester told him. Anton was probably asking for "help" to do his work for him.

"That was rude," Anton feigned offense. "You don't even know what I'm calling for."

"You want me to do your report for you."

"No, I want you to help me *edit* my report."

Lester accused, "You give me your notes and I write the report."

"I'm your boss, Lester. You're supposed to do my work for me."

Lester rolled his eyes. He corrected, "You're my team leader, not my supervisor. You're not supposed to *lead* from behind."

"Lester…"

"I'm home late because of you!"

"I'm sorry."

"No, you're not!"

Anton asked, "How can I make it up to you?"

For once in his life Lester saw an opportunity before missing it. He requested, "Give me tomorrow off."

"Why tomorrow?"

"Why not?"

Anton considered the request. "You'll have my report done by Sunday?"

"I'll have it done by Saturday."

"You haven't even seen my notes."

"Saturday," Lester repeated.

"Wow. Okay. Enjoy tomorrow."

"I hope so."

Lester returned to the tavern earlier than noon. He thought to sit where he sat yesterday but the seat was already occupied. "Choose," Lester thought he heard Dubious Merit… but when he turned the Mystic was nowhere in sight. Lester chose a spot but worried when the bully and friends entered the establishment. Lester relocated. He thought he heard Dubious Merit chuckle… but again the Mystic was nowhere to be seen.

Lester sat… and was startled to find the Mystic already at the table! "Mr. Freeman, thank you for coming."

"How did you do that?"

"Do what?"

"You just… appeared out of nowhere."

"That would be impossible."

"I didn't see you!"

"You did not see me." The Mystic was as eerily calm as ever. He waved for a waitress to come to the table.

"Mr. Merit," she already knew him by name. She smiled as if genuinely pleased to see him.

"Miss Rowling, my usual beverage and a sarsaparilla for Mr. Freeman, please." The waitress nodded and went off to do what was asked of her.

Mr. Merit put an envelope on the table. He nodded for Mr. Freeman to look inside it. Lester asked, "What is it?"

"Open it and see."

Lester opened the envelope. "A check for fifty thousand credits?" he found.

Dubious Merit snickered. He warned, "It would be best not to announce what is yours."

"Mine? What are you paying me for?"

"Quit your job and work for me."

"Doing what?"

The Mystic grinned, "The surprise is part of the deal."

There was a car key, a vehicle registration and an insurance form. "Is this real?" Lester held up the Vex driver's license with his name and high school picture on it.

"Yes."

"All my personal information is correct. Who are you?"

"Dubious Merit."

"Yeah, so you've told me, but who are you?"

"I am the friend of many."

Lester added, "When it suits you."

"Yes."

Lester put everything back into the envelope and slid it back to Mr. Merit. "Thank you, and I mean that, but I can't take any of this."

The Mystic knew, "It is 'too good to be true' and this is unsettling."

"There's a catch," Lester knew. "I'd rather not catch it."

Dubious Merit laughed. He smiled, "You are not a fool." He stood and as he did so Lester reflexively cringed. "Mr. Freeman, ask me any question and I shall answer it."

"Why me?"

"I watched as a man with the eyes of a predator was bullied by prey. I hoped to inspire your true nature."

"Why?"

"It would suit me." Dubious Merit left the envelope on the table as he made to leave.

"Mr. Merit," Lester called to him. Mr. Freedman held up the envelope.

"It was and is my gift unto you. The car is parked right outside." With that, Dubious Merit left the building.

Lester sipped his sarsaparilla in increments as he dwelt on the day's strangeness. He hoped he was not missing yet another opportunity. He laughed at himself when he realized, "I never take risks." He asked the one waitress, "Excuse me."

"Yes?"

"Who is Dubious Merit? He seems to be important around here."

The woman laughed. She explained, "He's a friend of Vincent Burdock."

"Who?"

The waitress whispered, "The gangster."

"Gangster?!" The waitress raised a finger to her lips. "Gangster?" Lester again asked.

"Don't worry: gangsters are 'legit' in this city as long as they keep the Vexites happy. Remember: this isn't really one of our worlds."

"Yeah."

The waitress asked, "Did he tell your fortune?"

"What?"

"Did you tell your fortune? Mr. Merit reads palms. I think he's an astrologer too and probably a few other magical things. He mentioned you were coming yesterday before you even came in."

"He did?"

The waitress nodded. "He told me a little man I would find cute would come in and sit with him." Lester blushed realizing the waitress found him cute. "You are cute," she confirmed. She patted him on the shoulder and returned to serving drinks.

Lester snuck past the bully and went outside. He saw a car parked with a note taped to its windshield that read, "Mister Freeman." Lester used the key and sat in the driver's seat. The vehicle was nice without being too fancy to worry about drawing undo attention. Lester drove home.

Annie Smith watched Lester park and get out of the vehicle. She asked him, "Company car?"

"No, it's mine."

"Really? I thought you were saving your money to start your own business."

"I didn't buy it." When Annie looked confused Lester explained, "I didn't steal it, you know. I don't steal... cars... or anything else... not even stationary."

Annie giggled. "Lester, I didn't think you stole the car."

"Yeah: of course not."

"How'd you get it?"

"A Mystic gave it to me."

"He *gave* you a car?"

Lester shrugged, "I don't know why either. He offered me a job and I declined the offer... but he let me keep the car anyway."

"What job?" Lester squirmed. "Lester, what kind of job offers you a car just for asking?"

"I don't know and I didn't want to know. I think he's a… gangster… of some sort or whatever."

"If he's a gangster you need to stay away from him! Lester, you're too nice of a guy to mess with people like that… especially *alien* gangsters. They'll kill you just because you look tasty. Some of them do eat people, you know."

Lester was already nervous about the whole thing but Annie's rambling was scaring him all the more. "I know," he told her. "I don't want anything to do with that kind of business."

"Lester, you took the car. They don't give you something for nothing."

"I didn't want to be rude! Annie, I told Mr. Merit 'no' and he insisted I take the car anyway. I wasn't going to tell him 'no' again."

Annie invited, "You're having dinner at my place tonight. We're going to talk about this."

"No, it's okay."

"Lester, we're going to talk about this. I want to hear you knocking on my door no later than six, okay?" Lester nodded. "You be there! I'm serious! I know a few things about gangsters and I can help you."

Chapter 2
"Dubious"

Lester knocked on Annie's door. A man old enough to be her father answered. "Lester?" the man smiled. Lester was too nervous to speak so he merely nodded. "Come on in."

"Hello, Lester," Annie smiled. She was still cooking. "This is my Uncle Vinnie."

Uncle Vinnie offered his hand. "Oh," Lester eventually noticed the hand and shook it. "Lester Freeman."

"Vincent Burdock." Lester recognized the name. He gulped. "What's wrong, kid? You've heard of me?" Lester shrugged. "Everybody's heard of me," Uncle Vinnie grinned. "I'm in the business of being everybody's friend."

Annie told the men, "I'll assume everybody washed their hands. Sit down, you two. Supper's ready."

The three humans prattled and ate. Uncle Vinnie eventually asked Lester, "What's this about you getting a car for no apparent reason?"

"I… I don't really know myself. A Mystic gave me a car."

"Who?"

"Dubious Merit." Uncle Vinnie nodded. Lester added, "I hear he's a friend of yours, Mr. Burdock."

Uncle Vinnie shrugged. "Like I told you: I'm everybody's friend."

"So you do know him."

Uncle Vinnie smirked. "Nobody knows him. My friends among the Mystics never heard of him until I asked about him."

Lester mentioned, "He said he's not from Mystique."

"Lots of Mystics aren't from Mystique. They're a confederacy of thirteen sovereign world-states, you know.

243

They still teach that in school, right?" Uncle Vinnie stared in silence as if awaiting an answer. Lester nodded. Uncle Vinnie continued, "Nobody knows this guy. I've sat with him for hours at a time and I still don't know him." Uncle Vinnie muttered, "He never offered *me* a car."

Annie worried, "Why would he do that: give Lester a car just because? Is he trying to involve Lester in some sort of trouble?"

"I don't know. This *Dubious Merit* is either freelance or he's with the Mutual Prosperity Syndicate. He's not with anybody else."

Annie told Lester, "The Mutual Prosperity Syndicate is an interracial gang run by a Penumbran."

"Bane the Ruthless of the Brightest Light is the top boss but our boy Sam Landquest runs things for the Syndicate here on Vex."

"Our boy?" Lester asked.

"He's human, Jingoan."

"Oh."

Uncle Vinnie told, "I'm too small a fry to ever even look Mr. Landquest in the eye so I won't be asking him anything about Dubious Merit."

Lester wondered, "What does that mean if Dubious Merit is with the Mutual Prosperity Syndicate?"

"It means you do whatever they tell you to do no matter what. *Nobody* and I mean *nobody* tells the Syndicate 'no.' Even the Fang Gangs kiss the Syndicate's ass." The *Fang Gangs* were the Vexite Mafia, notorious for their brutality.

Annie asked her uncle, "What would the Syndicate want with Lester?"

Uncle Vinnie laughed, "Nothing." He explained, "The Syndicate doesn't scrounge its boys off the street." He told Lester, "No offense."

Annie scolded, "Uncle Vinnie, I thought you knew everything happening in Noburg but you're not really telling us what we've been asking."

"What?"

Annie rolled her eyes. "Why is this mysterious Mystic interested in Lester?"

"I don't know."

"He gave Lester a car. Why would he do that?"

Lester mentioned what he hesitated to mention before, "He gave me a check for fifty thousand credits and knows my personal information."

"Wow!"

Annie asked, "What does it all mean? It can't be good."

Uncle Vinnie chuckled, "Fifty thousand credits *no questions asked* is *damn* good."

Annie pulled her uncle's plate of food away from him. "Hey!" he whined.

"You're not getting anything from me *no questions asked* so you'd better start earning your keep."

Uncle Vinnie laughed. He warned Lester, "She's the boss and you'd better remember that. She was telling everybody what to do when she was little."

"I did not!"

"Yes, you did. You still do." Annie looked at Lester and shook her head. Lester grinned, enjoying the melodrama.

Anton had his report on Saturday. On Sunday there was a knock on Lester's door. When Lester opened the door Anton whined, "I'm in trouble."

"Why?"

"My report is wrong, Lester. Why is my report wrong?"

"I used your notes."

Anton fussed, "Didn't you cross-reference anything?"

"I used what you gave me."

"Lester, you didn't even bother to think anything through. What's wrong with you?"

"I did someone else's job."

"Lester, I gave you your day off. I did expect you to earn it. I'll remember this next time you want a day off." Anton stormed off. His room was only a few doors down and he made a point to *slam* his door as he disappeared into his apartment. Lester wondered if the company discount was worth having Anton as a neighbor.

Late that night: there was a knock on the door. Lester thought it was Anton but no one was there when he answered. A package was on the floor.

Lester brought the package into his apartment. He locked the door before unwrapping the package. It was a box with a note, pistol and loaded magazines. The note read, "You must wield the power if you are to have the power" but it faded with each word read and the very note crumbled into dust. "That was weird."

Lester handled the gun. He would not load it for fear of shooting himself but he did appreciate the gift. "What's wrong with me?" he felt dizzy. He put the gun back in its box and he put the box in a drawer. He staggered to bed and went to sleep.

Morning: Lester was alone at a table enjoying his coffee after a pleasant breakfast... when a shadow loomed over him. He cringed as he looked up at the towering alien Dubious Merit. "Mr. Freeman," the melodious voice of the strange creature asked.

Though Lester would rather the alien did not sit with him, he gestured for the alien to do so, "Please."

Dubious Merit sat across from the human. "My gifts are for you but they are for me."

Lester whispered, "Why did you send me a gun?"

Dubious Merit smirked. "Give me a ride in the car I gave you."

"Where are we going?"

"I shall show you as I tell you." The Mystic just sat there staring into Lester's eyes. The alien was his usual calm, without giving off even the slightest vibe that he was in a hurry.

"Let's go," Lester wanted to get whatever was going on over with. The Mystic grinned.

Mr. Merit would point and tell Lester where to go and turn. "We're leaving the city?" the human worried.

"Yes."

"Why?"

"I shall show you what I shall not tell you."

Vex was a desert planet. The city of Noburg was a bustling city surrounded by wasteland. Mr. Merit pointed at a dirt road. Lester quivered, "Why are we out here? Where are we going?" The Mystic kept pointing. The human obeyed the unspoken command.

The car eventually came to a stop... in the middle of nowhere. "We are here," the Mystic smiled.

"Where?"

Dubious Merit got out of the car. Lester considered speeding off to make an escape but feared to do so. He got out. Mr. Merit gestured at the trunk. "You want me to open it?"

The Mystic smiled and nodded. Lester opened the trunk—and the bodies of men where stuffed inside! They were corpses of the bully and his friends. Dubious Merit chuckled. He stated, "It was a task getting them all in there."

The bodies had gunshot wounds. "What did you do?"

"Lester, my friend, the obvious is indeed obvious."

"Why?!"

"Why not?" Dubious Merit patiently waited for the human to regain his composure before mentioning, "It is believed Mystics do not use firearms. These men were shot... by the pistol with your prints upon its grip."

"What?!"

"Many witnesses saw them bully you. The weapon has your prints. The blood of the victims can be found in your vehicle. Lester, my friend, the circumstances do not favor you."

"You framed me!"

"Yes."

"Why?!"

"I want our circumstances to my advantage."

"Why?! What do you want?!"

"Our nature is our only impetus, my friend. Our circumstances adjust accordingly."

Dubious Merit got back into the car. Lester asked him, "Shouldn't we bury the bodies?"

"Why? Do you fear them being found?"

"Yes! You made it look like I'm the one who killed them!"

"Leave them to the desert. None on Vex shall mourn the loss of them. None live on this world who would seek to avenge them."

"My people won't stand for its citizens being murdered."

"Your people have no authority beyond the city limits. Your people are bound to the whim of the Vexites within the city limits. You have naught to fret." Lester was still flustered. Dubious Merit added, "Your people tend to be lazy. They seldom seek what they believe to be obvious. I have the pistol. I shall leave it for your authorities to discover should you defy me."

"Are you blackmailing me?" The Mystic grinned. "Why?"

"I require your services."

"Doing what?"

"I shall arouse your true nature and it shall serve me well... or I shall leave your pistol to be found by your people."

Lester fumed, "You really want me to remember that."

The Mystic reiterated, "Your people shall not bother to investigate beyond the obvious. They shall not seek the truth for your sake. I have the pistol and shall leave it to be found if you defy me."

Lester sobbed, "What do you want with me?"

"Your complicity shall suffice."

"Do I have a choice?"

"Yes."

"I do what you want or my own people bust me for murder."

The Mystic grinned, "Yes."

Lester just stood there not knowing what to do. He looked around and saw only desert. The city was just over the horizon. The Mystic sat still and silent, inhumanly calm and eerily patient. Lester sighed before getting into the car. He said, "Just tell me what you want me to do and let's get this over with."

"My friend, I see in your eyes what has yet to emerge. You may grow fond of your venture onward. After all, we are what we are regardless. Only the circumstances are for better or worse."

"Whatever." Lester started the car. He played music.

"I am fond of this," Dubious Merit smiled. Lester turned the music off. The Mystic laughed. "I am fond of you."

The internet was available wherever there was a Jingoan settlement. Servers on far-flung worlds had to be updated but there was always a portal opened between Vex and Jingo. The internet on Vex was as efficient as it was Jingo. Lester browsed. He wanted to know what he was dealing with.

The *Fang Gangs* were the indigenous organized crime on Vex. Smuggling, hired enforcement, prostitution and sexual slavery of human beings were their usual business. Their name was coined by Jingoans but embraced by the gangsters themselves. Females were the bosses and their sons the chief lieutenants, as was the norm in Vexite society in general. The female *Angst Infuriated* was the "Queen of Noburg," the boss of the Fang Gang that dominated the city. Her rival was the female *Passion Conniving*, who ruled the territory surrounding Noburg. Their feud was called the "Siege War" by Jingoan law enforcement.

Angst Infuriated was in business doing business with alien gangs. The *Greater Humanity Mafia* and the Golgothite *Silent Families* were among her best customers. The *Illicit Corporations* of the Delver race and the *Unsavory Guild* of the Mystics did business on Vex through her organization. She handled any interracial violence on Vex required by them. "He's not with the Unsavory Guild," Lester remembered Uncle Vinnie telling him about Dubious Merit. "Who else would he be working for?" Lester did not expect his internet browsing to equal genuine detective work but he found so many names he was surprised "Dubious Merit" was not among them. "Mystics don't use aliases," Lester checked. "It's considered bad luck. Bad luck?" Lester read that a name was magically significant and changing one's name, especially as a lie, weakened the identity from which a Mystic drew his power: according to Mystic mysticism. "What if he doesn't believe that?" Lester considered, but the notion did not ring true. "Hiding in plain sight," he happened upon. "He's hiding in plain sight."

There was a knock on the door. Lester sighed believing it was probably Anton. He cringed when he considered that it could be Dubious Merit. "Lester?" the voice of Annie called through the door. "Are you all right?"

Lester opened the door. "Hey," he feigned a smile.

"You looked nervous when you came home."

"When did you see me?" Lester questioned in the guise of a joke, "Are you keeping an eye on me?"

"I saw your car pull up."

"Oh. I didn't see you."

Annie muttered, "You never do."

"Sorry, what's that?"

"Nothing. May I come in?"

"Sure," Lester opened the door wide. "Would you like something to drink?"

"What do you have?"

"Beer."

"Lester, you don't drink! Don't start because of all this."

Lester shrugged, "The guys are always teasing me. They call me a 'milk baby' and... things like that."

"Lester, you're scared." Embarrassed that a woman would think he was scared, the man straightened his posture and shook his head. "Yes, you are. Don't hide from me. I want to help you."

Lester tittered, "You're uncle's a gangster."

"No, he's a business man and business has to do business with gangsters. There is a difference." Uncle Vinnie seemed rather "gangster" to Lester but he would let Annie believe otherwise.

"You were with him today."

"Your uncle?"

"No!" Annie whispered, "Dubious Merit."

"How do *you* know?" Annie shrugged. "No, seriously, how do you know?"

"My uncle's friends are keeping an eye on you."

251

"Friends? Gangsters, maybe?"

"Lester! You're in danger."

"Yeah, obviously: I've got gangsters following me around."

Annie nodded. "They didn't see your Mystic friend… and they lost sight of you."

"So?"

"Lester, my uncle's friends say this guy has all the skills of a Mystic assassin."

"What do you mean?"

"He's an illusionist and he knows when he's being watched."

"What am I supposed to do about it?"

"Lester, what did he involve you in?"

"Nothing. Well, he got me into trouble, well, maybe."

"What trouble?"

Lester did not want Annie inadvertently getting people to think *he* murdered half a dozen men. "Nothing."

"Lester, don't lie to me. You're not good at it. I want to help you."

"Why? Why do *you* want to help *me* with *my* problem?" Lester dared consider, "Are you in on all this?"

"No!"

"How do I know?"

"Lester, you've known me for almost a year."

"Do I?"

Annie sniffled. She stormed towards the door. "Annie, I didn't mean… Annie… I'm sorry." The door *slammed* leaving Lester alone with his troubled thoughts and feelings.

Lester was too upset about everything to go to sleep. He instead sat in his comfy chair with Spunky on his lap… until the little lizard hamster crawled up his shirt to sit on his shoulder. Lester dozed off despite his restless angst.

252

The next day was a long day of trying to concentrate on work while thinking about Dubious Merit, Annie and Uncle Vinnie. Lester wondered if he should apologize to Annie. He worried Uncle Vinnie might make him sorry if he did not.

Lester would look about wondering if anyone was watching him or following him. He even worried about the Vexite who "followed" him across the street. "I need to quit my job and get back to Jingo," Lester thought aloud while having lunch.

An older man overheard the thought and laughed. "I've been saying that for years," the eavesdropper told.

Lester asked him, "How long have you been on Vex?"

"I was one of the first. I was one of the guys who built this city. There was nothing and I mean *nothing* here until we got here. The lizards were living in tents or huts." The term "lizard" was a racial slur for Vexites but Vexites never seemed to mind hearing it. Jingoans still considered uttering the word crude and vulgar.

"Mr. Freeman," Dubious Merit seemed to appear from nowhere. He sat with Lester and smiled. "Your friends are quite interesting."

"Excuse me?"

"Annie Smith fancies you, my friend. Do you not notice the obvious?"

"I don't see how any of that is your business."

"Oh, it is very much my business. I must be mindful of those in the lives of my associates."

"I'm trying *not* to associate with you!"

Dubious Merit whispered, "They were found, the bodies."

"What?"

The Mystic grinned, "They were brought back into the city and given to the Jingoan coroner." Lester gulped. "People did see you leaving the city. They did not see me."

"What? You were with me!"

"Among your kind it is believed seeing is believing, is it not? If I was not seen would they believe you? Shall you insist that a *Mystic* used a *gun* and *shot* those men? The forensics shall show that the angle was consistent with your stature."

Lester whispered, "Is this just some sort of psychotic joke?!"

Dubious Merit sneered. Never before did Lester ever see malevolence in the Mystic's face. Never before did he ever behold anything so terrifying. The alien snarled, "You are with me now. My will is your only choice. Do you understand?" Lester nodded. "Tell me if you understand."

Lester choked, "I hear you."

"Oh, you shall do more than that, my friend. Quit your job. You need not fret for I shall pay you generously for your service. I shall come calling soon. Be ready." With that, the towering alien stood. He loomed over the human for a long, tense while, glaring at him before finally leaving the building. He vanished as he stepped out the door.

Chapter 3
"Shy and Anxious"

The Vexites were a race of savages and barbarians. Though hopelessly primitive by their restless nature, they were fond of the magic and technology of the advanced civilizations. Until tempered by the persuasive influence of the Penumbrans the Vexites were raiding and pillaging the frontiers of the empires. Though primitive, Vexite prowess and an uncanny knack for raids and ambush readily bested the forces of their victims.

The Vexites loved Jingoan technology more than magic or any other technology, especially the music, movies, television, automobiles and firearms. Other than swords, which the Vexites crafted themselves to an uncanny excellence, Vexite weapons were from the Greater Humanity Empire. Clothes made for them by the Jingoans were what every Vexite wore.

The bosses of the Fang Gangs wore a suit and tie if male and a dress or pantsuit if female. The thugs dressed casually, many of the males wearing sleeveless shirts or no shirt at all. Body armor without a shirt was common.

Angst Infuriated was a Vexite. She was the mother of two sons. She was the "Queen of Noburg" as the boss of the city's Fang Gang. She invited the bosses of the alien gangs to dinner.

Vexites with assault rifles, shotguns or machineguns guarded the grounds of Angst Infuriated's mansion. Male or female these guards were painted in the red and yellow warpaint of the Infuriated Fang Gang. They watched as the limousines of the expected arrived.

The Golgothite Yervand Willow of the Willow Family was the first to arrive. He and his bodyguards were black-haired humans with light olive complexions, as was typical of the breed of Golgoth. The weapons holstered under their coats were plasma weapons rather than firearms.

The Jingoan Chris Jackstone representing Mr. Simon Fink was the next to arrive. He was a black man and his bodyguards white or of mixed breeds, as was common among the humanity of the Greater Humanity Empire. All of them wore a suit and tie and a holstered firearm under the coat of the suit.

The Delver Lord Hammer of the Fringe Arms and Smuggling Corporation was the third boss to arrive. Delvers were a head shorter than most humans but broader and much heavier. Their thick and powerful arms were as long as their thick and steady legs. Like the Vexites they were pseudo-reptilian: scaly and warm-blooded; but the blood of a Delver was hemoglobin and orange whereas the green blood of a Vexite was a hemocyanin. Delvers were oviparous whereas Vexites gave live births.

A Delver's face looked as if chiseled from stone. Its eyes were brown within black. Lord Hammer wore robes. His body guards wore full suits of titanium alloy plate armor. Other than the needful gaps, the armor was impervious to blades and small arms. The bodyguards wore maces on their belts.

Wayward Certainty of the Unsavory Guild was the fourth to arrive. Though his people preferred beast-drawn carriages to the dangerously fast vehicles of humanity, the restless Vexites would not tolerate anything slow on Vexite streets. The Mystic arrived in a limousine driven by a human. Wayward Certainty was wearing a black robe. His bodyguards were male and female of his race and wore black, hooded cloaks. Though the hoods obstructed the eyes of their faces, they enhanced the view of their third eyes. The bodyguards wore talismans, swords and daggers for they were the warriors of a magically advanced civilization.

The *Queen of Noburg* wore a red dress and a red and yellow feather boa. Her sons wore dark red suits with yellow ties. The mother sat at the table and her sons stood on either side behind her. "Thank you for coming," Angst Infuriated smiled, showing her fangs. "Enjoy your meal." It was the custom on Vex to eat before a meeting under the axiom, "The hungry are restless in their hunger. Feed them or they shall feed themselves." The food served was a mix of Vexite and Jingoan whether the guests liked it or not.

"Are you worried about your rival?" Chris Jackstone blurted, as was the crude manner of Jingoans.

"Tell me about my rival."

"Maybe we should do that in private."

"No, Mr. Jackstone: Secret agreements arouse suspicion. I want my every guest to trust me."

Chris Jackstone coughed before stating, "Passion Conniving wants to do business with Mr. Fink. She is offering a better deal on *everything* and I mean *everything*. I like you, Ms. Infuriated, and I've convinced Mr. Fink to like you, but we'd both like you a lot more if we work some things out."

Angst Infuriated sneered, "Passion Conniving offers no such deals to the Fringe Arms and Smuggling Corporation or to the Unsavory Guild."

"You don't know that."

"Mr. Jackstone, I do know she has not. I do know she offers to favor the Willow Family as well. She seems to favor humans."

"Hey, I favor being favored." The Delver Lord Hammer rumbled a chuckle. Chris Jackstone explained, "I want the best deal. We *all* want the best deal."

"We all want what is best for ourselves."

"That's right, and you're not it... unless we work things out."

The Vexite snarled, "This is *my* city. We negotiate but on *my* terms."

"Yeah, I know the rules; that's why I'm talking to you."

"Mr. Jackstone," the melodious voice of the Mystic Wayward Certainty addressed the human, "Passion Conniving sells what is plundered. Bandits bring her loot and captives taken by raid and banditry. She sells the females of your race into sexual slavery. Surely Mr. Fink would not do business with the likes of her."

"Mr. Fink doesn't base his relationships on rumors." Lord Hammer guffawed in that booming voice of his race.

The Golgothite human Yervand Willow claimed, "Simon Fink already sells the daughters of his enemies into sexual slavery. He is shameless."

Chris Jackstone asked his hostess, "Why is this leftover of a dead empire at this table? Shouldn't there be a bald clone girl with spooky eyes sitting in that seat?" The Golgothite slammed a fist on the table. "Whatever, peewee," the Jingoan was unimpressed.

Angst Infuriated was thrilled by the intensity. She grinned at Mr. Jackstone, telling him, "You are a very bad man."

"That's why I've got lawyers."

"Mr. Jackstone, you may do business with my rival but it shall not be done within *my* city. The portals between worlds are *my* portals and nothing from *her* shall pass through them."

The gruff voice of Lord Hammer suggested unto Chris Jackstone, "There are other cities and other portals on this world. Use them."

"That would be more layers of others getting a cut of the profits. It wouldn't be worth it."

"I called this meeting," the *Queen of Noburg* reminded her guests. "*My* favor is your concern. I know who is already doing business with *my* enemy. I already know who is smuggling *her* merchandise into *my* city and through *my* portals. She is kept in business because of you. She is kept strong by you. Forsake her or you shall be unwelcome in *my* city. Do your business in *her* wasteland if *she* is so dear to you."

Yervand Willow implored, "Let's discuss this with Sam Landquest."

Angst Infuriated reminded, "For all its human bosses the one and only boss of the Mutual Prosperity Syndicate is a Penumbran. Lord Bane forbids his Syndicate from meddling with indigenous rivalries. Sam Landquest shall have no say on this matter."

Lester was watching the news on television when there was a knock on the door. Bringing Spunky with him on his shoulder, Lester answered the door. Anton was the one on the other side. "You quit?"

"Yes," Lester enjoyed telling Anton.

"Why?"

"I was tired of doing two jobs for the price of one."

"Lester, you should've talked to me. Why didn't you say something?"

"I did. I said 'I quit' and that was that."

"You didn't say anything to *me*."

"We don't have that kind of relationship."

"Lester, what are you doing for money?"

"I have friends helping me out."

"Who?"

"Bye, Anton. You have a good life." With that, Lester closed his door and locked it.

Lester was watching a cartoon when there was another knock on the door. It was Annie on the other side this time. Lester apologized, "I am so sorry. I… I would have come by earlier and… said something but I didn't know what to say."

"Lester, you quit your job."

"Yeah, I did."

"Why?"

"I got tired of doing two jobs for the price of one."

Annie shook her head. She questioned, "Lester, what is he getting you into?"

"Nothing… yet… maybe never."

"Oh, he means to get you into some sort of trouble!" Not wanting anyone, especially Anton, overhearing the details, Lester opened his door and gestured for Annie to come inside. "Lester, you need to get off this planet and back to Jingo! You need to report all this to the Imperial Bureau of Investigation!"

"No, that would be a *very* bad idea."

"Lester, this Dubious Merit is dangerous!"

"Oh, he's dangerous, all right. He does kill people."

"Lester, my uncle can protect you."

"Not from this."

"Yes! He's friends with… people… who can hurt people too."

"Annie, if I run away from this, our own police will come after me. I'll be busted for murder."

"What?"

Lester simpered, "You want me to call the Imperial Bureau of Investigation? They'll be glad I called. I'd be in handcuffs within the hour."

"Lester, what are you talking about?"

"He framed me, Annie. He'll plant evidence and I'll be busted for murder."

"But you didn't kill anyone."

"No!" Lester whispered, "He knows about you! Annie, he'll hurt you if he thinks you're a threat to him. Don't tell anyone what I'm telling you."

"Why did he frame you?"

"It doesn't matter. He's got me. I'll do whatever he wants… and hope I come out of it alive." Lester started weeping. "I'm sorry," he sobbed. Annie snuggled him and he hugged her back.

Annie promised not to tell. She said nothing about not investigating in the meantime. She did talk to her uncle but begged him not to garner attention on the matter. "Do you really like this guy that much?" Uncle Vinnie worried about his niece.

"Lester is a nice guy. We should help him."

"Why?"

"Good people help good people in need!"

"Are you sure he's really good? This Dubious Merit didn't randomly pick him out of a crowd. He chose Lester Freeman for a reason. You might not like the reason."

Annie challenged, "Then we find that reason."

Uncle Vinnie muttered, "Of all the boys you could be dying for it's this little freak."

"He's not a freak!"

"Whatever. I'm just saying…"

Dubious Merit had Lester drive him out into the desert. When he opened the trunk Lester worried there were more bodies. The trunk was instead full of gear and weapons. Lester asked the Mystic, "How do you get into my car all the time and no one notices?"

"Did I not tell you I was a scout in the Confederate Army?"

"So?"

"We hide in plain sight."

"Yeah, I've noticed."

"The Vexites have also mastered this skill. They used it against the Golgothites to devastating effect. Cunning shall prove our only edge."

Dubious taught Lester how to use a gun… which Lester thought was ironic considering that Mystics were a magically advanced race and did not use guns. "I was trained in the use of exotic weaponry," Dubious explained.

"I am also skilled in the operation of motor vehicles… but I would rather not drive."

"Why not?" The Mystic grinned and would not answer. "Are you worried about getting your fingerprints on my steering wheel?"

"Lester, my friend, I must train you now." For six days Dubious Merit taught Lester unarmed combat, knife and sword fighting, how to shoot and quickly reload firearms. "You learn quickly," the Mystic commended. "What I teach is already within your nature."

"I'm I getting as good as you?"

"Pick up a rock."

"Why?" The towering alien glared down at Lester. The human did as he was told. "Is this one big or small enough?"

"Toss it."

"Where?"

"Toss it." Lester shrugged. He tossed the rock. The Mystic drew a pistol and blasted the rock into powder with one shot while it was midair! "It is not speed and accuracy that is most deadly," Dubious Merit explained. "Your race is the weakest and slowest of all the Great Races yet you are two of the six Galactic Powers. Resourcefulness, my friend, is the ultimate edge."

Lester spent his day off pondering everything he was learning. Though he dreaded what Dubious Merit intended, Lester was actually enjoying the training. Against his better judgment he was actually grateful for being taught what he was being taught. He was flattered that the Mystic thought well enough of him to bother teaching him. No one in all of Lester's life expected him to amount to anything… except for Dubious Merit. Lester wondered if he should embrace a new life as the Mystic's partner in crime after all.

There was a knock on the door. Lester asked Spunky, "Who is it?" Lester answered the door. "Annie," he smiled.

"Lester, may I come in?" Lester nodded and opened the door wide. As Annie came into the apartment she said, "Dubious Merit is not with the Unsavory Guild, the Mystic gang." Lester shrugged. "He could be working for anybody. Does he say anything about what he means to do?"

"No."

Annie sat on the couch. Lester asked her, "Would you like something to drink?"

"Anything non-alcoholic, please."

"Golgothite tea?" Annie nodded. "Hot or cold?"

"Hot, please." Lester poured Annie a glass then heated it in his microwave oven. He would drink his own glass cold. "Lester, the more I learn about this guy the less I know about him."

Lester chuckled. He mentioned, "He did say he fought against our people on Bosky and alongside our people on Crux."

"Lots of Mystics did."

"Yeah."

"Lester, what do you do when you're out with him?"

"He's training me to be a killer."

"Don't grin like that," Annie scolded.

"What?"

"You're proud of it."

"No, I'm not!"

"Lester, you like what he's teaching you. You know he means to get you to kill people."

"Yeah, but he can't make me do something like that. He doesn't know humans if he thinks we're casual about killing people."

"Aliens are people too," Annie reminded. "Don't think it's okay if he wants you to kill aliens."

"I won't."

Annie choked, "You're a nice guy, Lester. We need nice guys. We've got plenty of bad guys already. Be a force of good in the universe, okay?"

"I will."

"Promise me."

"I promise."

Wayward Certainty of the Unsavory Guild was in his office when he asked, "Who is this *Dubious Merit* and why is he here?"

The female of his kind Feisty Grace responded, "We do not know. He tells he served on Bosky and Crux as a scout but our friends in the army do not know him."

"Ask the navy."

"The navy did not serve on Crux."

Mr. Certainty explained, "Marines do not need ships to serve. A heroic tetrad of marines may be sent anywhere."

The male Furious Serenity mentioned, "This Dubious Merit has done nothing worth our attention."

Mr. Certainty disagreed, "We hear tell of him yet he has done nothing. We know his name yet he is anonymous. We watch him yet we cannot find him. He who hides in plain sight does so with unfriendly intent."

Miss Grace considered, "He may be an agent of the Ministry of Vigilance."

"I am an agent of the Ministry and have always proven faithful. This Dubious Merit would be needless and redundant."

"Ask about him."

Mr. Certainty chuckled. He explained, "I *report* to the Ministry. It is not my place to ask anything."

Mystics are patient and contemplative by nature. The three pondered in silence until Wayward Certainty ultimately decided, "Kill him."

Mr. Serenity reminded, "He has done nothing against us."

"Nor shall he ever for he shall be dead. See to it." Mr. Serenity nodded.

Miss Grace warned, "We do not know who this would provoke against us."

"If they are acting in secret among us, they are already against us."

Two assassins stalked their prey. Hooded and cloaked they hid in plain sight yet kept to the shadows. They watched as Dubious Merit sat at window in a human business that served coffee. They watched and followed as he departed.

The expert assassins knew to watch for telltale signs. They were mindful if the target looked about or stopped to listen or seemed to be in a hurry. Dubious Merit was at ease. His stride and posture were casual. He wore a dagger but his hand never touched it. He was not wearing talismans.

The female Shy Gregarious was one of the assassins. Her brother Anxious Calm was the other. They hid and watched as Dubious Merit went into a Jingoan convenience store. Anxious told his sister, "This one is not our usual. He seems all too normal. Why must we slay him?"

"We do not choose our victims," Shy reminded her brother. "Assume he is dangerous." Anxious nodded.

Dubious Merit soon came out of the convenience store. Shy and Anxious followed him into an alley. Mr. Merit startled whistling. The assassins were glad for the noise for it helped hide their steps and breathing. They lengthened their stride and closed the gap. They drew their daggers… and lunged.

Dubious Merit dropped low and swiped his blade, disemboweling his assailants together. Shy and Anxious groaned and writhed. Dubious Merit left them to die in agony.

Chapter 4
"Lester's First Job"

Lester got in his car on his way to get groceries… and found Dubious Merit sitting next to him. "Whoa!" the human was taken back. "I never see you!" The Mystic grinned. Lester asked him, "Are you going to teach *me* how to be invisible?"

"Lester, my friend, to be unnoticed is to be invisible even if seen."

"Whatever. Are you going to teach me?"

"Yes."

Dubious Merit had Lester drive to an abandoned hotel. It was an old building left over from the early days of Noburg. The Mystic taught the human how to scale walls, pick locks and hide in nooks and crannies. "Do not look should you sense a stare, glimpse a movement or hear a noise," Dubious lectured. "Do not stop or hasten. Do as you were doing but listen and watch without looking or perking. Be ready without touching the hilt of your weapon."

"Why?"

"Your enemy is ready should he know you sense him. Let him believe you do not."

"That makes sense."

"Trust your feelings," the Mystic advised. "Intuition is infallible."

"Not always," Lester disagreed.

"Always," Dubious insisted. "It is your thoughts that cloud your feelings."

After hours of training Lester decided not to bother with getting groceries until tomorrow. As he drove he asked Dubious Merit, "You're not going to ask me to kill people, are you?"

"I shall not ask."

Lester snickered. He rephrased his question, "Are you expecting me to kill people?"

"You shall be true to your nature."

"What does that mean?"

"I shall not ask of you what shall come naturally."

Lester dropped Dubious Merit off in front of the Confederate Post Office. "You need not wait," the Mystic told him. "Good bye."

Lester went home. As he neared the door to his apartment the voice of Uncle Vinnie called, "Lester." Lester turned to face the man. "Let's go for a walk."

"I've been busy all day, Mr. Burdock."

"Doing what?"

"Nothing illegal."

"Not yet."

The two men stared at each other in tense silence. "Let's go for a walk," Uncle Vinnie repeated, but in a stern tone.

Lester glared back and told the man, "Come on in if you have something to say."

Uncle Vinnie tried to be intimidating… but Lester was not intimidated. "Okay," he conceded.

Lester opened his door but was mindful not to turn his back to Uncle Vinnie, remembering Dubious Merit's teaching, "Keep all before you lest to lure a predator when you are ready to make it your prey."

"Would you like a beer?" Lester offered.

"Beer? Kid, I didn't figure you drank beer."

"I don't, so I have plenty and might as well give it away."

"Yeah: I'll take a beer." Lester poured himself a glass of Golgothite tea.

"What are you getting my niece into?" Uncle Vinnie asked as if making an accusation.

"Nothing."

"She likes you, in case you didn't notice. She's worried about you and won't stop asking questions."

"I've told her everything I know."

"Really?" Lester nodded. "What did you tell her?"

Not knowing if Uncle Vinnie's "friends" were Dubious Merit's enemies, Lester responded, "I'm not at liberty to say."

"Why not?" Lester did not answer. Uncle Vinnie asked, "Are you his willing accomplice now?"

"Mr. Burdock, Dubious Merit was your friend before he was mine. Just ask him anything you want to know."

"That lefty was never my friend! He's not *your* friend! Kid, you're being pulled into a mess you can't handle. Work with me and I'll get you out of it."

"Talk to him yourself."

"I can't. He's disappeared."

Lester offered, "I'll ask him to talk to you."

"Yeah, you do that." Uncle Vinnie stood and went to the door. He turned to warn Lester, "Don't play games with people who don't play games." He then left the room and closed the door.

Dubious and Lester were together sitting under a shaded table at a rest stop out in the desert. "Ibrahim Blossom," Mr. Merit showed Mr. Freeman a picture of a man with black hair, brown eyes and a smirk for a smile. "The Silent Families of Golgoth were weakened when their empire was supplanted by the Concubines of the Great Seen Unseen. Mr. Blossom thinks to betray his employers by exploiting their vulnerability. He means to seize control of what has been placed in his care."

Lester worried, "We're not going to kill this guy, are we? I mean, I'm not killing people, especially people I don't know and who've never wronged me."

"My friend, would you kill to protect yourself?"

The human shrugged, "If I had to, of course." The Mystic grinned. "What?"

Dubious Merit assured, "Our task is not to slay Ibrahim Blossom. He is a Willow by blood and the Willow Family would rather not shed that blood."

"We were hired by the Willow Family?"

"You, my friend, were hired by the Willow Family. You accepted their payment in full."

"Me?"

Dubious Merit produced images, maps and floor plans as he shared his plan with Lester. They reviewed the plan during the long ride back to the city. "Why did we come all the way out here?" Lester wondered.

"You need the long ride. It shall provide the circumstances favorable for your meditation. Be ready."

"I will."

Lester parked a ways away from a two-story office building. He and Dubious Merit watched as Ibrahim and his body guards and a blond bimbo went into the building. The melodious voice of the Mystic remarked, "Golgothites are the most punctual breed of your species." He told Lester, "We are not to kill Ibrahim Blossom. His associates are not our concern."

"What? We're not going to kill people!"

The alien grinned and the grin frightened Lester more than anything ever had. The melodious voice of the inhuman entity assured, "I shall never ask you to kill."

"I don't want *you* killing either!"

The Mystic told the human, "Provide favorable circumstances and I shall oblige your wishes."

"Okay." Lester was relieved to hear what he took to be a promise. He would help the Mystic if for no other reason than to prevent needless slaughter. Lester made the call, "Let's do this."

"As you wish."

A Golgothite watching from behind a window in a building across the street watched as Lester picked a lock. The Golgothite aimed his camera at the intruder and reported, "A Jingoan is picking the lock to the south door. If he's armed, he's wearing his weapon under his coat."

"Acknowledged," a voice responded.

Dubious Merit told Lester, "Jingoans typically pummel a captive to ask him questions. Golgothites are too methodical for such barbarism. If we are captured, they shall employ elaborate means of inflicting pain."

"Torture?" Lester gulped.

"Yes."

Lester opened the door but Dubious led the way in. The human followed the Mystic upstairs. Lester noticed that his partner neither cast a shadow nor made even the faintest noise. They reached the top of the stairs. Lester looked away for but an instant… and Dubious Merit disappeared. Lester peeked around corners and into a room… but the Mystic had vanished.

Footsteps and whispers alerted Lester Freeman. The human drew his pistol, hoping not to use it. He wanted to escape.

A door behind Lester opened. A Golgothite stepped through and drew a pistol. The weapon shot a glowing, bluish white bolt of ionized gas at the intruder! Lester dove into a corridor. He *blasted* the Golgothite with bullets as the Golgothite came around the corner.

Firearms and their report were distinct from the plasma weapons used by Golgothites. Everyone knew these last shots were fired by a Jingoan. The tiptoeing became hurried footsteps. "He's on the top floor!" someone shouted.

Lester *blasted* the first Golgothite to reach the top of the steps. The others kept low. "Dubious!" Lester cried out. "Where are you?! Help!"

Golgothites wielding minicarbines poured into the corridors from rooms and the opposite side of the building. Their weapons *zipped* glowing bolts that *smacked* and *sizzled* whatever they struck. Lester blasted the assailing men. "Four already," Lester heard the voice of Dubious Merit. "You prowess is beyond what I reckoned."

"Where are you?"

Grunts and groans were followed by shots not at Lester. A man screamed. Lester held his pistol ready and dared to investigate. He found bodies of men he did not kill. Some of them were disemboweled but all of them were slashed. Lester watched as the last man dropped clutching his gory throat.

Dubious Merit wiped the blood from the curved blade of his dagger. He told Lester, "Your four and my dozen are all but six of them."

The Mystic kicked a door open. A glowing bolt shot at him but the alien nimbly dodged it. The bolt *smacked* into the wall behind him. "Drop it," the melodious voice of the Mystic commanded.

"I'm sorry!" the voice of a man sobbed. "Please don't kill me!"

Dubious Merit gestured for Lester to enter the room. Lester found Ibrahim Blossom and a naked blond woman hiding behind a bed. The Mystic asked Lester, "What are we to do with him?"

"We don't kill him."

"As you wish." The Mystic gestured at the cringing Ibrahim Blossom. Dubious Merit smiled and seemed to be waiting.

"Oh," Lester remembered. He told Ibrahim Blossom, "You know why we're here. You be a good boy… or we'll be back… and the next time we won't be nice. Do you understand?"

"Yes!"

272

Dubious Merit told Ibrahim Blossom, "Command what is left of your guard to allow our departure."

Dubious Merit had Lester drive around the city to nowhere in particular. "This is your moment of calm," the Mystic explained.

"What was I doing?" Lester disbelieved his own experience.

"You were acting true to your nature."

"People were trying to kill me!"

"Yes."

"No, they were *really* trying to *kill* me!"

"Yes."

Lester mumbled, "I killed people."

Annie was in her apartment watching television. The game show *We Dare You* was a contest of outlandish stunts with inglorious consequences. The master of ceremonies was the human Mortimor Morass: a comedian and actor few in his native Greater Humanity Empire found amusing but who the Vexites adored as hilarious. Mortimor moved to Vex to live among his adoring fans.

"Oh, that had to hurt!" Mortimor remarked as a contestant failed a nigh impossible jump while running an obstacle course. "He's going to need some tender loving care to the intimates! I hope he gets a girl healer." Vexite voices laughed. Vexites were the contestants and live audience. They liked their games rough and dangerous. Fortunately, the studio had a team of shamans readily available to administer the inevitably needed care.

We Dare You was a variety show of contests. The premise of this segment was a race that was a short run if a runner chose the most difficult route but a long run if he chose safer paths. Annie was not one for grim comedy but the stark madness of Vexite entertainment was strangely amusing.

Annie had a sixth sense. Her Vexite friends offered to teach her shamanism but she was reluctant to dabble in alien witchcraft. She had her "powers" if they were indeed powers and they served her well already.

Annie "heard" Lester's car park outside. She always knew when it was *his* car… because every engine sounds unique, maybe. She looked out her window and confirmed what she already knew.

Lester was walking to the door of his apartment when the door to Annie's opened. "Lester?" she addressed him. "Are you all right?"

"No."

"Come inside and let me get you something."

Lester shook his head, "Not tonight."

"Yes, tonight. You get in here now. I'll bang on your door all night if you don't."

Lester sat and started watching the Vexite game show. The screen went blank. Annie told Lester, "I need you to tell me everything. I'll go crazy if you don't."

"They tried to kill me," the man muttered. "They were *really* trying to *kill* me!" Annie did not ask who Lester was talking about. That he was talking was good enough for her. Lester rambled on, "I could feel the heat of the bolts and smell the ozone. What would those things do to me?"

When Lester became quiet Annie inquired, "Who tried to kill you?"

"Golgothites."

"Why were they trying to kill you?"

"Their boss was betraying his boss and we were there to tell him not to."

"They didn't kill you," Annie reminded.

"No. I killed them."

"In self-defense?" Lester nodded. Annie nodded as a hint for Lester to explain.

"Dubious Merit disappeared. I couldn't find him! The Golgothites found me... and tried to kill me."

"You killed them."

Lester snickered, "Dubious Merit slaughtered them."

Annie offered Lester a cup of hot tea. "Careful," she warned as his trembling hands spilled some of it. "It's hot." She watched Lester take his sips in silence before asking him, "Who was the boss?"

"Who?"

"The boss you were supposed to intimidate."

"Ibrahim Blossom."

"Did you kill him?"

"No. He's a Willow." Annie nodded. She figured her uncle would know all about this Ibrahim Blossom and what Lester's job was all about.

"Lester, I want you to spend the night." Lester's mouth gaped. Annie explained, "My sofa is a pull-out bed. I don't want you alone tonight, okay?" Lester nodded. Annie told him, "I'll make you a good breakfast in the morning."

Sam Landquest was the most important gangster on Vex and he was Jingoan but he worked for "the Penumbran" Mr. Bane the Ruthless. Chris Jackstone was the most important *Jingoan* boss on the planet. Vinnie Burdock met with Mr. Jackstone for lunch in an East Jingoan restaurant. "Yeah, I know who Ibrahim Blossom is," Mr. Jackstone told Vinnie. "He was working for me while working for the Willows before *Lester Freeman* scared the piss out of him."

"We're not talking about the same Lester Freeman," Vinnie chuckled. "Trust me, I know the guy. He would've done all the pissing."

Mr. Jackstone shook his head. He swallowed before confiding, "I have a girl on the inside with Ibrahim Blossom. She saw the whole thing."

"What did she see?"

"There was a Mystic with him."

"Dubious Merit," Vinnie identified.

"The Mystic used a knife."

Vinnie reminded, "Mystics don't use guns: it breaks their talismans."

"Whatever. Your boy Lester was the boss. He told the Mystic what to do and the Mystic did whatever he was told to do."

"No way," Vinnie disbelieved. "I know both these guys and I'm telling you: Lester was the bitch."

"Hey, my girl is a professional spy. It's her job to notice everything. She saw the boys in action. We both know the action is when it all gets real. I've already had my people look into both these guys and they found *nothing* on this *big bad* Dubious Merit."

"What about Lester?"

Chris Jackstone chuckled. "I think you're being played," he told Vinnie. "Don't be ashamed because he's probably one of the best."

"What do you mean?"

Chris Jackstone leaned close and whispered, "He's probably one of the Penumbran's secret killers. I won't touch him. I've already told my people to stop asking about him. Let's not figure out what we'd better not know."

"Talk to me, Chris. My niece is involved with this guy."

Mr. Jackstone hesitated before telling, "Lester Freeman was in For Now City a year ago."

"So was my niece: They worked for the same company. It was job-related."

"Whatever. Important people died *while he was there*. They were shot by the gun that matches the gun that shot six punks recently *here on Vex*."

"So?"

Chris explained, "The punks were seen getting in Lester's face the day before they went missing. I wouldn't be surprised if the gun is the same gun that shot Blossom's men."

"Lester Freeman killed people?"

"Oh, yeah: I know that for a fact."

"Why would he use the same weapon if he's so professional?"

"Why not? If he's with the Mutual Prosperity Syndicate then he's got nothing to worry about."

"Penumbrans don't like messy," Vinnie insisted. "If he's the Penumbran's boy, he won't leave loose ends."

"We don't know that. Maybe they want to leave a message."

"We're making too many guesses," Vinnie worried.

"No, I'm not. I'm leaving Lester Freeman alone. Vinnie, my friend, you stay out of that man's way."

"I can't. He's involved with my niece, remember?"

Chris Jackstone shrugged. "Good luck, my friend. Just don't mention me and you do whatever you must."

Annie insisted Lester take her out for a walk. When her warm, soft, delicate hand took hold of his hand, he responded in kind, mindful not to squeeze too tightly. The man and woman strolled past the windows of an electronics store filled with Vexite customers. "What would they do if we left?" Annie wondered. "Would they return to their old ways?"

"They haven't changed," Lester understood. "They were raiding and pillaging the Golgothites for the same reason they do business with us: they love human goodies.

They're not human so they can't make any of it but they'll take or buy whatever they can."

Annie mentioned, "Every Vexite I know personally is honest and friendly to a fault. I can't imagine any of them attacking and looting innocent people."

"We weren't 'people' to them until they got to know us. We were aliens: little monsters with interesting trinkets."

Annie snuggled up to Lester and cooed. He snuggled her and basked in her warmth. He wondered if they were dating. He hoped they were dating. He wanted this relationship to be more than friendship.

Dubious Merit was a master of hiding in plain sight. He knew to move gracefully and to not stare so as not to break the enchantment that concealed him. He followed without approaching. He watched without staring. He listened by *feeling* what was said.

Lester Freeman and Annie Smith kissed. Dubious Merit could feel the warmth and excitement and could not help but watch intently. The humans were too distracted by each other to notice him. The Mystic grinned.

Chapter 5
"Blood Money"

Lester came out of the bank and got into his car. He jumped in his seat and bumped his head when he noticed Dubious Merit already sitting next to him. The Mystic grinned. "That wasn't funny," Lester scolded. "Am I ever alone?" The grinning alien remained eerily silent. Lester accused, "You're invading my privacy."

"Lester, my friend, we have things to discuss."

"Yeah, like why did someone deposit a hundred thousand credits into my account?"

"Yes." The Mystic stopped grinning. He told Lester, "Your people call the Vexite Angst Infuriated the 'Queen of Noburg' and rightly so. She is the matriarch of the city's ruling Fang Gang. Her rival paid you a hundred thousand credits to kill her."

"What? No!"

"Yes. The deal has been made. Break the deal and you offend the Vexite Passion Conniving personally. She is the matriarch of the Conniving Fang Gang. She would mark you for death."

"I'll... I'll return the money."

"How will you do so? The manner of these transactions is indirect."

"You're in contact with these people, right? I mean, you're the one who gave them my account number."

The calm and melodious voice of Dubious Merit was that of a natural predator. It told Lester, "The transaction did not go unnoticed. The Infuriated Fang Gang is curious."

"What, about me? I didn't do anything!"

"The Vexites are warriors as hunters. They stalk their prey. They will find you. They will surely happen upon Annie Smith."

"No! Annie has nothing to do with this!"

"She has everything to do with you." Lester sobbed. Dubious mentioned, "The Fang Gangs are notorious for using their fangs in vengeance. They would likely maul Annie to death: all that *ripping* and *tearing* with *you* in mind."

Lester wept bitterly. "Please," he choked. "Don't let them do this."

The inhuman entity sat in cold silence for the longest while before eventually instructing, "We kill Angst Infuriated, her two sons and her niece. The rival gang moves into the city and assumes control."

Lester questioned, "Are you working for Passion Conniving? I thought you worked for the Willow Family."

"Yes."

"What do you mean?"

"Lester, my friend, I have been hiding in plain sight. Why do you not have eyes to see me?"

"I don't understand."

"Believe your own eyes, always. It is the thoughts that blind you."

"I don't care about all the mumbo jumbo! I care about Annie."

"Yes, of course."

"What do we do?"

Dubious Merit grinned. "Go where I tell you and we shall make our plans."

Lester and Dubious were riding in the busy traffic of Noburg… when a van veered into their lane right in front of them. The hatch-back flung open and a Vexite within the vehicle raised a machinegun. Lester slammed on the brakes and his car *screeched* to a halt as a stream of rapid fire shattered his windshield! He squeezed to the floor as bullets punched into the engine, ripped through the dashboard and shredded upholstery.

Dubious somehow slipped out of the car without anyone noticing. Unbeknownst to Lester, the Vexite never noticed the Mystic passenger at all… until it was too late.

The driver of the van noticed a Mystic reflected in his rearview mirror. The Vexite went for his pistol but a slash across his throat brought an end to that.

Lester kicked when his door suddenly opened. "Out of the car and into the van," the melodious voice of Dubious Merit implored. "Make haste."

Lester noticed the Vexite gunner sprawled between the vehicles. The Vexite was disemboweled and his green blood and greenish-gray guts smelled rancid.

Dubious closed the back hatch of the van. He opened the driver's door and plucked the driver out to drop unceremoniously onto the street. The Mystic then got behind the wheel.

Lester climbed into the passenger seat. The human amused the Mystic by reflexively buckling his seatbelt. "Holster your pistol," Dubious advised. "Appear calm that your countenance shall not garner undo attention."

"Right," Lester remembered his training.

Dubious drove into the flow of traffic. He remained calm as sirens blared and police cars sped by. He turned into an alley and parked between trucks.

The Mystic sat in silence. He studied the human as if looking for wounds upon him. "I'm all right," Lester assured.

"Good."

"Was that the Infuriated Fang Gang?"

"Undoubtedly."

"How did they find us so quickly?"

Dubious Merit smirked. He explained, "They knew you were leaving the bank."

"What?"

"My friend, the Queen of Noburg is ever vigilant. Her many eyes are always watching and her many ears always listening."

The Mystic got out of the van and started walking. Lester got out and followed after him. The human wondered, "What do we do now?"

"What I meant to do all along."

"What?"

"Lester, my friend, you shall be the man known for slaying the most powerful gangster of the Vexite race."

"I'm not an assassin."

"Yes, I know. I mean to give you my reputation. All shall fear you as they would fear me."

"Why?"

"Take heed, my friend: The death of Angst Infuriated may prove the salvation of your beloved female."

Dubious led Lester to the abandoned apartment complex where the Mystic taught the human stealth, climbing and lock-picking. "I have been residing here," the Mystic confided. "What we need is within my dwelling." The "dwelling" was a room on a top floor in a corner facing away from the city. The room was tidy but missing a section of wall.

Dubious showed Lester pictures and maps. "Her mansion is too heavily guarded," the Mystic explained. "Though we may be able to sneak in, one cannot hide from Vexites when they know to look. When we strike, we make haste."

"City Hall," Lester recognized.

"Yes. The mayor is Angst Infuriated's brother. She visits him, to conduct business and to socialize. Her sons and niece shall be with them tonight."

"Why? How do you know?"

"The five are a coven and tonight is the equinox. The Shrine of the Tree is within the City Hall. They shall be alone, naked and unarmed. Their guards will come but shall not be with them when we strike."

Lester fretted, "We're going to murder naked and unarmed people... while they're praying."

Dubious grinned, "Yes."

Lester seriously wondered, "Why me? This city is teeming with professional killers. Why bother setting me up so I have to do this? Why bother training me? Didn't you ever think you're wasting your time?"

"No."

"Really?"

The Mystic explained, "Your circumstances were indeed unfavorable but not your nature."

"My nature? I was a harmless guy living a harmless life because I wasn't inclined to do what I'm doing now."

"You were a dangerous man living a harmless life because you needed a reason. I gave you reasons."

Lester countered, "You don't know anything about me. Yeah, you've got my personal information but that's raw and really impersonal data. There is nothing about me dangerous except that you're putting me in harm's way."

"Lester Freeman, I knew you before I knew your name. I saw your glow and I followed it to you."

"My glow?"

"Yes."

"What glow?"

"Lester, my friend, the money is my reward but I do not do what I do for money. I joined the army for the thrill of adventure and the amusement of killing. Alas, the wars are over and my grim and restless nature vexes me."

"I'm not a killer."

"I am only a killer when it suits me. Yes, I slay for my amusement but never needlessly. You, my friend, languished being the man you never were."

"I am what I am."

"Yes and you need what you need."

"What?"

The Mystic grinned. He accused, "You ask what you fear to know. You hope to deny what I tell you."

"Maybe."

The alien chuckled. "Humanity alone denies its own nature. How can you be other than yourselves? I understand your nature and your circumstances yet I do not understand you."

Lester felt pity for what he suddenly realized was a truly soulless creature. The alien was humanoid and wore clothes. It was intelligent, skillful and eloquent. Its people had a culture and used tools—yet this creature was merely an animal true to its nature. Lester would be the man he wanted to be, no matter his nature or circumstances.

The Mystic put on talismans: a medallion, rings, bracers and a glossy black sash. He added a sword to his belt. This weapon was a short, somewhat curved, single-edged blade and a long grip. "The curved short sword is an assassin's weapon," Dubious Merit explained. "It is meant for use at very close quarters."

Lester already had his semi-automatic pistol but Dubious handed him a large revolver. "Your people call it the 'Mad Momma' for whatever reason. They say it is the 'sure thing to put a monster down' because of its power. It would be a more suitable sidearm for killing Vexites."

Dubious also provided Lester with a Jingoan fighting knife and a sub-machinegun. "No silencers?" Lester was surprised.

"Vexites *feel* the killing of their own whether they see or hear it or not. They shall be alerted regardless. Do not aim lest you are ready to shoot or else your Vexite target shall sense the danger."

"Roger that."

"Your ammunition is military-grade. It will penetrate body armor and maximize wounds. I inspected your weapons myself and they are in perfect working order."

"Thanks."

The Mystic smiled and Lester was surprised that it seemed genuinely friendly. He told Lester, "I have grown fond of you. May you prove worthy of my reputation."

Dubious and Lester made their way to City Hall on foot. They darted from shadow to shadow and kept to where there were few people. They waited as people passed by. "The Infuriated Fang Gang is watching," Dubious warned. Their eyes and ears are Vexite but other races as well."

"Obviously."

"Yes. The truth is always obvious. Noticing requires eyes to see and ears to hear."

"What does that even mean?"

"My friend, a creature of flesh is but an animal. As a creature of flesh we have our eyes and ears of flesh. As creatures of spirit we have eyes and ears of spirit—or we are blind and deaf in spirit."

The partners hid behind parked vehicles across the street from City Hall. "I don't see the guards," Lester told Dubious.

"You know to look. Why do you not see them?"

"Hey, I'm not a weird alien with freaky powers. I don't see things unless I actually see them."

Dubious Merit could see two Vexites: a male wielding a belt-fed machinegun and a female armed with a shotgun. He noticed another female perched on the roof and wielding a marksman rifle. The guards were *hiding in plain sight* as was a common skill among the warriors of Vex.

The Mystic pointed the sentries out to his human companion. "Wow," Lester was surprised not to have noticed them earlier.

"Remember what I have taught you, please. Do not return to the way of thinking that renders you blind and deaf."

"How do we get past them?"

"My skills are beyond theirs. Stay close to me. Move gracefully, with your weapon lowered and do not stare."

"Yeah, I remember."

Dubious Merit waved his hands. He waved at Lester then waved as a gesture to follow him onward. Lester remembered to "calm his heart and quiet his mind" so as to not break the spell. He was mindful to ignore to the armed Vexites as he passed them.

Dubious had Lester break into the main building. The Mystic led the way up the steps of a stairwell. Lester was mindful not to look away for fear Dubious would disappear again and leave him in a situation.

A tree was in the middle of a large, round room with a glass ceiling. "The shrine," Dubious Merit told Lester. "Our quarry is preparing for their ritual. We shall not strike till they are naked, on their knees, holding hands and facing the tree."

Lester was feeling sick and evil. He did not like himself for what he was about to do… even if it meant saving Annie. "I can't do this," he realized.

The Mystic seemed to be ignoring him. Dubious told the man, "You slay Angst Infuriated. It must be by your hand."

"Why?"

"You must save Annie from the wrath of Angst Infuriated."

"I'm going to murder someone over a misunderstanding, of all things."

"No."

"No?"

"Lester, my friend, I gave you your reasons to do what I require."

"What are you up to?"

Dubious Merit grinned, "I shall assassinate the matriarch of a Fang Gang and *you* shall be the one who did it."

"Whoa! I don't think Vexites will like some alien killing one of their bosses, even if they hate her."

The Mystic explained, "Among the Vexites it is honorable to slay warriors, whether in battle or by waylay. It is an affront to slay a matriarch. Her kin and followers are bound to avenge her even to their own death."

"Anybody left in the Infuriated Fang Gang will be after me."

"Yes." Lester gulped. The Mystic reminded, "You are their enemy. They shall find Annie Smith and realize she is dear to you. To hurt you they shall hurt her. They shall rip her apart with their teeth."

"I won't kill the matriarch."

"You were paid by the matriarch Passion Conniving. She will have you hunted and slain should you cheat her."

"I can live with that... even if it kills me."

The Mystic sneered and Lester cringed. The alien loomed over the human as he hissed, "Betray me and I shall do worst to Annie Smith than any Vexite would ever bother to do."

Dubious Merit looked down. Lester did not even realize that his sub-machinegun was already at the ready to spray the Mystic with bullets. "True to your nature," the inhuman entity grinned.

"Military-grade and maximizes damage," Lester reminded.

The Mystic slowly stepped back. He looked away... and disappeared.

"Annie," Lester worried. "Why didn't I shoot the bastard?!"

Lester hurried downstairs... none too quietly. A Vexite with a shotgun stepped out in front of him. Lester kept his own weapon pointing at the floor. "Hello," the human feigned a smile and waved.

The raspy voice of the Vexite questioned, "What are you doing here?"

"I'm trying to save my girlfriend."

Lester was disarmed and frisked. He was brought before Angst Infuriated and her sons Wary and Aggression. The matriarch wore a red dress and a red and yellow feather boa. Her sons were in dark red suits with yellow ties. "Lester Freeman," Angst grinned. Lester was unsettled seeing those fangs of hers. "Where is your Mystic?"

"He's probably after my girlfriend."

Angst Infuriated stepped up to Lester Freeman. "Mother!" Wary Infuriated worried.

The matriarch gently yet firmly grabbed the human by the chin and made him look up at her. "My death is not in your eyes."

Angst told one of her underlings, "I am not in the proper mood for the rite. Tell my brother and his daughter that we are returning to the mansion."

The underling asked, "Shall I tell of these unexpected happenings?"

"No. I shall explain later." Ms. Infuriated told Lester, "You shall explain to me now."

A female Vexite was opening the door of her car… when an arm suddenly seized her around the neck! A hand pressed against the back of her head. The attacker *snapped* her neck. The victim twitched but otherwise went limp.

Dubious Merit dumped the body of the dead Vexite into the trunk of her own car. He then sat himself behind the wheel of her vehicle and drove out into traffic.

Mystics are contemplative by nature. Dubious Merit realized that he had an opportunity to sneak into the mansion of Angst Infuriated while many of her guards were away. They would return with her but he would already be within her home waiting.

A human was Angst Infuriated's chauffer. He opened the door of her limousine as she approached. Armed Vexites climbed into vans or hopped into the back of a pickup truck. Vexites mounted motorcycles and rode ahead to scout ahead.

Lester sat next to Angst Infuriated. Her sons sat across from them. "Tell me everything," Ms. Infuriated demanded of the human.

"I did."

Angst Infuriated looked at her son Wary Infuriated. When he nodded, she smiled. Wary told his mother, "Dubious Merit is not with the Unsavory Guild. The Mystics have not turned against us."

"No," Angst Infuriated agreed, "but the Conniving may have seduced the Willow Family into a conspiracy against me."

"Mother, let us not be hasty. The Penumbran shall not abide war with the Golgothites. Let us voice our grievance to the Mutual Prosperity Syndicate. They shall investigate the matter. They shall arbitrate. Let us avoid needless incident. If we were wronged by the Willow Family they shall make amends."

"There is a conspiracy to kill me!"

"We do not know the involvement of the Willow Family in this matter."

"Look into it."

"Yes, mother."

"You," Angst Infuriated sneered at Lester. "I am ashamed I feared you." She then grinned and the sight of those fangs being so close made the human reflexively cringe. The Vexite giggled. She snuggled the little human, making him cringe all the more. "What should I do with you?"

"You can bite my head, for all I care," Lester blurted. The Vexites were startled but just as quickly laughed. Lester sobbed, "He's going to kill Annie Smith because I couldn't get to her."

Wary told his mother, "Annie Smith is the niece of my friend Vincent Burdock." He told Lester, "Our people are already watching Annie Smith as they wait for you. They know of your Mystic and shall kill him should he come."

"He's not *my* Mystic."

"Dubious Merit is his own Mystic," Angst told Wary. "Kill him."

Lester muttered, "Easier said than done."

Chapter 6
"Moment of Truth"

Dubious Merit had grown fond of Lester Freeman. The little human was cute for all his shyness and awkwardness. Lester was wiser than anticipated and his instincts amazingly keen. Dubious admired the man for his unexpected gall. "He bested me," the Mystic conceded. Dubious Merit was proud of his protégé. "Alas, I must rid my circumstances of him."

Mystics were patient by nature. Dubious watched as his prey and her entourage returned to the mansion. Dubious was pleased to see Lester Freeman was with them.

Lester Freeman and Angst Infuriated were together lounging in a posh living room. Human maids served drinks and snacks. "Nice place," Lester complimented. He thought the maids were comely but would not mention such a thing. The *Queen of Noburg* smiled. Lester asked her, "Where are your sons?"

"Aggression is leading the hunt for Dubious Merit. Wary is tending to business."

"Oh."

The female Vexite assured the man, "My son told me your mate is in her apartment watching television. She is safe."

"Good. Thank you so very, very much."

The Vexite giggled. She remarked, "You are such a skittish little creature. Why did the Mystic conscript you for an assassination attempt?"

Lester shrugged. "He told me I was 'glowing' or whatever that means."

"Yes. I feel your warmth."

"So, you know what he meant?"

"I know what I feel."

"Okay. I have no idea what either of you mean."

The Vexite giggled. She told Lester, "Vincent Burdock is a friend. We would not harm the niece of a friend."

"That's good to hear."

The Vexite added, "A friend must prove his friendship. We would call upon Vincent to do what he must." Lester gulped. He did not want to know whatever the monster meant.

Warding spells were easy enough to slip through. Keen senses were easy enough to avoid or distract. Sensors and alarms were useless. It was the uncanny intuition of the Vexites that gave Dubious Merit pause. Their primal instincts bested the honed skills of their civilized enemies throughout their grim history.

Dubious knew not to wait for Angst Infuriated in her bedchamber. She would be most sensitive where she was most familiar. It was a risk coming to her home but Lester Freeman altered the circumstances to where such a risk was now expedient.

Dubious Merit grinned. Though troubled by his loss of control over the little human, the Mystic was proud to have been the one to discover him. "May your training serve you well," Dubious hoped Lester would not prove an easy kill. The human was undoubtedly disarmed when captured by the Vexites. Still, he was human and the best of humanity was resourceful. The Mystic would not be gracious when the moment came. A moment of truth was never to be denied.

Dubious Merit was above, watching. Angst Infuriated was below, sitting. Lester Freeman was with the Vexite. Alas, Angst Infuriated was the Mystic's quarry. Dealing with Lester was a personal matter not to be bothered with... for now.

Angst was speaking to Lester... when all became strangely silent. Angst continued speaking but Lester no longer noticed her. He watched as a Mystic with a drawn sword leapt from above. "Look out!" the human barked. The Vexite looked up as a raised blade came down. Angst rolled out of the way and drew a pistol. She blazed away but her nimble assailant disappeared as suddenly as he appeared.

"The Mystic is in my house!" Angst Infuriated snapped at her guards. "Find him! Kill him!"

Angst kept her pistol raised. "Your back to mine," she told Lester.

"I don't have a gun."

"You have eyes to see!"

Armed Vexites, male and female, scoured the mansion. A male was suddenly cut across the back. As he groaned and dropped to his knees, the female with him turned around—and was disemboweled. "He is over here!" a male with a shotgun found the bodies. A stab in the back dropped his body to the floor with the others.

Angst did not like the sound of Vexite voices grunting and groaning. She could hear bodies and weapons dropping to the floor. She glimpsed a shadowy form darting from shadow to shadow. "He is below!" she called to her guards.

More guards came into the room. "This way," a female waved for her matriarch to follow.

"The human comes with us," Angst insisted. The underling nodded. "He is to be protected."

"Yes," the underling understood. The Vexites were a simple race unaccustomed to extraneous formality or explanation.

Rapid fire and shotgun blasts where mixed with clattering, screams, grunts and groans. Angst and Lester were brought to the limousine. "He is not yet dead?" Angst noted the continued shooting.

"Away with you, my boss!" the faithful underling slammed the door of the limousine. Her voice told the driver, "Hurry to where you are to go!"

"Yes, ma'am," the human voice of the human chauffer responded. Motorcycles ridden by armed Vexites took the lead.

Lester sat next to Angst Infuriated. The Vexite was sneering but in cold silence. As they neared Lester's neighborhood the human requested, "I live near here. Could you drop me off?"

"Reginald!" the matriarch barked at her chauffer. "Pull over." The limousine pulled to the side of the road. Angst glared at Lester and told him, "Get out."

The human hurriedly got out. "Thank you," he told the seething crime boss.

"Close the door."

"Yeah," Lester closed the door. The limousine sped off.

Lester walked to the apartments. As he climbed the stairs he worried Angst Infuriated may not have told her watchers not to kill him when they saw him. No shots rang out so he assumed the message was sent.

Annie was at her table putting a puzzle together one of its many pieces at a time… when there was a knock on her door. She answered the door, "Hey!"

Lester pushed his way in. He closed the door and locked it. "What's wrong?"

"I turned on Dubious Merit."

"Is he after you?"

Lester told Annie, "He said he'd be after *you*." Annie cringed and trembled, clearly taken aback. Lester sobbed, "I'm sorry."

"Let me call my uncle," Annie picked up her phone.

Lester explained, "The Infuriated Fang Gang is after Dubious Merit now. He wanted me to kill their boss and I didn't. I couldn't… kill somebody who never did anything to me."

Annie raised a finger to her lips for Lester to be silent. Lester heard the voice of Uncle Vinnie greet, "What's happening, sweetie?"

"There's a problem."

"Anything you don't want saying over the phone?"

"I don't see why not."

"What's wrong?"

"Lester's at my place."

"Really? Why?"

"He'e protecting me. I don't want to be alone right now."

"Whatever," Uncle Vinnie conceded. "Wary Infuriated assured me the boy's all right."

"That's not the problem."

"What problem?"

"Dubious Merit."

There was a long, tense pause in the conversation. "Lester's with you?"

"Yes."

"Give him the phone." Annie handed Lester the phone. Uncle Vinnie asked, "What's the problem?"

Lester answered, "Dubious Merit is on the loose and he wants to kill me and Annie."

"Why does he want to kill Annie?"

"Does it matter?"

"No. Hand the phone back to Annie."

"Yeah?" Annie took the phone back.

Uncle Vinnie told his niece, "The Infuriated Fang Gang has people watching you. Stay in your apartment and they'll kill anybody who tries to get in."

"All right."

"I'm on the other side of the planet but I'll be there as soon as I can."

"Okay."

"Stay in your apartment! Keep the door locked! Don't let anybody in! Do you hear me?"

"Yes."

"Do you *hear* me?!"

"Yes!"

"Good."

Five Vexites were hidden and watching. Two of the five were female and the one was the leader... until a Mystic squeezed the life out of her. "Patience?" a male called to the leader. A bluish beige hand with only four digits snatched him over the mouth. A blade sunk into his belly and sliced it open.

Dubious Merit knew where the Vexites were hiding. He found them days ago and they always hid in the same spots. It was easy enough to silence them. Lester and his mate were soon to perish... with none to help them.

Annie took Lester's hand. "Stay with me," she pled. Lester could see the fear in her eyes but there was also a glint of confidence.

"What about your uncle? He might not like finding us together."

"Lester, don't leave me alone. Please."

The man nodded. He asked, "Do you have a gun?"

"No."

"You have knives, right?" The woman nodded. "Let's have a look at those knives."

The man and woman were together in the kitchen scrounging every knife Annie owned. "I wish I asked for my guns back," Lester bemoaned.

"Wishing isn't going to help us right now," Annie emphasized. "Let's use whatever we've got."

Lester tried to reassure her, "He may not even come. The... the Vexites outside might scare him away."

"Or kill him," Annie hoped.

Lester remembered when he was attacked and Dubious made short work of the attackers. He remembered the ceaseless shooting, grunts and groans. He seriously doubted Vexite goons were the ones to take down Dubious Merit. "He isn't human."

"What?"

"Nothing."

Lester and Annie barricaded the door. They locked every window.

Dubious Merit made his way up the steps to Annie's apartment. The Mystic could feel the presence of Lester Freeman with that of Annie Smith: they were together. "Lester, my friend, forgive me." The Mystic knew the human "heard" what was "said" as a thought. Dubious Merit was telling what he thought. "I must avenge or I am bested. My profession is its reputation. I must take back the reputation I gave you."

"Lester?" Annie snapped the man from his trance. "Lester!"

"What?"

"You disappeared."

The man insisted, "I was right here the whole time."

"No, you weren't *with* me with me."

"What?"

"Lester, what's wrong with you?"

"Nothing!"

"You looked like you were in a trance."

"I don't know. Maybe I was."

"Does he have power over you?"

Lester found a meat cleaver. He answered Annie's question, "Not anymore."

Dubious Merit stood before the door to Annie Smith's apartment. He drew his sword with his left hand. He closed his eyes and waved his right hand. The door was barricaded on the other side. Dubious slid his blade back into its scabbard.

Lester had Annie turn off the television. She whined, "The silence is driving me crazy!"

"He hides in noise," Lester explained. "He uses every distraction to *his* advantage."

"What if he doesn't come tonight? What if he doesn't come at all?"

"Like you said; wishing isn't going to help us right now."

The man and woman snuggled together on the couch. Lester told Annie, "I'm so sorry for getting you into this."

"You didn't. I did."

"Whatever. I'm sorry."

The man and woman snuggled for a long, silent, blissful while. The threat of death seemed to make the moment all the more tranquil. "This isn't what I thought I'd be getting into when I came to an alien planet," Lester commented. "I was told 'it's like here, but not here' and was left to figure out what all that gibberish meant."

"Noburg is like home in many ways," Annie turned Lester's remark into a conversation, "We built the city and everything in it."

"True. Well, there is alien architecture here and there. Little Mystique is totally alien… except for the streets and traffic."

Annie snuggled all the more. Lester was enjoying the snuggling. He mentioned, "I was paid a hundred thousand credits to kill an alien crime boss."

"You're a paid assassin?"

Lester nodded. He shrugged, "Well, I was paid but I'm not an assassin. I still have the money."

"What are you going to do with it?"

"I don't know."

Annie warned, "You shouldn't touch blood money."

"I didn't. *It* touched *me*."

Humans had a nasty habit of *breaking* things to get things done. Mystics preferred finesse. The window was locked but transparency is visibility. The Mystic could *see* that the window was locked shut. His third eye saw it otherwise… and the latches became as he envisioned them. Dubious Merit opened the window, knocked out the screen and slipped into the bedchamber.

Annie was in the bathroom using the toilet. Though afraid of being alone, her modesty was stronger than her fear. "I want to take a bath," she said through the door.

"Go ahead."

"I'm scared to."

Lester felt guilty actually hoping Annie would invite him to take a bath with her. "I, uh, I see your… dilemma."

"If I leave the door open, will you promise not to peek?"

"Annie, I wouldn't see you through the shower curtain."

"I mean when I get in and out."

"I promise not to look when you tell me not to look."

"I don't want you going anywhere!"

"I won't go anywhere."

"Not even to your apartment just to get something! Lester, please don't go!"

"I'm not going anywhere. I'm here as long as you need me."

A door barely and slowly opened. Lester was in the kitchen making tea. He was unarmed and his back exposed. Now was the moment to strike.

"I'm not going to take a bath," Annie decided. The toilet flushed. Dubious used the flush to hide the opening of the door. His sword was drawn and he lunged!

Lester spun around and flung hot tea into the Mystic's face! Dubious Merit stumbled. Lester picked up a chair and broke it over the Mystic's back.

Dubious Merit snarled and lunged. Annie *screamed* as she stepped out of the bathroom and saw an alien swiping a sword at Lester. She threw her remote control at Dubious Merit, distracting him. Lester grabbed another chair and ran it into the alien, knocking him down. Dubious kicked the chair away and hopped back onto his feet.

Annie hurled a ceramic statuette at the Mystic. It bounced off harmlessly, but it proved a distraction. Lester struck Dubious with the chair repeatedly. Annie kept snatching things and throwing them. The Mystic was being overwhelmed.

Lester snatched up the meat cleaver and hacked the Mystic's shoulder, drawing blue blood but not even grunt from the victim. The soulless eyes of the alien glared at the human. Lester renewed the hacking. Dubious Merit slumped to the floor. Annie plunged a knife into the alien. Lester kept hacking.

Lester and Annie snuggled on the floor and stared at the sprawled alien and all the blue gore. "Is he dead?" the woman asked.

"I hope so! He'll be pissed if he isn't."

Someone tried to barge through the front door but the barricade held. "Annie Smith!" an unfamiliar human voice called through the door.

"Come in!" she responded. She was not quite in her right mind.

"You're uncle sent us! Are you all right? You're not answering your phone."

"Where's my phone? I don't know." Annie looked at Lester. He nodded so she responded, "I'm all right!"

"Is the door blocked?"

"Yes. We had a problem… but we think he's dead."

Lester remembered Dubious Merit explaining, "Resourcefulness is the ultimate edge," but only now did he understand the lesson.

Printed in Great Britain
by Amazon